THE SUMMER AND THE MAY

THE SUMMER AND THE MAY

Lucinda Hart

Published by Vulpine Press in the United Kingdom in 2023

ISBN: 978-1-83919-543-3

www.vulpine-press.com

To Sylvia Matthews (Dee)
1923 – 2010
This one's for you, of course

Helston: its name means the stone of hell.

Legend says that St Michael the Archangel encountered the Devil over the skies of south-west Cornwall. The Devil bore a huge black stone to block the mouth of Hell. In the conflict the stone fell onto Helston and its broken shards were used to build the Angel Hotel, which still stands in the main street today.

That is the legend, but not the truth.

St Michael the Archangel did meet the Devil, and the Devil did bear a stone. Their battle did not take place over Helston, but some miles to the south, where turbulent seas thunder against jagged rocks at the very end of the world.

The Archangel defeated the Devil and banished him to Hell. He dropped the Devil's own stone into that gaping black mouth and sealed the entrance to the underworld for ever. As the stone fell, its reverberations shuddered the coastline, and a giant wave engulfed the sand and rocks. The entrance to Hell was now barred by both stone and by sea, by rock and by water.

But over millennia, the earth exhales and moves, then settles once more. Tectonic plates rise and fall. And cracks appear in the doorway to Hell.

The Wild Hunt is coming: shouting, horns, drums, whistles.

Twig hears the mummers in the narrow, twisted streets above St John's. Their cries are like white noise buzzing somewhere behind his eyes. Twig staggers; he almost falls into his neighbour, who steadies him, probably presuming him drunk or ill. Heads turn as the whistles become louder, more strident. The drum's tattoo drives Twig's heart faster; he feels the growing pressure in his chest and ears.

He is coming, Twig thinks, closing his eyes. And so is she.

Twig does not want to see, but his eyes flick open. He gasps, gags. The writhing figures before him are wild-eyed wraiths with tattered cerements trailing behind them, and wilting blooms in their skeletal hands. Twig can hardly breathe for the stench of decay. The tangle of dancers ebbs and flows across his vision. In the centre of the circle, a black, horned figure turns slowly to face him.

He is here.

Twig's legs shudder. Before he falls, he must find the sacrifice. The Devil shimmers before him, shrouded once more by handmaidens. As they hide his face with shivering leaves, Twig sees a flash of colour across the circle. A slender girl, gowned in the gold and green of the summer and the may, ribbons fluttering from the tambourine she holds in her hand. She smiles as though she sees Twig, but he knows she cannot, that she dances to a different tune, moving in another sphere to the company of the dead.

Twig holds the image of the girl's laughing face as he crumples to the ground. He has seen her; she is here.

1

Caroline Tripconey unhooks a bright key fob from the pegs in the hall.

"Frank? Boys? are you coming?"

"Do we *have* to?" Four-year-old Andy moans from the living room.

"We do," his father says, zipping up a hoodie. "I don't want Mummy lifting anything heavy, with the baby inside her, and there's no way we're leaving you two here alone."

"It's only next door." Jonny pokes Andy. "We can play in the garden while they do the stuff. Hey, Mummy, we can go through the secret tunnel and meet you there."

"No." Caroline tweaks a sticker out of Jonny's blond hair and he yelps. "We'll all walk round together. Come on, Andy."

Andy is sitting cross-legged on the floor, gazing at the bright cartoon on the TV. Caroline grabs the remote and snaps it off. Andy wails and pushes at his glasses, but allows his mother to haul him up and shove his feet into abandoned trainers.

The early evening sun is silvery-gold, but the wind from the ocean is fresh. Frank strides ahead and unlatches the garden gate. The cliff road is an uneven track, one car's width, bordered with tamarisk, bluebells, and wild garlic.

"And over we go!" Frank jumps across a bumpy mauve vein in the ground that marks a geological fault line.

First Jonny, then his little brother, take exaggerated leaps over the dark seam.

"What have you got to do, Mummy?" Jonny asks as Caroline ushers them towards Nick Hersch's bungalow.

Beyond this house, the track peters out into a narrow coast path by the towering rock outcrop Carrag Luz. Caroline stops a moment, gazes round the sweep of Mount's Bay to the distant snake's head of the Land's End peninsula.

"Mummy?"

2

"I told you before. People are coming to stay here and I've got to make up the beds and Hoover round, make it nice for them."

"Them?" Frank asks. "I thought it was just this girl."

"Well, yes, to start with, but Ellen's brother's coming later, with the son, I think."

"There's the sun." Andy points to the sky.

"You two play here on the front lawn where we can see you," Caroline says. "Daddy'll be watching."

She climbs the stone steps set in a steep grassy bank. On the lower lawn the boys are already racing about. Caroline unlocks the front door and stoops to collect some mail. It looks like junk but she won't bin it just in case. Not that she has any idea when Nick Hersch will be back here. His ex-wife, Ellen, told Caroline he would be in the States for some months, painting the portraits of Hollywood stars. Ellen explained that her brother Tim and his two step-children would love to escape the dust and noise of Bath for a break in Cornwall, and that Nick had said they would be welcome at his house. But now it seems Tim's step-daughter Verity is coming alone.

"She arriving tomorrow?" Frank asks, as he trails behind Caroline into the front bedroom.

"So Ellen said. I haven't actually heard from Verity at all. I told Ellen I'd be at home and could let her in."

"Bit lonely for a young girl on her own." Frank stops flapping out a white duvet cover and glances at the boys on the front lawn.

"The others might join her later, I think. You know what Ellen's like. Going on and on, and changing the subject all the time."

Frank grimaces and smooths down the covers on the double bed.

"I told her I'd lock the studio." Caroline says, adjusting one of Nick's vivid abstracts. "I much prefer these to his portraits."

"Portraits are pretty dull," Frank agrees, then, "Hey, she'll be here for the Flora."

3

Suddenly there's a long loud wail from the garden. Frank shoots out of the house and stumbles on the steps as he leaps down.

"What's up, Andy, old sausage?"

Caroline watches from the higher level as Frank crouches beside Andy and squeezes him close. She can't hear Andy's jumbled words.

"Dunno," Jonny calls up to her. "He was fine, then just started yelling. Shut up, Andy."

"I won't be long," Caroline promises and whisks back inside.

She quickly finds some towels to leave on the bed, locks Nick's studio of shrouded easels and stacked canvases, and runs the Hoover through the living room and hall. So much for not doing heavy work, she thinks, glancing through the door to where Frank and the boys are gazing out to sea watching a tanker.

"All done." She locks the front door and comes down to join them. "OK, what are we having for tea? Pasta?"

Andy has stopped crying, though his eyes are still pink and blotchy behind his spectacles.

"Pasta, yeah." Jonny runs on ahead to the gate and shoots through onto the cliff road, ignoring his father's warning shouts.

A deep primal rumbling, and the ground judders underfoot. Caroline wavers, but doesn't fall. Jonny dashes back to the others, eyes startled. A moment later the rumbling stops and the ground is still.

"What was that?" Jonny shouts.

Andy buries his face in his mother's tie-dyed skirt, heaving with fresh tears.

"It's just another of those earth tremors," Frank says. "You know, like the other week."

"Isn't that when the ground opens up and…"

"Not always, Jonny. Sometimes it's just a little rumble, and no damage."

4

Caroline's pulse has shot up. She feels like something ancient is stirring underground, vibrating through her body, more powerful even than the kicks of her unborn child. Instinctively she drops her hand to her swollen abdomen.

~

"To the monument!" someone cries. "The monument!"

Little John's horn, the whistles, the relentless drum.

Ahead of her, up the slope, Verity can see the Devil. He seems to be further and further from her. Two flower maidens appear on either side of her; one rattles her tambourine, the other screams the call of the Hal an Tow. Verity feels the flare of goose flesh on her arms.

"He waits for you."

Verity lifts her eyes once more. Standing on the crest of the hill, gilded by the morning sun, stands the Devil, watching her stumble up the rise towards him. The two girls melt away into the greenery that borders the house doorways.

The Devil holds out a black gloved hand. She reaches for him. His grasp is firm; her legs steady. She looks up to his face. Pewter eyes behind the mask, as he bows over her hand.

"Maiden, will you join my dance?"

~

A sunny spring afternoon in Bath.

Tim Hurford walks slowly from his flat in St James Square to open Cosmos after lunch. It only takes a moment to reach Margaret's Buildings, the tiny pedestrianised street of galleries, craft shops and cafes. The windchimes outside his shop tinkle softly as he unlocks the door and flicks the sign to *open*.

Cosmos still smells of the patchouli joss sticks Tim was burning before he closed up to see Verity off. He takes a fresh stick from the packet, holds a lighter to the tip. A tiny flame glows for a second until he blows it out.

He's tried to raise his twin step-children to be adventurous, fearless even, but something nags inside his heart. Verity has just left Bath, behind the wheel of the Getz she shares with her brother, Jack, for a holiday alone in the far south-west of Cornwall.

True, it is at his sister's ex-husband's house, and Ellen tells him the neighbours are on-hand and friendly, but he feels uneasy about Verity being so far away by herself. It's ridiculous, he knows, but he can't shake it off. Ellen rather forced the situation when she came to stay a few weeks earlier. Tim could see Verity's interest ignite at Ellen's description of Nick's house on the cliff at Mullion, the views across Mount's Bay, the changing skies at sunset.

The place is empty till the end of May, Ellen had said. *Why don't you guys go down? Nick won't mind.*

Tim explained patiently about his hypnotherapy clients that he could not abandon, and reminded her that Jack couldn't just walk out of university on a whim, that it isn't always possible to simply disappear out of one life and into another. But Ellen showed Verity pictures of the bungalow, the wild garden, a tortured outcrop of rock on the cliff, and Verity said, *I really want to go.*

The door to Cosmos opens and two girls come in. They're about Verity's age, but clearly tourists. Tim nods at them and busies himself tidying up the display of crystals, finding comfort in the smooth lozenges of amber and the startling cold of fluorite. The girls wander round the shop, tweaking paddles on windchimes, running fingers through the trays of tumblestones, stroking the feathers on dreamcatchers, and then drift out again, one of them already scrolling through her phone.

Tim reaches in his pocket for his own mobile and sends Jack a quick message.

Verity on her way now. Really hope you can come down with me in a few weeks.

As he pockets his phone again, he notices the display pack of Tarot cards has slid into a heap. He gathers them together, gently knocking them into a block. A lot of people handle this deck. Tim does not like absorbing the energy from them. As he is about to replace them on the velvet display cloth, the pack falls from his hands.

"Shit," he mutters, crouching down to retrieve them.

He stops a moment. Only four cards are face up.

The Moon.

The Fool.

The Magician.

The Devil.

Tim stares at the four images a moment. There's something there he should understand, but he can't fathom it. He scoops up the cards, reforms the pack and sets it down on the velvet.

~

Verity turns left out of the gate and onto the cliff road. The tamarisk-covered wall crumbles down into the springy grass and weeds of the cliff top. A narrow path winds on along the coast towards Mullion harbour and its island, a dark wedge on the silver ocean.

Another track has been trampled down to Carrag Luz, the rock outcrop on the cliff edge. She scrambles up the lower ledges. Beneath her feet the rocks are worn smooth, patterned with green and saffron lichen. She can see now that one of the upper rocks is firmly embedded on the crag, but the one on the left is balanced on a pointed edge, poised to fall. Placing her hands on the solid boulder, Verity edges closer to the abyss.

The cliff falls sheer to dark mauve water and churning silver eddies. The tide's in, rushing far up the beach below, leaving only a slim sickle of pale sand. There's a narrow cove between the beach and Carrag Luz, and the sea roars into this funnel, waves exploding with a crack onto the shining rocks and skerries. Verity feels a moment's giddiness and sits down on a rocky ledge. From here she can see Nick's bungalow, the tamarisk hedge, the hump of her car like a glossy beetle.

She has only been in Mullion for a couple of hours. When she arrived, she knocked at Caroline's, next door, as Ellen had told her to. Caroline let her into Nick's bungalow, gave her a whirlwind tour, and fuzzed her mind with information about bin collections, immersion heaters, and washing machines.

Verity noticed her pregnancy, and asked when she was due.

"Another couple of months," Caroline said. "But I'm feeling this one more than the others. Come round for dinner tomorrow night, meet my husband and the boys."

Verity's not sure how long she sits there, with her back to the rocks and the sea. She listens to the disjointed rhythm of the ocean below, feels her eyes close. She could fall asleep here. With great effort she opens her eyes, suddenly remembering she hasn't even let Tim or Jack know she has arrived safely. The sun is dropping to the horizon, staining the sea with its molten blood. She stands and makes her way down from the rocks, and back through the long grasses to the stony cliff road.

Back at the house she sends two quick messages then mutes her phone. She doesn't want to be disturbed with questions about the trip, about the house, about *anything*.

Caroline has made up the front bedroom for her. It has a high ceiling and white walls, hung with three bright canvases. The paintings are abstract: thick swirls of paint applied with a knife. She's surprised to see the signature *Hersch* in the corners; she thought Nick was a portrait painter. She knows where his studio is; it's behind the locked door on the corridor and leads out onto the front veranda. There is an unidentified key on the fob Caroline gave her which she thinks may be for that door and she wonders if Caroline meant to remove it but forgot.

"So, what did you find out?" Frank asks Caroline as he makes tea for them to take to bed.

They haven't been able to talk much since Verity's arrival as the boys were fractious and argumentative. Andy threw toys across the living room. Jonny thumped Andy who wailed and cried, inconsolable for what felt like an age. Finally, they fell asleep, Andy's face still puffy from tears, but Caroline hasn't been able to find out what started it all.

"Not much." She splashes milk into her tea, thinks back to her brief meeting with the girl next door. "She's young, early twenties, I think. Seems fairly capable. She obviously knows Ellen pretty well, but not Nick."

"And her family's coming later on?"

"So she says. Her step-father and her brother. He's at university; Newcastle, I think."

"Where's the mother in all this?" Frank opens the cupboard and helps himself to chocolate biscuits.

"She's dead. I thought you knew."

"Christ, no. Glad you told me if she's coming round tomorrow. Was it recent?"

"No, some years ago. Ellen said it was cancer. Don't know what sort."

"She and her brother have lived with their step-father then, all this time?"

9

"They're very close to him. I don't think their biological father was ever on the scene."

"Did you tell her about the earthquakes?" Frank asks suddenly.

"No, I forgot. I should do, shouldn't I?"

"Tell her tomorrow. Just in case."

~

Verity wakes in the big white bed, disorientated for a moment. She reaches for her travelling alarm clock on the bedside table. Just after ten. The alarm hand is still set at seven-thirty. She twists it at random. Seven-thirty belongs to Bath, to opening up Cosmos for Tim, to then. This is Mullion time; this is now.

She pads out of bed and across the hall into the living room. There's a window seat in the huge front bay. She slides down on it. Today the sea is a harder, brighter blue. Round the bay she can see the Land's End peninsula, and the crenelated crag of St Michael's Mount. She turns to the left. Carrag Luz. There's the huge teetering rock at the top, and the mossy ledge where she sat.

I could spend hours at this window, she thinks, gazing out across the wide jaw of the bay, watching the clouds chasing in, the colours of the sea.

At last, she rises and turns on her phone.

Messages from Tim, from Jack, from Caroline.

Come for dinner about 7, Caroline has sent. *What are you doing to-day?*

Going to the beach, Verity taps back.

Tide should be out and you can get into the second bay.

An hour later, Verity lets herself out of the gate and turns right onto the cliff road, then stops, looks back. Carrag Luz is behind her, the outlines of the rocks ever so slightly hazy in the sunlight. Something ruffles the shaggy grasses; Verity sees the white scut of a rabbit.

10

If she can see the beach from Carrag Luz, she must be able to see Carrag Luz from the beach. She walks past the Getz under its canopy of tamarisk, past Caroline's gate, and the two cars parked outside her garage. Verity glances into a shabby Peugeot: there are children's seats fastened in the back, and scrunched-up wrappers on the shelf below the rear windscreen.

She can smell the wild garlic in the verges. Suddenly the hedge drops, and she's standing on the edge of the cliff, with only a tatty wire fence between her and the abyss. The road has come in a curve. She's above the headland that separates the main beach of Polurrian from the second tidal bay. She takes a step closer to the edge and looks down. The tide is ebbing beyond the headland, leaving a shiny glaze on the sand. In the second beach the sun flashes on water caught in crevices and dips of rock.

The cliff path joins the tarmacked road and she takes steep left signposted for the beach. Now she can hear the soft boom of the sea. She comes out from under a twisted umbrella of spindly trees, then the valley opens up, and there's the beach below her, pale and shiny. There are people stooping to pick up shells, splashing and shrieking in the frothy shallows far out.

Verity runs down steps cut in the cliff and, a moment later, is on the beach. A stream gushes out from the valley, spreading into an intricate delta. She pulls off her pumps, and feels the soft sand under her toes.

As she walks further into the cove, she stops and gazes up at the giant cliffs above her. There's the great shoulder of rock between the beaches, but she can't see the distinctive form of Carrag Luz. She can make out a few fronds of tamarisk on the cliff top, and then she sees it: a jagged silver tooth. It's Carrag Luz from below – completely different: rougher, wilder, petrified.

The kitchen in Tim's attic flat looks across into the back of the Royal Crescent. He loves this jumbled view of uneven sash windows and jutting extensions. It's much more interesting than the immaculate grinning façade of the buildings. A red and blue hot-air balloon glides past with a roar of fire. Tim slides a bottle of Shiraz out of the wine rack and twists it open.

The flat is quiet without Verity. He's used to Jack being away in Newcastle, but Verity has never left home, and he feels her absence acutely. He wonders whether to get onto Jack and see if he can get away from university a little earlier to come to Cornwall.

Tim gulps the first mouthful of wine and his phone buzzes.

"Ellen, hi."

"Verity's all settled. Caroline called me this morning. Have you heard from her?"

"From Verity? Yes, she texted last night when she got there. I wrote back but I haven't heard any more."

"Give the girl some space. She'll be fine with Caroline and Frank."

"I'm feeling lonely without her already. Stupid, I know. She'll up sticks for good one day."

"It's Cornwall not Antarctica. And you're going down soon anyway. What were you doing at her age, huh? Travelling round India, and we had no idea where you were and Mum thought you were dead half the time."

Tim laughs, tops up his glass. "I know, I know. It's just I have this responsibility to Rosie. I promised I'd look after them. Anyway, what about you?"

"I'm going out to LA to see Nick for a bit."

"Jeez, why did you two ever get divorced?"

12

"More to the point why did we ever get married? He'll be back at the end of May. Let's all get together somewhere…Cornwall, Bath, London, wherever."

"That'll be good."

Tim hangs up the call, with a cold sliding feeling between his shoulders.

Frank answers the door to Verity's ring. He appears older than Caroline, and looks dishevelled as though he has been crawling around on the ground with the two boys.

"How do you do? I'm Frank." He offers his hand for her to shake and she follows him into the hall.

On a low table is a vast collection of rocks and crystals. Verity recognises amethyst, agate, rose quartz and turquoise, and there are other stones too, rougher darker chunks from the beach.

"These are beautiful." Her hand hovers over a spiky amethyst.

"The crystals are Caroline's. The boys and I have added a few rocks we've found. Serpentine, gneiss, and the like."

Verity is about to say something about Tim being a healer who uses crystals and Tarot cards, hypnosis and runes, but she holds back. Not everyone understands. Instead, she says, "My brother would love these. He's at uni doing geology."

"He's joining you soon, I hear?"

"Not sure. Tim is. Jack might not be able to take the time. But he did mention that there's some interesting geology down here."

Frank looks about to speak but Caroline comes out of the kitchen, a bright pink apron tied over her bump.

"Frank, introduce Verity to the boys, and fix her a drink. I won't be long."

13

"Of course, I'm sorry. Chardonnay OK? The kids are watching TV. Come on through."

The glass is cold as fluorite in Verity's hand as she follows him into the living room. Two small boys, one lanky and blond, the other dark with thick glasses, are watching *In the Night Garden*. Frank snaps the screen off.

"Dad. It was nearly over."

"Jonny, Andy, this is Verity. She's staying next door for a few weeks. Remember we went to sort out the house for her?"

"You live in the magic garden." Andy shoves at his specs.

"They play in Nick's garden," Frank explains.

"I'm not in the garden exactly," Verity says. "I'm in the house. You like the garden?"

"I like the pond," says Andy.

"Loads of places to hide."

"Will you play with us there?"

"You mustn't bother Verity. She's here for a holiday."

"We can show her the pond," Andy suggests.

"Have you got a pond too?"

"Daddy says we can't have a pond."

"Or a dog." Jonny glares at Frank.

"There are fish in your pond," Andy tells Verity.

"Nah. The Loch Ness Monster."

"Bears too."

"Bears? In my garden?"

"Yes. Bears. That's why there's that stuff on the pond."

"The netting," Frank translates. "I told you, Andy, it's to keep herons and gulls out. Not bears."

"I saw a bear there once. Watch out for bears."

"OK troops," Caroline calls. "Time to eat."

14

Caroline settles the boys with plastic beakers of juice and mashes up the insides of their jacket potatoes with butter. Frank offers Verity an oval platter of cut chicken and refills her glass with wine.

"Now, have some salad." Caroline heaps leaves and cucumber onto the boys' plates, despite their grumbling. "And I want it all eaten up. Are you going to have some chicken?"

She suddenly feels exhausted and over-heated. She reaches behind to untie the apron. Her hair is sticking to her face and her underarms feel slippy with sweat.

Jonny and Andy were easy pregnancies, but this third one is wearing her out. She knows in her heart this will be her last child and at moments like this she is glad not to have to go through it all again.

"Am I right that you and Jack are twins?" she asks Verity, and gulps mineral water to cool down.

"We are. And born under Gemini."

"That's brilliant. Who's older?"

"Me. By a few minutes. I call him Little Brother if I want to annoy him."

"I do that too," Jonny says and pokes Andy. "Little Brother."

"You were talking about Jack doing geology before dinner," Frank says. "I was going to tell you about the earthquakes – well, tremors – we've been having."

"What, *here?*"

"Yes. On the cliff. It's to do with the fault line. You've seen that on the road?"

"No, you'll have to show me."

"It's a darker vein running through the road. I'll walk out with you when you go and show you. Where the Lizard serpentine meets the schist. The join runs though the cliff."

"I'll have to get some pictures for Jack."

Caroline watches Frank talking to Verity. She's a beautiful girl, with swinging dark hair and cool eyes – are they blue or grey? You are silly, she snaps silently to herself. He's only being friendly.

"You going to be here for Flora Day?" Frank asks.

Acid bubbles up Caroline's throat; she puts down her knife and takes a cold mouthful of water to ease the burn.

"Caroline's in the Hal an Tow, that's the mumming play. She's done it for years."

"What is it?"

"You must come," says Jonny, sliding a cucumber disc under the skin of his potato.

"It's the feast day in Helston," Caroline says, as her throat calms. "The Hal an Tow is the story of St Michael and the Devil. St Michael fought the Devil in Helston. There's also St George and the dragon, Robin Hood and so on. Good winning over evil. I'm Mary Moses, the Earth Mother Goddess figure."

Frank is swiping the calendar on his phone. "Three weeks yesterday. Hey, why don't you do it too? There are lots of extra parts."

"I don't know," Verity says.

But she does know. She will be in it, the Hal an Tow. She must be in it. The mummers are waiting for her to join them.

"The first rehearsal is on Thursday evening," Caroline is saying. "Come with me, if you like."

"You can keep an eye on her for me," Frank says, gesturing to Caroline. "I told her she shouldn't do it this year."

"I've done it for years. It's even more important that I do it now. Fertility; that's what it's all about."

"What could I be?" Verity asks.

"There are plenty of maidens and tree spirits and so on. Always room for another one."

Caroline watches Frank and Verity amble down the path to the gate. The street lights of Penzance sparkle amber across the bay. Just beyond the town Tater Dhu lighthouse pulses three times. Further out the single flash of Wolf Rock. Caroline can no longer see the two figures behind the tamarisk hedge. Frank will be pointing out the dark line in the bedrock; Verity will be bending down to see the change in the half-light.

Jonny and Andy are squabbling somewhere behind her. Caroline tugs the curtain across the front window and turns back to deal with her sons. A moment later Frank bounds in again, squeezes her to him.

"She seems OK. I hope she will do the Hal an Tow with you. You should be taking it easy. I know this time it's been harder." He rests his hand on her stomach and Caroline feels her tension ebb down into the ancient rocks beneath her feet. It's only the pregnancy spooking her. Or the earthquakes. Or something.

Verity lets herself into her garden, climbs the steps to the front door. Before she takes off her jacket, she goes down the back corridor, past the locked studio, to the end bedroom. She remembers seeing a framed geology map on the wall there; perhaps she will see the fault lines scratched into the earth.

The map seems out of place with the series of red and purple abstracts on the other walls. Verity stands in front of the plate glass. There's Mullion Island, that clover-shaped rock just offshore. She traces the cliff path from the island and harbour to where a dotted line bisects the cliff: the fault line. She notices an inset box in the blue expanse of the bay. Wolf Rock lighthouse, even further out, more remote, too remote for the scale of the map. That was the lighthouse she

17

saw flashing on the far horizon. Her eyes find the promontory and Carrag Luz, and the two bites in the cliff that mark the beaches at Polurrian below.

Something flickers in her peripheral vision and she spins round, but it's only her reflection in the long, mirrored wardrobe. She turns off the light, and walks down the passage to the hall. Through the glass front door, she sees a single white pulse from the lonely Wolf Rock lighthouse. She tugs down the blind at the door, closing off the night.

~

Jack throws his mobile down on the bed. Another message from Tim asking if he will be going to Cornwall in a few weeks' time. He'd like to see Verity – until he went to university, they'd rarely been apart – and Tim too, but he simply can't be arsed. He has work to do, an evening job in a bar, and he's recently met a girl at the gym he'd like to know better and ask out, and it's all too much effort to get on a train for Bath and then travel down with Tim in the car.

He picks up his phone and scrolls through pictures of Verity. They are both tall, but unalike in looks: she is dark and slender; he is fair and stocky. He wonders how she is getting on at the end of the world. It's a weird place to go really. Especially as she will be alone for several weeks. But Verity was never afraid of her own company. If she couldn't have Jack, she'd just as soon have no-one.

The phone rings suddenly and he jumps. Verity. Of course. He was thinking about her and she called.

"Hey. How are you?"

"Yeah, I'm fine. Listen. You'll like this. I'm living on a fault line."

"You what?"

"There's a fault line in the cliff. The neighbours have shown me. And there's more. They've been having earthquakes."

"What, in Mullion?"

18

"Yes, on this very cliff."

"Well, I haven't heard of any earthquakes."

"They're only little ones. So far. Anyway, thought you might like to know that if you were thinking of coming?"

"I didn't say I was," Jack starts. "I've got stuff up here to do. I don't know. OK. I might."

He hangs up, feeling like his own life is balanced on a fault line. He would like to see Verity, but it's a long way, and he doesn't want to walk out of his life just like that. And yet he feels a tiny twinge of unease imagining his sister, his other half, alone at the end of the world.

⁓

Verity hears the splash-splash of rain as it falls on the uneven path outside her bedroom. She rolls over to see the clock. It's just after eleven. She's slept for over ten hours, and she feels heavy and groggy.

By the time she has showered and dressed, the rain has stopped. The sky over the bay has lightened. She unlocks the front door and pads out onto the step. The garden is vibrant with the scent of the rain. Water beads hang off the ends of leaves like ripe fruit, before falling, so quickly, yet so slowly as though freeze-framed, to the sticky black earth below. Verity smells the loam, the perfume of the rain.

Across the bay, the Land's End peninsula is a deft watercolourist's mark, dark lavender, almost translucent. Verity shades her eyes, scans the horizon. There is it, a tiny hair, an eyelash: Wolf Rock lighthouse. She steps onto the lawn. Wet grass darkens the hems of her jeans, soaks through her slippers. It feels like she's wading across the grass to the flower bed. Snails are out, on leaves and longer grasses, shells curled like complicated sweets. At the edge of the lawn she stops, gazing out across the huge vacuum of the bay. It feels like she could be sucked in, swallowed, devoured.

The horizon has blurred. She can no longer define the delicate brushstroke of Wolf Rock. A rhombus of steely mauve marks the shape of rain coming in. Verity turns her back on the bay, the snails, the rain, and pads back to the house.

~

Later that afternoon, Verity is walking back from the village shops with two bags of groceries. She wishes she'd taken the car, as the plastic handles are cutting into her palms.

The road crests before she reaches the hotel, and the blue-mauve bowl of the bay opens below. She hears the sound of a car engine coming up behind her.

"Verity," Caroline calls through the open window. "Hop in. I'll give you a lift."

"OK thanks." She squeezes her shopping into the footwell beside Caroline's woven tote bag, and finds a corner for her feet. "Hi Jonny, hi Andy," she says to the two in the back.

Jonny is wearing a school uniform jumper and has a backpack on his knees.

"We've just been to collect Jonny from school," Caroline explains.

"You like school, Jonny?"

"S'all right. Sometimes."

"Yes, you do," his mother says. "I've tried to get Andy into nursery so he can get to know the other kids before September but he gets so upset. I can't do it. Jonny loved it, but Andy's...I don't know. Andy."

"Can we play in your garden?" Andy asks as they pull up outside Caroline's garage.

"Of course, you can some time. If you mum agrees."

"Can we do it now?" Jonny unclips his seat belt.

"I can show you the bears."

"There aren't any bears, Andy. Sorry Verity."

20

"Please."

"All right," Verity concedes. "Come round for a bit now, and your mum and I can have a cup of tea while you explore."

The boys run on ahead over the fault line. Verity gathers her bags once more and Caroline rings Frank at home to tell him where they are.

"He's got a bit of time off now." She drops her phone back into her tote bag. "He's just set up the new computer system at the university, so he deserves a break."

The boys are racing up and down the grassy bank on Verity's front lawn.

"Can we go round the back now?" Jonny asks Caroline.

"No, you stay where we can see you from the front window."

Jonny groans and shoves Andy who staggers down the slope.

"Too much in the back," Caroline whispers to Verity.

Verity agrees. The steps to the upper lawn are cut into the stone wall, little more than a stile. There is a pond, and a huge copse of bamboo. Plenty of hiding places for small boys. Too many.

"They've made a way through from our garden," Caroline says as Verity shoves her meat and salad into the fridge. "I'll tell them to leave you alone."

"It doesn't matter. As long as you know where they are. You go on. I'll bring your tea."

When she carries the two mugs into the front room Caroline is tapping on the glass and gesturing to the boys not to trample on the flower beds.

"D'you know what you're having?"

"Not officially, but I think it's a girl. This is my last. No more after this one. It hasn't been so easy this time round."

"The whole thing seems terrifying to me," Verity says.

21

"Ah, the boys were easy. This little one…I've felt so tired, and jumpy too for no reason. Everything is fine with the baby. She's always moving and that. It's me not her."

Jonny and Andy have stopped running. They're both hunched over the edge of the flowerbed where Verity stood earlier watching the snails, and the rainwater dripping off the leaves.

A loud squeak from Andy.

"What have they found now?" Caroline sighs and hauls herself up.

"Probably a snail. There were lots this morning."

Andy scrambles up the bank to the window. He's crying behind his glasses. Caroline starts for the front door. Verity follows, a sudden fluttering in her chest. When she steps out onto the lawn Caroline and the boys are all by the flowerbed. Caroline has her arm round Andy.

"What is it?" Verity goes over to them.

"A rabbit," Caroline says. "A dead rabbit."

"What's happened to it?"

"I don't know. Hawk maybe or cat."

"He's dead," Andy wails.

Verity looks over Jonny's shoulder. The rabbit is on its side in the dark damp earth under a rose bush, with its ears still pricked up. There's a crimson gash in its side, blood smeared on its fur. She can see one eye: cloudy, half-closed.

"We can't leave him here," says Jonny.

"I'll deal with it." Verity doesn't even know if Nick has a shovel she can dig a grave with. There isn't a shed; maybe the tools are kept in the locked garage. Frank does the mowing; he and Caroline should know.

"It's the circle of life," Caroline says to the boys. "Creatures are born, and live, and die. Sometimes people kill them for meat, sometimes other animals kill them. It's just how it is. Come on. Let me get my stuff and I'll take you home." She spins the boys round towards the door.

"It might be here," Andy says.

"What might?"

"What killed it."

"Perhaps it was a bear," Jonny mocks.

"Of course, it's not. Don't go giving yourselves the heebie-jeebies." She turns to Verity says quickly, "I'll take them home to Frank and come back with a spade, OK?"

When they leave Verity collects the mugs from the living room and takes them back to the dishwasher. The rest of her shopping is spilling out of the bags on the kitchen floor. She sorts out fruit, chocolate, pasta sauce, a packet of rice and a bottle of Merlot. There's a rap on the front door.

"What have you done with it?" Caroline is holding a muddy spade. The sky has clouded over.

"Nothing. I was in the kitchen."

"It's gone."

"It can't have."

Verity follows Caroline to the flower bed. A couple of raindrops catch her face.

"It was there, by that bush."

"It was." Caroline shoves the spade into the earth, gazes round their feet. "Well, it couldn't have got up and run off."

"I guess whatever killed it came back for it. Perhaps the boys frightened it off."

"I suppose."

Verity touches the earth with the toe of her shoe. It's dark from the recent rain, but it doesn't look bloody. There's no fur, no disturbance. It's as though the rabbit had never lain there.

23

Later, alone again, Verity puts on her jacket and ventures back into the garden. She walks slowly along the lawn edge, looking out for any scuff marks or blood, but still there is nothing. If she and Caroline had not seen the rabbit themselves, she would have dismissed it as Andy's imagination, or a trick of Jonny's.

The Land's End peninsula is bruised with cloud. A distant growl rumbles round the bay. Verity jumps at the thought of an earthquake; a second later she realises it's only thunder. The sea is steely and choppy; waves are curling and breaking offshore. In her peripheral vision she sees a flicker of lightning. She glances up to Carrag Luz, hunched on the cliff edge, its boulders strangely pale in the afternoon storm. She walks back up the slope to the front door, closing and locking it with relief, spooked in the garden, by more than the thunder. Something just isn't right. Dead animals don't vanish into nothing in a matter of minutes.

She strokes the extra key on the fob. The key she thinks Caroline forgot to remove.

The studio is large with French windows leading to the veranda. Roman blinds are pulled close, letting just a faint light in from the garden. The air is stale. A huge canvas is shrouded in a sheet against the side wall; others are propped face-in against each other. Two easels are pushed together, legs interlocking. In the corner there's a stained sink, with shelves beside it where Nick keeps his brushes and jars. Large pots of acrylic paint are aligned like rainbow chessmen underneath. The wooden floor is splattered and specked with colours, and even one blue footprint.

The door sighs behind Verity. She reaches out a hand to stop it closing. She's being stupid, because she has the key in her hand but even so she shoves a stool against it to prop it open. A brighter flash of lightning comes through the narrow slits of the blinds and, a few seconds later, the answering growl follows.

The shrouded painting might be what Nick was last working on. How long ago was that? Tentatively she approaches the canvas and reaches up to remove the sheeting. It falls, fluttering round her feet, revealing a massive block of white. Verity gasps, steps back. It's not a block of white, she realises, it's many whites: cream-whites, icy blue-whites, even dirty snow-whites, all layered on thickly, erratically. She gazes at it, waiting for something to emerge. There's something there, she's sure, but she can't see it.

The next roll of thunder is further away. Verity drapes the sheet over the huge white painting, and backs out of the studio.

Tim wakes, lies still, lets the familiar city sounds calm his pulse. It's quiet outside tonight, this morning: only a couple of distant cars, no ambulance, no drunks.

It's just gone three.

His whole body aches, as though he's been in a fight. He remembers no visual images from his dream, just a sense of – what exactly? Fear yes, but something else too, something nearer awe, and an adrenaline rush. The muscles in his left arm and shoulder ache, like when he took up squash again after many years. His right hand is stiff and tight. It feels like he's been holding something, wielding something. A flash of deep memory, atavistic memory, sparks and dies in his mind

He turns uncomfortably on his pillow and, in the half-light, sees a pale scattering of cards on the carpet. Very quietly, as though afraid to disturb someone, something, he sits and lowers his feet to the floor. The pain in his arms forgotten, he reaches down to the four cards.

The Moon.

The Fool.

The Magician.

The Devil.

They are cool in his hands, these cards. He holds them loosely, and checks the bedside table. No, he did not bring a Tarot pack to the bedroom. These four cards – the same ones that spilled on the shop floor – have appeared by themselves. Tim hunkers down under the cover again, acutely aware of the cards just inches from him. His eyes drift shut and he relaxes his aching arms. Suddenly he jolts awake. There is one more card on the floor, by his door. He can't reach this one from the bed. He pads across the rag rug and scoops up the final card.

The Empress.

Tim stands with the card in his hand, his thoughts blurred. How does the Empress fit in with the others? She is a fertile woman, who represents the cycle of life and death and rebirth.

Tim can't find the connection between the five cards. He drops the Empress on top of the others, rolls his aching shoulders, and gets back into bed. He imagines he will not sleep, as neurons fire ideas around his brain, but he does, and when he wakes in the morning, there are no cards beside his bed.

~

"Got your dancing shoes on?" Caroline asks.

Verity glances down at her faded pink Converse boots. "I'm really not much of a dancer…"

"You don't have to be." Caroline unlocks the Peugeot. "It's not difficult. Really."

"Tell me more about it so I don't sound stupid," Verity says, as they bounce along the cliff road to the junction by the hotel.

"St Michael fought the Devil in Helston," Caroline says. "The Hal an Tow celebrates his victory. There's also St George and the Dragon, Robin Hood and Maid Marian…all the legends where good defeats evil."

"And this is done at dawn, you say?"

"Not exactly. Half eight on Flora Day morning. We do it in seven locations round the town."

"I tried to Google it today," Verity says. "But the internet jammed."

"Don't Google it. It's much better to experience the Flora yourself like this."

The Community Hall echoes with voices and laughter when they arrive. It's chilly inside, and smells like a school changing room.

Caroline takes Verity's wrist and drags her into the throng. People break off their conversations to greet Caroline. Two men are mock fighting with lances. There's a group of girls, Verity's age more or less, in the corner, and Caroline steers her to join them.

"Hi girls," she says. "This is my friend, Verity. She's new this year. Can I leave her with you?"

A couple of the girls know Caroline; one asks after Frank and the boys, the pregnancy. Others continue their own conversations. Verity leans against the wall, knowing she looks as awkward as she feels. She wishes she hadn't come.

Someone bangs a drum, and yells for quiet. Verity looks round the circle for Caroline. She's with a huddle of other women. The men have dropped their spears. The dancers face each other across the arena, and suddenly Verity can feel the expectation crackling in the air with the buzzing from the strip light overhead.

~

"So?" Caroline asks when they have said their goodbyes and are walking back to the car.

"Kind of amazing," Verity says, jangling her tambourine. "Costumes next time. I suppose you know what you're wearing?"

27

"Luckily it's a fairly shapeless gown," Caroline laughs. "If yours needs any altering or mending, I can give you a hand with it. Some of them are fairly shabby."

Verity gets into the car with the tambourine on her knees and Caroline quickly calls Frank to tell him they are leaving Helston.

"Something I thought was a bit odd..." Verity starts, as Caroline fires the ignition. "The Devil. That guy who played the Devil..." She hesitates, trying to remember if the portly, shambling man was a friend of Caroline's. "He didn't seem right for that part."

"Ah, he won't be playing the Devil on the day. We never know who the Devil is. They always have somebody else, anybody, doing it at the meetings. That's part of the Hal an Tow."

"No-one knows who the Devil's going to be? Not even St Michael?"

"Well, obviously some of them know who it is. I guess he might be one of them. Archangels' privileges."

It's getting dark now. Verity falls silent, thinking back over the Hal an Tow meeting, how, once the dance began, the girls standing beside her stopped talking to each other, and welcomed her into their circle, and how, as the evening drew on, and the twilight fell, the dancers were reflected in the uncurtained windows, like distorted transfers on the glass.

"Did you ever find that rabbit?" Caroline asks suddenly.

"No. Something must have taken it away. Is Andy all right about it now?"

"I think so," Caroline says. "Andy's an imaginative kid, and he has such poor vision. I did explain to him again about the circle of life, and all that, but I do worry that he frightens himself sometimes."

"Like the bears, you mean?"

"Yes, he probably saw something in the undergrowth, or a shadow, and thought it was a bear."

Across Mount's Bay, Penzance is a hazy blur of street lamps. Verity finds the lighthouse she saw before: three white pulses. Then, far out to sea, comes the bright flash of Wolf Rock.

Caroline brakes, and goes down to second to take the sharp left onto the cliff road. The car bounces on the rocky track, and Verity's tambourine jangles again. The road curves, and there is Carrag Luz, pale, almost glowing, against the twilight sky. Wolf Rock flares again. A gull swoops low over the cliff, ghostly, silent.

The car judders, scrapes, drags along the stones.

Have you got a puncture? Verity is about to say, when the car stalls. The ground grates beneath the tyres and Caroline's headlights dip and waver. Then all is still.

"It's an earthquake," Verity says.

"Yes."

Caroline opens the driver's door. Verity can hear the angry surge of the sea below. Caroline walks a few feet along the road in the pale spill of her headlamps. Verity gets out too, still holding the tambourine.

"Shall I walk ahead of you?" she offers.

"I think it's OK. Let's just get home." Caroline starts the car, and stalls once more. "Stupid woman," she mutters to herself, firing it again, flicking on main beam which washes Carrag Luz in cold blue.

Something moves in the undergrowth – a rabbit or shrew – and Verity jumps.

"They're nothing really," Caroline says as she parks. "Nothing at all compared to what people get in other countries. We don't even have any damage. They're only tremors."

"What about the sea?" Verity asks. "D'you think there could be a tsunami?"

"It would need to be much bigger than that," Caroline says. "That was just like the others we've had, but I was a bit spooked because I was driving."

Verity says goodnight to Caroline and walks the few yards to her own gate. She pauses again at the fault line, that thick mottled vein in the earth's flesh. It must be the source of the earth tremors. She jumps over it quickly, stops, turns. Back across the fault is the lit crescent of bungalows, and the bright windows of the Polurrian Hotel. Where she stands is her own darkened house and Carrag Luz. She is separated from the rest of Mullion by the fault, by geology. Quickly she runs up to her door and into the hall, snapping on the light as she goes.

Frank has put the boys to bed, but they're wide awake because of the earthquake. Caroline stays in their room, until she judges them to be asleep. She tiptoes out of the bedroom. Frank is in his office. Caroline stops in the doorway to ask him if he'd like a tea or a glass of wine.

"What you looking at?"

He glances up from his laptop.

"I was Googling earthquakes. I don't like it. We shouldn't be having this many, so close together. And yet it seems no-one's heard of our earthquakes. There's only one mention on the local BBC site."

"Perhaps they're so localised we only feel them on this cliff," she suggests.

"If the epicentre's the fault line, surely it would radiate out at least to the village?"

"I don't know," she says. "They can't be very powerful. There's been no damage. The cliffs haven't subsided anymore."

"It's still a weak cliff."

"Cup of tea?" Caroline asks, not wanting to dwell on the earth tremors. "Glass of wine?"

"Wine would be great."

Caroline goes into the kitchen and pours a glass of red for Frank and makes a tea for herself. Frank takes his drink into the living room, and she hears the sounds of him changing channels: a few bars of ABBA, gunfire, applause, some boring guy droning on.

Tim has been out for a few drinks with friends in Bath. He's only had a couple of whiskies, before changing to mineral water, and he's left because too many of the others were getting drunk and boring. He moves swiftly through the city's nocturnal cast: the girls hobbling on high heels, the young men shouting, the crusties and beggars, and the loners like himself. His mobile rings in his pocket.

"Tim, it's me."

"Jack. How are you? You heard from Verity?"

"Yeah. She seems fine. She tell you about the earthquakes?"

Tim stops. A taxi groans by with a grind of gears. He feels dizzy suddenly, disorientated, his shoulders ache once more for no reason.

"Tim?"

"Uh. No. What earthquakes?"

Tim knows, in that instant, that these earthquakes are important, crucial, dangerous. He closes his eyes as Jack goes on about a geological fault and earth tremors, and a peacock feather's eye flashes behind his closed lids.

"Are you coming down with me?" he interrupts Jack. "I understand she's doing the dance in Helston. Why don't we go down for that? Can you get back to Bath by then?"

"I'll see what I can do," Jack says at last.

Tim knows Jack isn't enthusiastic. He wants to bark at him *Verity needs you. She needs both of us* but he is unsure where that thought came from, and the words alone will not be enough for Jack.

31

It's something about the bay. Verity gazes for hours out of the huge front window, watching the swell of the sea and the rain systems.

On Saturday morning she calls Tim, who has left her several messages. She feels bad as she hits his name in her contacts.

"I'm coming down for Flora Day," Tim tells her. She can hear the breath of panpipes playing on the stereo in Cosmos.

She bites back an impatient retort. There's no discernible reason why she doesn't want him and Jack coming, just that two men in the house will be noisy and bossy and will try to drag her away from her window vigil.

"What about Jack?" she asks, hearing the wariness in her voice. "Is he coming?"

"I hope so. He'll let me know nearer the time. Sorry, I have to go. There's an order just arriving."

That afternoon Verity walks up to Carrag Luz.

She swishes through the long grasses to the crag. In the sunlight she can pick out the dark and light flecks in the serpentine, the saffron-gold and khakis of the mosses and lichens. She settles on the ledge where she sat before. The stone is warm from the sun. On Polurrian beach, the sea is peeling back across the sand, leaving a shimmering wet film. Shouts carry up from the cove to where she sits. She watches people running into the water shrieking, a kid digging in the soft sand. Waves suck at the promontory separating the beaches. The smaller, tidal cove is still cut off by the sea.

It's just gone high tide, Verity thinks. I could walk down tomorrow morning, and it would be low tide. I could walk round to the second beach, stand under Carrag Luz, look up to its raw twisted face.

When she gets back to the bungalow, she pads along to Nick's studio, key in hand. It's a warm sunny afternoon. This time she'll open the Roman blinds, let some light in. There's nothing to spook her in the studio, but she finds that she's holding her breath as she opens the door, as though she's expecting something to leap out of the shadows.

Inside, she tweaks the blinds' cords, and sunlight slices into the room. She unwraps the white painting once more. She's never realised the depths and differences of whites before. It's a white painting, but she can see a whole spectrum in it. There's a curve in the foreground and to the right. It looks familiar. She steps backwards towards the windows. It could almost be the bay, the view from the front of the house. The whole bay painted in whites.

What made Nick do that?

She could understand nuances of blue, green and mauve – the colours of the cliff – or the dark steels and purples of a storm making landfall on the cliff, but she cannot think what the white might represent.

She drapes the painting again, and gently pulls out one of the canvasses propped against the wall. There's writing on the back in dark blue paint: *Carrag Luz*. Verity slides it out, turns it to face her. It's not abstract, but distorted. The rocks are painted as though Nick had positioned his easel on the cliff path by the fault line, depicted with almost careless slashes of grey, white and blue.

Why hasn't Nick hung this painting in this house?

She's distracted by a buzzing from the window. It's a fly. She must have disturbed it when she opened the blinds.

The French windows open onto the stone veranda above the lawn. There's a key in the lock. She opens the doors wide. Behind her the studio door slams, and she jumps. She steps out onto the veranda. There's something there at the far end: brown-grey and red. Fur and blood.

It's the rabbit's corpse.

33

Verity recoils. She doesn't want to go near it, and certainly doesn't want to touch it. It will be decaying, writhing with maggots; it will smell. She doesn't want to ask Caroline for help either. She glances down to the flower bed, to the rose bush, where Andy first found the rabbit's lifeless body. She'll have to find some kind of spade, or wrap her hands in newspaper or something. She looks back down the veranda, and there's nothing there. No twitching fur, no smear of blood on the stone.

Verity turns again, surveys the garden, as though someone's hiding there with the dead rabbit in his arms. That's ridiculous, she scolds herself, and takes a step towards the end of the veranda.

Something thuds and she spins round. The garden gate has swung back into the shrubby wall.

I know I shut it, Verity thinks.

It's not that windy. The catch must be faulty. Unless someone's just escaped from the garden. Verity looks back along the veranda. The stone is still clean; there's not a trace of anything. She scrambles down onto the lawn, and slides down the grassy slope to the gate. There's no-one on the cliff path. She checks both ways.

Jonny and Andy, she thinks, retracing her steps into the garden. They must have come into the garden, and run away, meaning to spook her. But they wouldn't touch the rabbit. Andy wouldn't go anywhere near it.

She goes into the studio through the French windows, locks them behind her, and tests the handles. Then she lets herself onto the corridor, and locks the studio. As she walks down to her bedroom, she can't help glancing over her shoulder.

~

Verity wakes early on Sunday. She's had an uneasy night, though she can't recall her dreams at all.

34

Half an hour later and she's on the cliff path. The scent of wild garlic rises from the fuzzy white flowers in the verges. There are blue-bells too, soft and denim-coloured. It seems overnight the flowers have bloomed and multiplied. When she turns back to look at Carrag Luz, she sees the flank of cliff beside it is bruised mauve with bluebells.

The cove is fully exposed, the sea far out. On the right are slabs of black rock, draped with seaweed streamers. But it's not that side of the beach that interests Verity. She pulls off her boots and socks, lets the soft sand between her toes. As she nears the headland the sand becomes wetter and firmer. There are shells – creamy scallops, tiny pink butterflies – and black, white and sepia pebbles. The lower crags of the headland are knobbled with barnacles. Verity walks towards the very end of the promontory. The sea is nearer now, but still, she can see right round into the further bay and, beyond that, to Mullion Island. She feels vulnerable walking round the edge of the rocks.

The second bay is much smaller, narrower, less friendly. There are dark boulders jutting up from the sand. Verity raises her eyes to the cliff where the bare rock blends into grass, to the frail wire fence at the very top. Very slowly she turns her head to Carrag Luz. She's ready for its twisted ragged face, but it still makes her start.

At the water's edge she rolls up her jeans and runs into the shallows, gasping and hopping with the cold. Unconsciously, she starts walking back through the water back to the main beach. There are people there; Verity is no longer alone. The water feels warmer here and she stops, wades out a few feet, until she can feel her rolled-up jeans getting wet. She feels she has stood here, in the frothing water, before. Something half-remembered.

Tim backs down the step ladder. Over his head the new metal chimes toll with a gentle boom. He reaches for the paddle and silences them.

The noise unnerves him. He hesitates a moment, wonders whether to climb up again and remove them.

No, he is being stupid, letting metal tubes spook him.

It is more than that.

Tim folds the step ladder and returns it behind the desk. The tea light glowing in an amethyst holder suddenly puffs out. Tim glances sharply to the door in case it has blown open. It is closed, but suddenly the new chimes, those long deep metal tubes, resonate against each other as though an unseen wind were swirling through the shop.

He snaps his lighter at the blackened wick of the candle, and a tiny flame glows. The chimes still, and he can only hear the gentle background music. His soaring heart calms behind his sternum.

Call me, Verity, he urges silently. But he does not have the twins' connection she shares with Jack, and his phone remains silent.

He sells crystals and a CD, some candles and prayer flags, and still he has not heard from her, so he flicks the door sign to *closed* and calls her. He is almost surprised when she answers.

"How are you?" he starts. "I was worried about you."

"Don't worry about me," she says, but he doesn't sense any warmth in her voice, it seems more of a warning.

"What are you up to?"

"Oh. This and that. Beach. Walking on the cliffs. Chilling out. Taking it easy."

Tim wants to ask her to stay in touch before he hangs up but it goes against everything he has taught the twins over the years. A young guy is peering through the shop door. Tim waves and strides over to open up. As he opens the door wide for his customer he winces at the sharp pain in his arm once more. That is part of it. He just can't explain how or what.

~

36

Verity is barely aware of the days drifting by. She walks on the cliff, disturbing the insects amongst the bluebells, or scrambles down to the beach where the sand is cool and soft underfoot, and the brutal face of Carrag Luz looms overhead. She curls in the window seat watching the hazy horizon and the white sails of yachts in the bay.

One afternoon she is dozing there, half-conscious; she jumps awake at a loud thumping on the door. Voices. Her name: *Verity*. More thumping. A young voice saying *her car's there*.

She shoves her feet into her slippers and runs to the hall. Yes, it's Jonny and Andy on her doorstep. She gulps down a surge of relief but, as she opens the door, she sees tears behind Andy's glasses.

"What's up, boys?" she starts.

"I told you she was here." Jonny pokes Andy.

Andy wails.

"Why are you crying, Andy? Is your Mum OK?"

Premature labour, waters breaking, sudden bleeding, no ambulances; Verity panics for a moment thinking of all the possibilities.

"The bears are here," Andy says.

"Hey, Andy." Verity crouches down, puts an arm round him. "There aren't bears here anymore. Really."

"The bears have killed them."

"Killed what?" Verity straightens, senses a prickling of fear, remembers the rabbit.

"The fish," Jonny explains.

"They might kill *you*," Andy says.

"Where's your Mum?"

"At home," Jonny says. "We came into your garden. We've got a secret way through. I can't show you because it's secret."

"No," Verity agrees. "You couldn't do that."

"The bears –"

"We'll show you the fish," Jonny offers.

37

"OK, you show me." Verity closes the door and follows the boys round the side of the house.

It's shadowy here and she shivers in her T-shirt. When they come out into the back courtyard Jonny runs up the stone steps to the upper lawn.

"I don't want to go up there," Andy says.

Verity glances up to where Jonny stands by the pond.

"All right, Andy. You stay here. Stay right here."

Verity scrambles up to Jonny.

"There, look."

Verity looks.

There are dead fish: four – no, five – of them. Their bright tangerine bodies look obscene on the stubbly grass.

"It's not bears," Jonny says.

"No, it can't be bears. It must be birds. Gulls or herons."

"How?"

"How?" Verity repeats.

"How'd they get them?" Jonny points. "The net's there."

He's right. The protective net is intact over the pond and weeds.

"There...there must be a hole or something."

"Come on!" Andy cries from below.

"We're coming, Andy. There must a tear, just enough to get a beak in."

"So why hasn't it eaten them?"

Verity stops, turns back to the nearest fish. It's perfect: there are no beak or claw marks on its scaly body.

"I don't know," she says at last.

"Come *on!*"

"OK, Andy."

She and Jonny run down the steps and join Andy on the paved terrace.

"I don't know what killed the fish," Verity says to Andy. "Let's get you both home now. Your Mum will be wondering what's happened to you."

As she says this, she hears Caroline over the wall shouting for the boys, her voice rising when they don't answer her.

"Caroline," Verity shouts. "They're here with me. I'm just bringing them back."

"We can go back the secret way," Jonny says.

"I think we should go the normal way," Verity says. "I want to know you get home OK."

"It's quicker our way," Jonny says.

Andy pulls himself away from Verity and dives under the shrubbery.

"Andy," Jonny grumbles, following him. "You've ruined the secret."

Andy mumbles something, then calls for his mother.

"Jonny, Andy," Caroline says in the neighbouring garden. "What were you thinking of – Andy, what's the matter?"

Verity walks slowly round her bungalow to the front door. She can hear Andy squeaking about bears, then Caroline's reassuring metronome. Suddenly she stops. No doubt Caroline will be round in a moment, wanting to know what frightened Andy, wanting to see the dead fish. Verity spins round, and runs round the back of the bungalow and up to the higher lawn. The neon corpses have vanished. She walks up to the edge of the pond. The netting is intact. There's a pointed water snail on the edge of the brick-work. As she stands there, there's a bright orange-red flash in the dark water.

This is ridiculous. As soon as Andy left, the dead rabbit disappeared, and now *this*. What was it Caroline said about Andy's vision and imagination?

He can't be imagining these things, Verity thinks. *I've seen them too; so has Jonny. Caroline saw the rabbit.*

Verity trails across the upper lawn towards the bamboo plantation. Suddenly she's apprehensive to go behind it, to let it obscure her view of the house.

Don't be so stupid, she tells herself, and quickly walks behind the tall spiky shoots.

The very top of the garden runs up to a dilapidated stone wall. There's nothing there, not that she's sure what she was expecting to find. She walks down the grassy slope at the opposite side of the garden back to the terrace.

But what about the rabbit on the veranda? Andy wasn't here then. She glances down the courtyard. With no effort at all, she can imagine the dead rabbit beside the kitchen door. *But, of course, it is not there. I must have imagined it on the veranda,* she thinks silently. *I was spooked, and I thought I saw the rabbit, but there was never anything there.*

She is surprised that Caroline doesn't call round or ring up to find out what happened in the garden, and relieved as she doesn't know what to say. There were dead fish – she saw them, and so did the boys – but only moments later they had disappeared back into the water, leaving no sign on the grass.

~

Thursday night, and the next Hal an Tow meeting.

Verity's driving this time. They have only just turned right off the cliff road when Caroline says it.

"What happened at yours the other day? Andy was so upset. Jonny said your fish were dead."

"Yes, two of the fish had somehow got out of the pond," Verity starts. If she denies everything it's disloyal to the boys. "I've got rid of them."

"That's a shame. Do you need new netting?"

"No, it's OK. There was just a small hole, and I think I've fixed it."

"Jonny said there was no hole. He couldn't understand how the fish had jumped out or been caught."

"The hole was at the other end. We didn't look too closely because Andy was so upset."

"You're not having much luck with the wildlife, are you?" Caroline says.

Verity and the other flower girls crowd into the costume store. Verity's still holding her tambourine, and it jingles softly at her side. The room is stuffy and windowless, and the racks of clothes smell musty like a charity shop. One of the Hal an Tow organisers is handing over long pastel gowns to the girls in front. When it's Verity's turn the woman unhooks a long yellow and green dress and shoves it into her arms. Verity is surprised at how heavy the gown is. She squeezes out of the costume store to the main hall, where the dancers are still milling and talking.

It's dark outside the windows. Robin Hood calls a goodnight to everyone and strides out of the hall, followed by two Merry Men and the violinist. Caroline's talking animatedly to St Michael, who has propped up a peacock-blue and silver shield against the wall.

Verity finds a space and unfurls the material in her arms. The gown has a bodice of dark green, with a full golden skirt and short capped sleeves of pale yellow. It smells stale. It needs a good wash straight away. She holds it against herself. It should fit.

Two of the other girls come over to Verity to compare costumes. One has been given a gown of pink flowers, the other lavender and cream.

41

The girl with the flowered dress is stretching the waist, muttering "It'll never bloody fit."

Seeing Caroline kiss goodbye to St Michael, Verity peels away from the other girls. Caroline's holding her own long green dress. The mummers wish them goodnight, and they step out into the twilight. Verity's pale dress seems to glow with its own translucence.

"Do we wear our costumes next week?" she asks Caroline.

"Oh no," Caroline says. "No costumes until the day."

"And no real Devil?"

"And no real Devil."

The light, the light. The light is all around Verity, and no matter how much she screws up her eyes she cannot escape from it.

Verity opens her eyes, and still the light is there. She closes them and the lids burn red and stinging. Something is not right. This time she opens her eyes slowly. The bedroom light is on: the central ceiling light. She checks the clock. Almost three in the morning. Her heart rate quickens. When she goes to bed, she doesn't put the main light on, only the bedside lamp. She fancies she can hear the electrical buzzing of the bulb, then a fly blunders towards her, woken by the light, as she is.

She swings her legs out of bed, pads barefoot, as quietly as she can, to the door. The hall is in darkness; so is the living room. The fly whines past her ear. She hesitates, her hand on the bedroom light switch. The brightness has frightened her, but will the dark frighten her more? She presses down, catching her breath.

The bulb expires.

So, the switch works. She knows she did not turn on that light earlier. Did she walk across the room in her sleep and turn it on? She

42

still hears the drone of the fly for some moments until it settles somewhere waiting for daybreak. She does not sleep for a long while.

By Friday evening Verity's dress has almost dried. She'd put it in the washing machine, crossing her fingers that the green wouldn't bleed into the yellow. Wet, it was even heavier. She dragged the clothes horse into the back courtyard and hung it out in the sun to dry.

It's still cool and a little damp, as she carries it inside before the snails come out. She goes into her bedroom, snaps on the lights. Immediately she recalls standing there in the early hours, her breath in her throat, her hand on the switch, afraid of the light and afraid of the dark.

She takes off her clothes and pulls the dress over her head. The cool material on her skin brings up sudden gooseflesh. She tugs down the heavy skirt. Only when she has fastened the zip and tied the yellow sash behind her does she raise her eyes to the mirror.

"*Robin Hood and Little John* –" she starts to sing, then stops, embarrassed in the empty room.

Quickly, she takes off the dress and puts on her own clothes. She felt charged, alive, wearing it: a feeling for the Hal an Tow, not for standing alone before a mirror. She slides the gown onto a hanger and hooks it on the front of the wardrobe.

When she goes to bed, she turns on both bedroom lights until she is ready to sleep. Then she pads across the room and turns off the ceiling light. She walks backwards to the bed. The bedside lamp is hot and bright on her face. She cannot sleep with it on. With a click she kills it.

In the darkness, the room feels airless as a tomb. Her Hal an Tow dress glows palely on the wardrobe, and for a second it makes her think of a body swaying gently on a gallows. She turns her back on the dress, and faces the side window, where green darkness glows at the curtains' edges.

Thunder.

Verity hears a lazy faraway growl through her dreams. A sudden bright flash of lightning. She shudders awake into the roar of more thunder. The lightning is relentless.

No, it's not lightning.

The bedroom light is on and the house is shaking. Verity is awake in an instant, flattened against the bed's headboard. The ceiling lampshade swings crazily from side to side. Verity's dress slides from its hanger and lands in a crescent of green and gold. There's another groan, a wild cry from the centre of the earth, and then quiet. Verity doesn't move. The lampshade still sways. A low thrummimg coming closer. It's the fly again, swooping round the room. At last Verity slides her feet into her slippers. There's a flicker behind the curtains.

There *is* lightning, as well as the earthquake.

She pulls aside the curtain. It's almost dawn. Abstractly she remembers it's the first of May, daybreak on Beltane. A crack of thunder closer this time. She drops the curtain, and faces the lit bedroom.

There must have been a power surge from the earthquake or from the storm. Somehow, instead of killing the electricity it's revived it. She turns back to the window, moves aside the curtain.

There are no lights on next door.

She goes to the door and opens it carefully, quietly. The hall light is on. So is the living room light. She pads into the hall, aware that the fly has followed her. Through the panes of the front door, she sees another pulse of lightning over the bay. She runs through the house. Every light is on. It has to be something to do with the earthquake. In the far bedroom she hesitates.

Something is wrong.

44

The geological map has fallen from the wall. Verity picks it up. It's heavy. She lays it across the bed. The lightning still flickers sporadically, but the thunder isn't coming any closer. The glass has cracked across Mullion. She traces the line with her finger, suddenly sees that the crack follows the fault line bisecting Polurrian Cliff.

It's early, ridiculously early, but Tim calls Jack anyway. It goes to voicemail.

"Jack, it's me," he begins, then hangs up. This is not a conversation for voicemail.

He walks unsteadily, clutching onto the walls, the doorframe. In the bathroom he slides open the sash window. It's so high up no-one can see in. He stands there naked, gulping the breeze, watching the early traffic. At last, he moves away and tugs the shower curtain along the bath. The rush of water fills his ears, his brain.

The pain through his body is receding. It no longer hurts to breathe, but he vividly recalls the violence of his dream, the way he was ripped apart as ferocious white light surged through his body.

When he is dressed, he checks his phone. Jack has not called back, but another half hour has gone by. This time Jack answers groggily.

"Bad night," Tim says.

"What – you or me?"

"Me. I'm dreaming again. It's agony, violent. I woke up in such pain."

"Sure you haven't been smoking something?"

"Jack. You know my dreams. You know what happened when Rosie died. The other times. You know I can see things, sense things. This is about Verity. I should never have let her go on her own."

"She's doing all right."

45

"The earthquakes," Tim shouts suddenly. "The earthquakes down there, the dream…it was like I was the earth being split apart…got to be something to do with the earthquakes."

"They're only tiny. Not even national news. Don't worry about it. Look, I'll message her in a bit, OK? Why don't you give her a call?"

"I bloody hope you're going to come down with me. I think I'm going to need you."

Jack hesitates. "I'll see what I can do," he says at last.

~

Verity is surprised to see that it's half past eight. She must have slept again. The bedroom looks normal. There are no lights on that should not be. Her Hal an Tow costume is still on the floor, exactly as it fell.

She gets out of bed, picks it up and slides it back onto its hanger. She follows her earlier footsteps to the far bedroom. There is the map where she left it on the bed, the crack in the glass. There doesn't seem to be any other damage indoors. No other pictures have fallen from the walls; somehow the washing up on the draining board is still there.

It's very strange.

She opens the back door and stands in the sunshine in the back courtyard. There are no fallen tiles, no broken glass, nothing.

She washes and dresses quickly, and is about to unlock the front door when her mobile rings in her bedroom. It's Tim.

"Tim. Hi."

"Is everything all right?"

"I think so," she says, then "Aren't you out celebrating Beltane?"

"Have you had any more earthquakes?" Tim says, ignoring her question.

"Why?"

"Have you?" he demands.

"I think there was one in the night," she improvises at last. "By the time I was properly awake it was over. There doesn't seem to be any damage."

"What time at night? Was it almost daylight?"

"Maybe. Why? What is all this?"

"I don't know," he says. "Just that I had this…. awful dream. I think it was about earthquakes, and I wanted to make sure you're OK."

"I'm OK."

No, I'm not OK, she thinks. Weird things are happening. Dead rabbits and fish. Lights coming on. I'm not all right. Why can't I tell him any of this? Because he'll insist I go home.

"I was thinking I might –" The line goes dead.

Verity checks her screen. No signal. She waves the phone over her head a few times, but no bars appear. At last, she drops the phone on the bedside cabinet.

~

"…Jack says he'll try to come with me. We'll come down on Friday for Flora Day. Verity? Are you there?"

Tim takes this phone from his ear. No signal. That's ridiculous. He never has a problem with signal in the attic flat.

~

Verity stops on the cliff path, takes a few steps towards the knotted thread of the fault line. It looks just the same. There is no gaping hole in the road, severing her from the rest of Mullion. The bluebells and wild garlic are undisturbed in the grassy verge. The car is fine. It has no flat tyres or cracked windows. If it weren't for the geological map and the electrical surge there would be nothing to show for the earthquake.

She leaves the fault and starts walking to Carrag Luz. Both boulders are still balanced on top of the crag. Verity cannot understand how the more precarious of the two is still there. Surely the vibrations would have sent it over?

The sunlight makes the horizon hazy, and she cannot discern Wolf Rock. The bay shimmers silver-blue. Beyond Carrag Luz she can see soft waves breaking on the outer skerries of Mullion Island. She scrambles onto the crag. The sea has flooded into the second beach, eddying round the black headland. A rabbit zigzags away down the cliff; for a second she remembers the dead rabbit and its unblinking eye. Then suddenly, as she leans over to watch the rabbit's scut disappearing into the bluebells, she sees a human below her on the steep grassy cliff above the sheer rock face.

The figure is lying in the bluebells and grasses that fall down to the sea. She can see long pale hair. She thinks it's a man, but she can't be sure from above. She grips the rock beside her, suddenly dizzy.

The man – if it is a man – does not seem to be aware of her standing on the crag above him. She hesitates. He might have fallen. He might be injured. He might be contemplating jumping into the shimmering blue void. Or he might simply be enjoying some quiet time on the cliff.

No. No-one would choose to lie on a slope like that.

Verity looks for a rabbit track, or any indication of how the man got there, but there is nothing. She's about to call out, afraid of startling him, when abruptly he stands, unfolding long limbs. He's wearing white: white jeans and a shirt. He gazes out across the bay, then turns to look up at Verity.

"I did not think I would be alone for long."

"I thought you were hurt," she says.

"Not hurt," he says, climbing swiftly through the grasses and bobbing bluebells. "Not anymore."

Verity stumbles back from the edge of the cliff. The man strides effortlessly up the cliff, and climbs onto the rocky shelf where she stood a moment ago. Only feet apart they face each other on the crag.

He looks young, about Verity's age. His hair is long and loose over his shoulders, bright as sunlight. In his white clothes he seems to glow against the blue of sea and sky. His skin is pale, and his eyes, cool and observant, are the silver-grey of granite. His feet are bare, unstained with grass or blood.

"You're not hurt, then?" Verity stammers, embarrassed under his even gaze. "I couldn't have climbed up the cliff like that."

"I know this cliff well."

"Do you live in Mullion?" Verity asks, stepping down to the grass, anxious to move away from the precipice.

"I have been away."

The wind lifts his hair, and it shimmers like a halo. Verity gazes up at him, on the rock. She should move right away from this isolated, dangerous crag, away from this strange man, but she cannot turn away from him.

"Why are you out on the cliff?" he asks.

"There was an earthquake in the night," Verity says. "I came to see what had happened to the cliff, if anything had changed."

"A lot has changed."

"It looks much the same." She gestures to Carrag Luz, the bluebells.

"It is very different below."

Verity says nothing. If he is trying to get her to follow his footsteps down the cliff face, she is not going to do it. She takes another step backwards from the crag, feels swaying grasses brush her legs.

"I should be going now," she says reluctantly, crazily wishing he would contradict her.

"Yes," he says. "And I am just going to stay here alone."

"Goodbye then," Verity says, looking one last time into his silver eyes. "Please be careful."

She starts walking away from him, feeling his gaze on her back.

"There is no danger. There will not be another earthquake."

Where the grass track joins the cliff path Verity turns back. The man raises one hand to her, then leaps further up Carrag Luz. Verity almost cries out, but he stands still on the very top of the crag, aflame with the sun on his hair.

She drags one foot after the other along the rutted cliff path. When she reaches her gate she stops, looks back to Carrag Luz.

The man has gone.

～

Verity has only been in the house a few moments. She's standing at the window, too restless to sit. There is no-one on Carrag Luz.

Did he jump? Surely someone would have seen him from the beach below?

She hurries back to the front door. She can be in the cove in ten minutes if she runs.

The stones of the cliff path hurt her feet through her thin soles.

I should never have left him there. I could have saved him, stopped him, stayed to talk to him, led him away from that crag.

She stumbles past a group walking down the cove path. Loose stones skid beneath her and she nearly loses her footing. At last, the path tumbles onto the beach. The valley stream sucks over the sand. The tide is high.

Down here, the sea is rougher than it appeared from above. Spray arcs over the headland. The second cove is completely flooded by the green-blue swell. Verity runs the few yards to the breakers. The rocks below Carrag Luz are black and shiny; water pours over them with each thrust of the ocean.

There is nothing white, no broken body.

"Stupid woman," she says aloud, but the sea crushes her words.

Of *course*, he didn't jump.

She is aware of her heart rate, the sweat under her clothes, and the blister on one foot from running. She is about to retrace her steps to the path, but instead she stops, looks above Carrag Luz's terrible face.

No, it cannot be.

She shades her eyes from the morning sun. There he is, tiny on the top of the rocks.

In that moment, Verity knows he is looking down into the cove, and that he has seen her.

Verity is exhausted by the time she reaches the Polurrian Hotel. Her foot is burning with the blister. She hobbles along the cliff road. Caroline is trying to settle the boys in the back of the car. Frank is standing on the seaward side of the road, gazing across the bay, talking on his mobile.

"There wasn't anyone, Andy, darling," Caroline says reassuringly.

"There was!" Andy wails as Caroline shuffles awkwardly out of the open back door.

"Hi," Verity says.

When she stops walking, she can feel a relentless pulse in her wounded foot.

"There was!" Andy cries again. "I saw him. He was all white."

"White?" Verity asks. "Who was all white?"

Caroline pulls a face. "Andy thinks he saw someone from his bedroom window very early this morning. He got spooked by the earthquake, that's all. You must have felt it? It was the worst yet."

"Yes," Verity says, but she hasn't been listening. "Maybe Andy did see someone. On the cliff path perhaps."

"He was in the garden," Andy shouts.

"Shut it, Andy." Jonny jabs Andy. "There wasn't anyone."

"Don't do that, Jonny. Oh, come on, Frank." Caroline scowls at Frank's back, moves towards him. He laughs, says yeah, that's it, that's it.

"If he was all white, that'd make him a ghost," Jonny says. "There's no such things as ghosts."

"Yes, there are, but he wasn't a ghost."

"What was he then? A snowman?" Jonny shrieks.

"He was like…"

Verity watches Andy's face through the open car door. He's screwing up his eyes behind his glasses, trying to find the word.

I know what he was like, Verity wants to say.

"An angel," Andy says at last.

"An angel," Verity whispers.

"Angels have wings, stupid."

"Not all the time," Andy says.

"Sorry, sorry," Frank says. "Hi, Verity."

"We must go," Caroline says. "We're going to Sainsbury's."

Verity says goodbye, takes a few painful steps towards the fault line.

"You hurt your foot?" Frank calls after her.

"It's nothing," she calls back.

"You'd better be all right for the Hal an Tow," he says. "This time next week it'll all be over."

All be over. Frank's words seem so desolate. Verity crosses the fault line. There is no-one standing on Carrag Luz. She can hear the car growling away down the road. Her garden gate is open. She can't have fastened it properly when she ran out.

In her bedroom she flops down on the bed. She doesn't even have the energy to tug off her shoes. Her mobile cheeps by her head. She reaches up with an aching arm, trails her fingers over the cabinet surface, finds cool plastic.

Tim.

She reads his message three times. He's coming down at the end of the week for Flora Day. Jack has agreed to come too.

This time next week it'll all be over.

On Sunday morning, Verity wakes early and walks to Carrag Luz.

There's a fine mist obscuring the Land's End Peninsula. She can see the dark shoulder of the headland, but the beach is hidden by cobwebs of sea fret. She reaches out a hand to the huge rock beside her. It has a sheen of damp, like sweat. She leans forward into the white nothingness. There is no-one below the crag. She straightens quickly. She feels she is being sucked into the void. She turns her back on the rocks and gazes towards the cliff road, but there is no sign of life, no figures forming out of the mist. She feels truly alone in the suffocating, dazzling whiteness.

Once home, she goes straight to the living room and slides onto the window seat. The mist parts and she can see Carrag Luz.

Of course, he is not there, she tells herself angrily. She stands up and strides out of the room.

You met – no, encountered *– a strange man on the cliff one morning. It doesn't mean you will ever see him there again, and anyway, why would you want to?*

53

There was something very wrong with him. He was unbalanced, possibly crazy. Andy saw him too, in the garden. In the garden? That can't be right. On the path maybe.

Verity wishes she could go round to Caroline's and ask Andy about the man he saw. Caroline dismisses Andy's words as his imagination, but Verity knows he was right.

~

"So, he's making you come too?" she says to Jack on the phone.

"I said I would. It's not I don't want to see you, you know that, just I've got a lot on, and I'm at the other end of the country. But you know Tim. And he's convinced something awful is going to happen."

"To him or me?"

"You, of course. The damsel in distress at the end of the world. He's been having dreams again."

Verity is silent. Tim's dreams foretold their mother's illness, her death.

"He probably just misses me," she says at last.

"Sure, he does. And he's worried about those earthquakes. Any more?"

"There was one the other day." Verity smiles to herself, remembering the beautiful blond man. She is just about to say something to Jack about him when the line screeches. Jack's voice is cut off.

Verity throws down her phone.

They're coming. She can't stop them.

Jack is like flotsam on Tim's wave.

She feels her jaw tighten. She doesn't want either of them here with their shouting and fussing. She'll never be able to find the man on the cliff. And they'll make her go back to Bath. As hot tears of frustration burn her eyes, she vows not to answer the phone to either of them.

Verity doesn't see her neighbours for several days.

Sometimes in the early evenings, she hears the boys shrieking in their garden. Once she went out into her own garden, and waited near their secret tunnel, hoping the leaves would rustle, and Andy would slither through so she could ask him about the angel he'd seen. But neither Andy nor Jonny came into her garden. Caroline may have told them to stay away, but more likely they are afraid to come round because of the rabbit and the fish.

She walks up to Carrag Luz, and down to the beach. On Wednesday she drives into Helston and buys green, lemon and white ribbons for her tambourine, and a pair of cream pumps to dance in.

She has not answered calls from Tim or Jack, and has replied to their messages with curt texts. She knows she is being unfair to them, especially to Jack, who doesn't even want to come to Cornwall, but she can't help herself.

A gentle tapping wakes Verity on Thursday morning. She opens her eyes. It's like an irregular clock, a failing heart. The curtains are half drawn. A dark flash at the window. She sits up quickly. It's a butterfly, a Peacock.

Verity stumbles to the window in her bare feet. She feels a dusty crunch under her foot. She glances down. There are moths crumpled on the carpet, dead moths, their soft wings frozen. She jumps back, aware of the Peacock's insistent beating on the glass.

"OK, OK," she mutters to the butterfly, and opens the window wider.

The butterfly swoops towards her face, then taps again on the glass. Verity scoops it out into the sunshine. There's a dark dusting of wing scales on her palm. She crouches down and gently pulls back the fore-wings on one of the moths, revealing bright amber with a dark band.

The window was only open a few inches overnight. How could all these moths have got in? Something must have attracted them. She looks round the room. There are no flowers. There's no foliage outside on the wall; if there were she wouldn't open the window at all for fear of snails and slugs getting in.

Oh Jesus.

She slams the window shut. She won't sleep with it open again.

It's still early but she's wide awake now. She showers and makes tea, then swings her bag onto her shoulder and sets off for the village shops. As soon as she steps out onto the cliff road, she hears a car approaching. Caroline is parking the Peugeot on the tarmac strip. Andy's in the back.

"Just taken Jonny to school," Caroline explains as she opens the back door.

Andy bounces out of the car.

"Did you have a party?" he asks Verity.

"Party?" she asks, aware suddenly that this conversation with Andy is important, important like the time when he told her he saw an angel.

"Last night. In the night. You had a party."

"Andy, what are you on about?" Caroline scolds, shouldering her handbag, checking the screen of her mobile phone. She holds out a hand to her son. "Come on, let's go in."

"I know you had a party," Andy says to Verity. "I saw all your lights on. Was the angel at your party?"

"Angel," Verity whispers, seeing again those cool silver eyes, the sun-flamed hair.

Caroline shakes her head. "I don't know, Andy-kins. Let's get you inside." Andy takes her outstretched hand. "I'll call you later about tonight."

"Tonight?"

"Hal an Tow rehearsal."

Verity stands still in the lane long after Caroline and Andy have gone through their gate. At last, she crosses to the seaward wall, tangled with grasses, brambles, wild garlic and bluebells.

She starts walking to Mullion. Andy saw lights on in her house. Something must have disturbed the electricity again, but there was no storm, no earthquake. Nothing woke her until the butterfly. But something had attracted those moths to the narrow open window.

Light.

Jack usually enjoys travelling but he can't settle. He's sprawled in the aisle seat with his rucksack by the window, hoping no-one asks him to move it. The last thing he wants is the company of a stranger. A previous passenger left a tabloid on the seat. He flicks through it, hardly noticing the shouting headlines. He doesn't want to read; he doesn't want music. He just wants this trip over with as soon as possible.

The industrial north Midlands slide past the grimy window. Jack's heart rate is high. He is more affected by Tim's dreams and warnings than he'd confess to anyone. He hasn't liked Verity's sharp – often mis-typed – messages. For some reason she doesn't want either of her men to come to Cornwall, and for some reason Tim is adamant they must go.

Jack settles back in the seat and closes his eyes.

"It will be nice to see Tim and Jack tomorrow, won't it?" Caroline asks. "Perhaps we could all meet up for a drink on Flora Day?"

They're leaving Helston. The last Hal an Tow meeting is over. Next time Verity sees her fellow dancers they'll be in their costumes: gowns, swords, shields, ribbons, and flowers.

"Verity?" Caroline asks.

Verity gazes out of the passenger window at the milky twilight.

"Yes, of course," she says at last.

"You don't want them to come?"

"I'm enjoying the time on my own. They want me to go back."

"Going home after a holiday is always horrible."

"That's the thing," Verity says. "This doesn't feel like a holiday. This feels like real life. I feel I belong here. In Mullion, on the cliff. I feel I'm being uprooted from my home."

"You'll have to move down."

"I guess."

Verity hasn't thought of this. But it wouldn't be the same in a poky flat in Helston, looking for a job just to cover the rent. She wouldn't be out on Polurrian Cliff, watching the sea surge into the gully below Carrag Luz.

"I can't leave without—"

Without seeing that white-gold man again. The angel.

"I just don't seem to have done much," Verity finishes lamely. "I've spent all my time on the cliff and the beach."

"Can't you persuade them to stay on?"

"No, Tim has to get back for work, and Jack to uni. Tim says we'll be going in a few days."

She'll be back in Bath, and this time will fade like a sun-bleached paperback. She'll fall asleep to the wail of ambulances, not the sea. Even the rain will taste different: dusty as the city pavements. One day she might smell wild garlic somewhere, or see a bruise of bluebells, and she'll remember the crumbling cliff, the vast crag, the shape of the rain squalls driving into Mount's Bay. She will see a flash of sunlight on gold, and think of the angel on the cliff.

Time will pass.

Caroline's daughter will be born; the boys will grow up; Andy will forget that he too once saw an angel.

"Cribbage?" Jack asks, dropping the board down on the kitchen table with a crack.

"Go on then." Tim splits the last of the wine between their glasses.

"Nothing from her?" Jack starts shuffling the pack.

"No. I left a message while you were in the shower. Said you were here, that we were coming tomorrow, that we'd head back Sunday or Monday."

"Bloody hell. I've come all this day just for a long weekend."

"I've got work."

"Suppose I could stay on with her. You take your car back and she and I drive up together later."

"No."

Jack freezes, holding the pack for Tim to cut.

"I want her home. Away from down there. Something is badly wrong. I told you. Please believe me. You know I…you remember the other times. I'm not bullshitting you. I'm scared. We must stick together, you and me, and get her home. We all travel back at the same time."

"OK. Whatever."

Tim picks up his hand, quickly puts two sevens aside. He glances back at the four left: three tens and a five. Nothing else. Jack cuts; Tim turns up the top card.

Tim's counting fifteens in his dreams. Somehow more and more cards fly towards him from an unseen dealer's hand. He can't pick them up quickly enough and they scatter across the table. Queen, ten, five, eight, seven, seven, the Moon, Ace, nine, six, nine, the Fool, ten, King, two, the Magician, four, Ace, five, the Devil, the Empress.

He starts awake as the relentless counting chant seems to burst out of his head. His stomach is roiling; he's sweating so much his hair is wet. The room tilts as he stumbles out of bed. He's cold and shivering. In the bathroom he slams the door, not even caring if he wakes Jack, and vomits over and over again. He hasn't put the light on, and an amber wash seeps into the room from the street lamps far below on Julian Road. Tim slides up the window and freezing air hits his skin. He's still counting over and over in his head. No, he's not; some incubus is squatting between his ears chanting the numbers.

At last, he screws up his eyes and pulls the light cord. He flinches at the blue-white glare. The fan comes on with a grumble. Tim washes his face, cups water in his hand to drink. When at last he meets his reflection's gaze in the mirror he's shocked at how haggard he looks. He snaps off the bathroom light.

Back in his room he inhales some lavender oil to dispel the nausea, He pulls on a thick jumper. Still, he shivers, and still his stomach heaves. Half an hour later he returns to the bathroom and brings up more bile.

"Tim, you OK?" Jack taps on the door.

"No," Tim says.

"Can I get you anything?"

"I'm going back to bed."

Tim doesn't go to bed. He pads into the kitchen and runs water into a glass. The cold water shocks his stomach. He pours the rest away and stumbles onto the settle. The cards and crib board are still on the table. Tim reaches out for the pack, turns them upside down and fans them out. They're just playing cards.

There's a faint growl of early traffic. He opens the sash and tastes the morning. If he cranes his neck to the east, he can see the first mother-of-pearl luminescence in the sky. He doesn't know how long he sits there in the cold. Eventually he realises he is shaking and slides the window down again.

"What's up? It's freezing in here."

"It must've been the Indian last night."

"Can you manage tea?" Jack lifts the kettle to check the water level and flicks it on. The red light burns in Tim's eyes. Jack clanks two mugs onto the worktop. "Toast?"

"No thanks."

Jack makes tea and shoves a mug towards Tim. Even the delicate fragrance of Earl Grey is fluttering his stomach. He drinks. The tea feels thick and rough like an animal's skin. He stands up, the room sways and he staggers, half-falling into the table.

"We can't go today," Jack says.

"See how I am later."

"You can't go like that. I could go. Get me insured on your car...the train...whatever. I can go."

"I told you. We must stick together."

Jack says nothing. Tim sees his indecision. He understands. One minute he's saying Verity is in danger, the next he's saying Jack should stay with him.

"I have to be there. I have to go. I'm the one who can help her."

His guts lurch and he stumbles up. He just makes it to the bathroom before the thin black tea bubbles out of his mouth.

~

When Verity wakes, she glances to the floor. No moths. Nothing. The window is closed.

It's her last day alone in Mullion. She doesn't want to check her messages but she needs to know how long she's got before her solitude is splintered.

Call me. Please. Tim's not well. X

Not well. Those words. *I'm not well*, Rosie had said to the twins, when her cancer was diagnosed. Not well. It can just mean a cold. It can mean something else.

"We won't be coming today," Jack says when she calls him. "He's throwing his guts up. Said it was the Indian we had last night, but I'm OK. It's not the Indian."

"What is it then?"

"Don't you remember? When Mum...he had the dreams and he was vomiting. It's just the same."

"Dreams?"

"He's been dreaming again. He thinks it's because of something happening to you. I said it was probably the earthquakes."

"I'm fine. There's no need for either of you to come. I'm really happy here. I have a car. I can come back when I want to."

"We'll be coming. I'm just not sure when. And Verity?"

"What?"

"Please take care. I know I usually dismiss Tim's ramblings but...please be careful till we get there."

As Jack ends the call his screen flashes white. The background picture of him and Verity has gone. It's just bright angry white. He jabs at the screen, scrolls up and down. White behind the icons. He hits gallery and swipes through his pictures. Friends at uni, geology samples, a huge burger with a paper Northumberland flag stuck in it. He swipes on. All his pictures of Verity have turned into white boxes. He clicks her contact details. The number is still there, but the picture gone to white. Like she has disappeared.

"How long can you stay?"

"As long as you need me." Jack sits down on the edge of Tim's bed.

"I can't travel today."

"Of course not."

"Can you stay on for a week? We could go next weekend?"

"Can't we go in a few days?"

Tim tastes bile and snatches at the bowl on the bedside table. He retches, but nothing comes up.

"I've got commitments. Work. And I need more time to prepare."

"For what?"

"What we have to do." Tim closes his eyes, take deep shuddering breaths. "Maybe this is all right. That we wait. We plan. We work together, you and me."

"I could go…"

"Stay with me. I need you."

Jack squeezes Tim's hand. It's freezing, but his hair is greasy with sweat.

"Let me get you more Paracetamol."

"Please."

Jack stands and takes Tim's old water glass to refill.

"And Jack?"

"Yes?"

"Please stay with me. We need to work together."

Twig shoulders through the crowd to the front door of the Angel Hotel. As he steps out under the porch, he feels the sudden chill of the May evening on his skin.

He gazes up and down Coinagehall Street. The shop doorways are framed with garlands of laurel and bluebells. There are pennants strung between the upper floors, criss-crossing the street. Drinkers straggle out of the many pubs. There's noise and colour all round him, but Twig stands still in a cold dark pocket.

The evil has come to the Flora.

It is already here. And the girl, the sacrifice. She is somewhere nearby.

A group of girls totters down the hill towards Twig, all exposed gooseflesh and tattoos. One wobbles on her heels and stumbles into him. He breathes the stale smells of alcohol and tobacco.

None of them. No, she is not in Helston, not yet. But she will come tomorrow to the Flora, where the evil is waiting for her.

Verity shivers. It's six o'clock on Flora Day morning.

She slips on her dress. It's cool and heavy against her bare legs. She twirls once or twice in front of the mirror, watching the skirt billow. She brushes her long hair and picks up her ribboned tambourine. It jangles discordantly in the empty bedroom.

Suddenly, she understands – though how she understands this she does not know – that the waiting is over.

At last, she moves away from the mirror, knowing that when she returns everything will be different, she will be changed.

She picks up her rucksack with her own clothes bundled inside, unlocks the front door and steps out into the garden. Dew dampens the hem of her skirt. The lawn below is mottled with scattered bluebells. She gazes down at them. It's as though a giant hand has plucked the blooms from the cliff and thrown them over the tamarisk hedge into her garden.

64

The sky is a white-mauve, the air cool as peppermint. She runs down to the gate and onto the cliff path. By the time she reaches Caroline's she has forgotten the bluebells.

~

Twig darts behind the Guildhall. It's early, but the crowds are already thick. People are eating: he can smell pasties, onions, chips. There are metallic balloons: flaring suns, crescent moons, dinosaurs.

As he starts down the dip of Church Hill, he can hear the distant silver band of the early morning street dance. The dancers will be passing through St John's very soon, and then the way will be clear for the Hal an Tow.

Twig's heart kicks a warning. He must find the girl.

He cuts down one of the alleys that lead to St John's, that hidden square where the Hal an Tow begins. He's not watching where he's walking, and another man cannons into him.

"I have to be somewhere," he says to Twig.

Twig glances at him. He's fairly young, slim, clean. He doesn't look or smell drunk, but he's unsteady on his feet, and his eyes look unfocussed.

"Where do you have to be?"

"I don't know. But they can't do it without me."

"Can't do what?" Twig asks.

~

"Where the hell is he?" shouts St George.

"Anyone seen the Devil?"

The mummers are gathered outside the Community Hall, uneasy and flustered.

The Devil hasn't arrived.

Verity glances round the ring: Mary Moses in a long green tapestry dress, a bunch of sycamore wands in her hands; St Michael in silver armour and a peacock blue cloak; St George in gold and red; the orange scaled dragon whose mask is opened in a perpetual roar; Robin Hood and his men; sailors, tree spirits, and flower maidens.

One of the organisers is tapping a mobile phone urgently. Little John climbs onto the wall, glances up and down the hill.

"We can't go without him," he says, jumping down.

"We need to go *now*."

"Someone else will have to do it."

"There is no need."

Verity starts at the new voice.

Everyone turns.

The Devil strides through the mass, gowned in purple and black. His mask is silver with curled horns. The air seems to crackle around his form. The tree dancers stumble backwards out of his way.

A crescendo of whistles, drums and tambourines. Little John's horn. The saints raise their lances to the sky.

"To St John's!"

~

"The Hal an Tow's coming," Twig tells the man.

Behind him, up the hill, he hears the horns, the whistles, the shouts. The sounds, primitive and ancient, prickle his skin. His muscles tighten for flight.

"The Hal an Tow?" the young man gasps. "That's what I have to do. I'm the Devil. They can't go without me."

Twig glances up the lane. Already he can see the banners, the sycamore fronds. The whistles and cries are louder, louder. She's here somewhere.

"They can't be coming. I'm the Devil."

Twig staggers away from the man. As he looks back at the approaching mummers, he sees above the faceless blur of trees dancers a pair of silver and black horns, evilly curled and glinting in the sunlight.

"The Devil's there," Twig manages to croak, before turning his back on his companion, and sprinting down the hill to St John's, the Wild Hunt thundering behind him.

Verity scoops up her skirt and runs down the lane.

Cries and whistles explode around her.

She sees people framed in the garlanded doorways, on the pavements, leaning out of casement windows; she sees them frozen for a second, then they are gone, and her feet are shooting onwards. Sometimes she catches a glimpse of the curled black horns, and then the Devil is hidden once more with leaves and banners.

The Wild Hunt is coming: shouting, horns, drums, whistles.

Twig hears the mummers in the narrow, twisted streets above St John's. Their cries are like white noise buzzing somewhere behind his eyes. Twig staggers; he almost falls into his neighbour, who steadies him, probably presuming him drunk or ill. Heads turn as the whistles become louder, more strident. The drum's tattoo drives Twig's heart faster; he feels the growing pressure in his chest and ears.

He is coming, Twig thinks, closing his eyes. And so is she.

Twig does not want to see, but his eyes flick open. He gasps, gags. The writhing figures before him are wild-eyed wraiths with tattered cerements trailing behind them, and wilting blooms in their skeletal hands. Twig can hardly breathe for the stench of decay. The tangle of dancers ebbs and flows across his vision. In the centre of the circle, a black, horned figure turns slowly to face him.

He is here.

Twig's legs shudder. Before he falls, he must find the sacrifice. The Devil shimmers before him, shrouded once more by handmaidens. As they hide his face with shivering leaves, Twig sees a flash of colour across the circle. A slender girl, gowned in the gold and green of the summer and the may, ribbons fluttering from the tambourine she holds in her hand. She smiles as though she sees Twig, but he knows she cannot, that she dances to a different tune, moving in another sphere to the company of the dead.

Twig holds the image of the girl's laughing face as he crumples to the ground. He has seen her; she is here.

Verity feels the magic hit her bloodstream like a drug. Two silver blades cleave the air: the cloaked saints, Michael and George. She glances left and right looking for Mary Moses. They have become separated in the rush down to St John's.

There she is, beside the fiery dragon, a sheaf of sycamore in her arms.

Tree spirits swirl in a circle, ivy leaves and flowers fluttering from their headdresses. Verity cries the responses to St Michael's shouts, raises her ribboned tambourine and her face to the sky. Through the throng of trees, maidens and green men strides a tall figure, cloaked and masked in black and purple with twisted silver horns. Verity's arms drop to her sides, the cry dies in her mouth as the Devil stops and gazes at her. For a moment she loses her bearings. The tree dancers engulf the Devil in a mass of sycamore fronds and he is lost to her.

The town crier rings his bell. Six drum beats, then the reedy tune.

There is a sudden movement in the crowd.

A young red-haired man has fallen to the ground. Cameras flash across the arena. Another maiden gives Verity a nudge, and she starts to move round the ring. She barely sees Robin Hood wed Maid Marian in the greenwood or St George defeat the dragon with his sword.

She's looking everywhere for the Devil, who seemed to look through her soul with his silver eyes. Whenever she spies a glimpse of black, a tree dancer or a flower girl skips across her vision. The circle breaks once more, and the Devil leaps into the centre, sinuously evading St Michael's blade.

Shockingly, Verity wants history re-written, wants the Devil to defeat the Archangel this day in Helston.

The Devil knocks aside St Michael's arm; the crowd gasps, breaths hovering in the air until at last the saint thrusts his sun-flashed lance through his adversary. The mob roars and punches fists to the sky; the grove of trees flows round the Devil, shrouding his slain form with leaves and flowers.

~

A voice in Twig's ear above the screams of the crowd.

He finds himself on his feet once more, but supported by a man's strong arm. In his spare hand the man waves a mobile phone camera at the mummers. He says something to Twig. Twig can't hear; his ears feel they are about to explode. He manages to nod, mouth something back to his rescuer. The man lets go of him, as the dancers surge towards them. People stumble back as the troupe forces through. Twig draws in air. Blackened bruised corpses barge roughly into him, exhaling the breath of the grave. A flurry of twisted limbs, distorted faces. And then he sees her again – the girl, the sacrifice. Her skirts swirl as she runs after the Devil. A green ribbon escapes from her tambourine. Two crones appear on either side of her. They grab her arms, drag her up the slope. Twig can't move. He can do nothing for her; he can only watch as the lovely young girl is hauled out of his sight. He bends down, reaches for the trampled green ribbon by his foot.

~

"To the monument!" someone cries. "The monument!"

Little John's horn, the whistles, the relentless drum.

Ahead of her, up the slope, Verity can see the Devil. He seems to be further and further from her. Two flower maidens appear on either side of her; one rattles her tambourine, the other screams the call of the Hal an Tow. Verity feels the flare of goose flesh on her arms.

"He waits for you."

Verity lifts her eyes once more. Standing on the crest of the hill, gilded by the morning sun, stands the Devil, watching her stumble up the rise towards him. The two girls melt away into the greenery that borders the house doorways.

The Devil holds out a black gloved hand. She reaches for him. His grasp is firm; her legs steady. She looks up to his face. Pewter eyes behind the mask, as he bows over her hand.

"Maiden, will you join my dance?"

Verity feels the burn of tears in her eyes. Her legs are aching, unused to running up and down hills. The seven dances through the town have blistered her feet. Now, outside the Guildhall, its frontage garlanded with laurel, gorse and bluebells, the town crier rings his bell, the saints raise their spears, and the Devil crumples to the ground for the last time.

This time next week it'll all be over, Frank had said. That time is now.

The circle of dancers implodes. Jonny races into the arena, throws his arms around his mother's hips. All around Verity, the dancers are talking and laughing, rattling tambourines, their costumes now mingling with the many colours of the crowd. St Michael and St George stride past her. Frank follows Jonny with Andy in his arms.

Verity is aware that Andy seems distressed about something, and she imagines the crowds frighten him. Frank tries to distract him, pointing to a youth holding a glittering swarm of helium balloons. Jonny and Caroline go over to join them, and Verity watches the family group, suddenly feeling alone, an outsider.

She spins around, looks up and down the street. She cannot see the Devil anywhere. He can't have just disappeared, she thinks, feeling unexpected tears starting to form.

Frank hands a note to the balloon man, who pulls out a turquoise fish for Jonny. Jonny unfurls the string, and the fish jumps on its line. The balloons swing round in a swirling storm, and suddenly there he is: the Devil, standing alone, in front of the Guildhall, watching her through the dark slits in his mask.

Verity thinks she speaks, or at least makes some noise, but then the balloons billow again, as Caroline ties a metallic Duggee to Andy's wrist. Verity moves, stumbling into a man with a plastic pint glass. Beer spills on her dress. She mutters an apology. The balloon man is walking away, his wares streaming behind him, and standing where the Devil stood only a moment before is a man so different, so unexpected, that this time Verity knows she cries out.

The man outside the Guildhall is the man she met at Carrag Luz, the man with the sun-blazed hair, the white clothes, the silver eyes: the eyes behind the Devil's mask.

The man inclines his head in acknowledgement, then weaves through the crowd down the main street.

"Verity," someone is saying. A woman's voice. "Verity."

Verity stretches on her tiptoes but she cannot see over the heads of those in front of her. He is so distinctive, surely she can discern him amongst the hordes, but she cannot see that long pale hair anywhere.

"Verity," Caroline says again.

Verity turns. *He saw me too*, she thinks. *He saw me and he knew me. He would have seen me all the time behind that mask. He held out his hand for me.*

71

"Yes, St Michael is an angel," Frank is saying to Andy.

"No, no," Andy says. "My angel." He points at Verity, and Duggee judders as his arm moves. "Her angel."

~

In the Community Hall Verity peels off her dress. It smells of beer. One of her dancing shoes has worn through on the sole. She unknots the ribbons from her tambourine, and stuffs them into her rucksack. She tugs on jeans and T-shirt. Her back is damp with cooling sweat. She combs her hair with her fingers and laces up her Converse.

Caroline, still wearing her Mary Moses dress, is talking to Maid Marian and Robin Hood. Verity slings her gold and green gown over her arm and carries it through to the costume store. As she enters the darkened room, she jumps and gasps. The Devil is standing in the half-light. No, it's just his mask, empty, hanging on the back wall. She moves forward, and reaches out to touch the glinting horns. Voices are coming closer, and she drops her hand.

It's the dragon and a couple of tree spirits. Verity slides her dress onto a rail, sad to be leaving it here in the dark, wondering who will wear it next year. The dragon hooks up his roaring mask.

"Why was he late?" he asks the women he's with.

"Don't know," one of the women says.

"He was a brilliant Devil whoever he was," the other says.

Verity pretends to be smoothing down her dress on its hanger, hunting for something in her bag. When the others have gone, she stands once again before the mask, expecting for a second to see those silver eyes behind the slits.

Frank and the boys are waiting for her when she steps outside. The sunlight dazzles her and she wishes she had brought sunglasses. Andy is picking at the string round his wrist.

"Caroline takes forever to say goodbye to everyone," Frank sighs.

72

Verity smiles, but she feels trapped. She wants to leave the others and forge through the crowds herself looking for the man, the angel. She wonders how she can suggest she goes off alone for a while. Every moment that goes by makes it harder for her to find him again.

Jonny is bouncing up and down on his heels, bored. Verity glances back towards the hall. There's still no sign of Caroline.

A crowd comes out.

At last Caroline emerges with St Michael.

Tim, Verity thinks randomly; *I wonder how Tim is. I should call him.*

Frank starts walking towards Caroline. Jonny is kicking a Pepsi can.

"Where is he?" Andy asks Verity. "Where's the angel?"

Verity gazes down at Andy's upturned face. Behind his glasses, his eyes meet hers. Caroline says he has poor vision, but Verity thinks he sees more clearly than anyone.

"I don't know, Andy," she says.

"Are you going to find him?"

Verity glances at Frank, Caroline and St Michael, who are having an animated discussion. St Michael is gesturing with his sword arm.

"Yes," she says. "Yes, I am."

Frank peels away from the other two to rescue his boys.

"That was all very weird," he says to Verity. "Do you know who the Devil was?"

"No-one does," Verity stammers.

"Well, some of them do, but it's all hush-hush, you know. Apparently, the guy who was supposed to be doing it just turned up at the hall after the dance had finished. He was kind of spaced-out. Caroline reckons he was drunk. Anyway, he'd missed it all, and no-one seems to know who played the Devil."

Caroline appears beside Frank, and reaches down to cuddle Andy.

"Very strange," she says.

"Can we go to the fair, Daddy?" asks Jonny.

"Let's see what Verity would like to do," Caroline says.

"Oh, well, I'd just like to have a look round...the market, and all that. What time are we going home?"

"Let's meet up about twelve," Caroline says. "I think we'll all have had enough by then. I'm on my mobile, Verity."

"I want to go with Verity," Andy cries.

"Verity wants to have a look round by herself." Caroline takes Andy's hand and spins him round.

Would I find him if Andy were with me? Verity wonders, as the other four walk away.

Andy turns once, his loose child's mouth forms a word: angel.

~

Twig stands still a moment, lets the crowds flood round him.

Someone bangs a buggy into his legs. He hears random words of strangers' conversations: *at least the sun's shining; horses; she lives in Mullion; yes, next weekend.*

He cannot find the girl.

He saw her with her friends after the Hal an Tow. The boys had balloons tied to their wrists. She saw the evil behind the mask of balloons. The boy – the little one – he saw it too. All those who see it are in peril.

Twig fingers the tin whistle in his shirt pocket, calmed by the slim metal tube. He starts up the hill once more, the faces of the crowds swarming before him: open mouths, shifty eyes, stale breath. Suddenly, he sees the two balloons. There are the boys, and their parents. The mother – Mary Moses – rests a hand on her abdomen. But the girl is not with them. She must be somewhere alone, vulnerable. Twig turns again, and darts downhill, stumbling between dithering

74

pedestrians and market stalls. The road bends to the left at the monument, and the market straggles on to the very bottom of town. He hears the insistent drone of the silver band, marching with the children's street dance. Over the rooftops he can see the arc of the Big Wheel in the fairground beyond. And suddenly he sees her.

~

Verity has hurried down the market, hardly stopping to look at the stalls. Frozen images and smells tell her what she has passed: candy floss, ceramics, hot dogs, hardware. She is not interested in the market, only in the man, the Devil – the angel – who held out his hand to her, who knows her. She does not know what she will say to him when she finds him, but she has to find him.

He is so beautiful, so ethereal. She feels a longing, a desire, ancient as time, and as powerful.

She stumbles to the side of the road, glancing left and right. Incense catches in her throat, smoky and musky. The stall beside her sparkles with tumblestones, dreamcatchers, medicine wheels and crystals.

Tim, she thinks again, for a brief second, then the name and the face in her mind evaporate.

There's an arched Gothic mirror at the back of the stall. Verity meets her own gaze in one of the three pointed panels of glass. Her hair is awry; she looks breathless. Behind her tousled reflection is a shimmer of white.

Verity whips round.

The man lopes through the crowd, his long hair blazing in a sudden sun beam. He moves so fast, slicing through the milling people. Verity runs up the hill, bumping into shopping bags and people. A fat woman swears as she shoulders past her. The man is ahead of her, his white shirt luminous, silver-blond hair tumbling down his back.

Verity pushes on up the hill. He has stopped moving. People fan out around him. He is still, then he turns to face Verity. His silver eyes watch her, appraise her, as she stops before him. There are only yards between them now. Verity fancies, in those seconds, she sees in his eyes that same longing, that same desire. She steps forward and stumbles, nearly falling, as someone barges roughly into her. She staggers, finds strong hands on her arms, holding her steady.

"Do not look at him." Her assailant is a young man with bright auburn hair and moss-green eyes.

"Get off me," Verity cries, tugging her arm from the man's grip. She sees a tin whistle in his shirt pocket. His breath smells of tobacco.

"He's gone," the piper says, following her gaze up the hill. "Stay away from him."

Verity scans the crowds up the street, cleared to the sides for the children's dance. She cannot see the beautiful white man, the angel, anywhere.

"If you don't look for him, you won't see him."

"What do you think you're doing, crashing into people like that?"

"I'm sorry. I had to. Go and find your friends. Stay away from *him.*"

The piper gazes at her for a moment, then slips away into the crowd. Verity finds herself shoved to the side of the road, beside a stall selling jams, chutneys and honey. People around her are talking loudly. Across the street a man juggles with flaming torches. The sound of the silver band comes closer and closer, and then the long, long line of children dressed in white. Verity sobs. Suddenly, there is white all around her, but the man she seeks is gone.

~

Frank moves Andy's hand from the balloon string tied round his wrist. Andy's been picking at the knot for ages. Caroline, who said she was

76

feeling tired after the Hal an Tow, has found a renewed energy now she's bumped into a friend from Helston. They've dissected someone's divorce, someone else's critically ill child, someone's problems with car insurance. Jonny's jigging up and down, tugging at Frank's sleeve.

"I'm bored, Daddy. Can't we go to the fair now?"

"Caroline," Frank starts. "The boys want to go to the fair. OK if I take them down?"

"Sure, of course," Caroline says. "Keep an eye out for Verity on your way down."

"Come on, then. Let's go to the fair. Andy, you'll lose that balloon if you don't stop fiddling." Frank checks the knot at Andy's wrist and leads the boys down the hill.

"Where is he? Where is he?"

"Where's who, Andy?" Frank shouts over the insistent band, trying to shelter Andy from the crowds watching the children's dance. Duggee catches on a woman's hat; Frank apologies as he unhooks it.

"The angel," Andy says.

"Shut it, Andy," Jonny says. "There's no stupid angel."

"Jonny, Jonny," Frank warns, knowing Jonny's mockery can make tears burst in Andy's eyes, but Andy doesn't cry now, just mutters to himself.

"There is, there is. Verity knows."

Oh, bloody hell. Verity. Frank's supposed to be looking out for her. But what if he finds her? She won't want to go the fair; she's probably poking round the market stalls, maybe she just wants some time alone. As they pass one of the pubs a gassy breath of beer spills out onto the street.

"I want candy floss," Jonny says, pointing at pink blooms of spun sugar hooked up under a striped awning.

"You won't like it," Frank says. "It's really sweet."

"I want it. Last year you said I could have it this year."

"All right, all right." Frank's beginning to wish they'd just stood like lemons next to Caroline. He buys candy floss for Jonny. "D'you want anything, Andy?"

Andy shakes his head. It's not like him to not want a treat. Frank's about to ask him if he's OK, then thinks better of it. Andy's bored, and probably tired, doesn't like the crowds, and there's nothing he can do about any of it right now.

"I don't like this," Jonny says, his mouth turned down at the corners.

"I said you wouldn't," Frank says, wondering where there's a bin he can shove the candy floss in, and wishing he had some wet wipes for Jonny's sticky fingers.

"I want the toilet, Daddy," Andy wails.

Frank swears under his breath. They're nearly at the bottom of the hill. There are public lavatories only a few yards away.

"D'you really need to go, Andy?"

"Now, Daddy, now."

Frank scoops up Andy in his arms, and strides down the hill.

"Where can I put this?" Jonny waves the candy floss.

"I don't know, Jonny."

Jonny shrugs and dumps the candy floss in a plastic crate of DVDs in front of a market stall.

Verity sees Frank marching towards the lavatories with Andy in his arms. Andy's balloon is gently knocking on Frank's head. She sees Jonny, some yards behind them, doing something by a DVD stall, then running haphazardly through the crowd to catch up. She calls out to Frank.

"Verity," he says with relief. "Would you wait with Jonny while I take Andy...what have you done with that candy floss?"

"I dropped it," Jonny says.

Frank opens his mouth, immediately silenced by an anguished *Daddy, hurry up* from Andy.

"I didn't exactly drop it," Jonny tells Verity, as Frank and Andy disappear into the Gents. The public lavatory smell makes Verity feel queasy.

"Drop what?" she asks.

"The candy floss," Jonny explains. "It was gross. I put it in that DVD box." He points to the stall on the corner of the street, where a man is effeminately dropping a ball of candy floss into a Tesco carrier bag. "Don't tell Daddy."

"I won't," Verity promises and laughs with Jonny.

Frank comes back out with Andy.

"Are you sure you don't want to go, Jonny? I don't want to have to come back."

"All right, I'll go," Jonny sighs theatrically.

"Leave Andy with me," Verity says quickly, taking Jonny's fish balloon from him. The string is warm from his hand and sticky from the candy floss.

"Andy," Verity begins, and her heart is jumpy with the enormity of the question she's about to ask this four year-old boy. "Who is he?"

Andy doesn't answer, just fiddles sullenly with the knot of his balloon string. Verity glances behind her to the grim concrete portal of the lavatory. A guy shambles out with his flies open. Verity squats down to Andy's level, and feels her rucksack sliding uncomfortably off her shoulder.

"The angel. Who is he?"

"He's an angel."

"Where's he from?"

Andy doesn't answer.

"Andy, please."

"I don't know," Andy cries. "You know."

79

A hand tugs the fish out of Verity's grasp. Jonny grins at her and glances over to the DVD stall.

"We're going to the fair," Frank tells Verity. "Would you like to come with us?"

"Where's Caroline?"

"She met up with a friend."

Verity looks up and down the street, but she can see neither the angel nor the fiery-haired man who crashed into her, uttering his abrupt words of warning.

"I'll come to the fair," she says, trying to sound enthusiastic.

What's the chance the angel will be there? The last time she saw him he was walking up the hill. She glances once more over her shoulder, then follows Frank and the boys. The market straggles on with clothes, towels, pewter jewellery, pet food, wooden carvings, a fortune teller, hot dogs, more candy floss.

"Can I have an ice cream?" Jonny asks.

"Not after the candy floss," Frank says.

"But I didn't eat the candy floss."

"Can I buy them one each?" Verity asks.

Frank gives her a despairing look. "On the way back, then," he says. "I don't want them throwing up at the fair."

"I won't throw up," Jonny shouts. "He might, though."

"Won't."

"Yes, you will."

"Shut up, both of you, or we're not going to the fair, and you won't get any ice cream."

Jonny scowls and kicks Andy's heel. Andy plods on, unresponsive. Jonny prods Andy.

"He's here," Andy says, as they go into the dusty arena of the fairground.

The air is hot with diesel. Power cables snake across the cracked mud, and Jonny stumbles. Music pounds from somewhere, something with a heavy bass line. Girls in micro minis are loitering by the Waltzers. A boy is carrying a huge teddy bear, almost as big as himself. Frank shoves the boys into a queue for a small space-rocket ride.

"I want to go on that," Jonny points at a huge carousel with vivid horses dipping on twisted golden poles.

"You're not big enough," Frank says. "You going to have a ride, Andy? I can hold your balloon."

"Don't want to," Andy says.

Frank glances at Verity, as Jonny spins off in the Lunar Jet.

"Are you all right, Andy?" he asks at last.

"Hmmm." Andy says.

Where is he? Where is he? Verity wants to demand of Andy.

As Jonny whizzes past she glances around the fair. The Big Wheel soars overhead, coloured lights blinking on and off. The centrifuge is taking off, rising like an alien space ship; beyond that, a monstrous eight-limbed nightmare ride is rearing up, spinning upside down. The fair is muscular and colourful; there is no white, no ethereal beauty. The pink lights on the carousel, a woman's hennaed hair, a girl's lime-green miniskirt, the red painted Big Wheel against the hard blue sky. If he appeared here, he would be so shockingly different, everyone would turn their heads to his unearthly form.

Verity tries to see a flash of white between people's heads, behind the carousel, but there is nothing beyond the roar and heat of the fairground.

She moves away from Frank and Andy, and walks over to the carousel. As it slows into its final circuit, the horses' features solidify into awful beauty: bared teeth, flared ears, wild eyes. The carousel stops. The horse beside Verity has no rider. She steps closer to look at him. He is painted black with purple and silver decoration. There is a sheen

81

on his flanks as if he has been ridden too hard and for too long. His long nose is outlined with a delicate tracing of silver, which frames his slanted eyes.

"Andy, you stupid –"

"Jonny, just don't. Andy, you can share Jonny's balloon."

"No way. He'll lose it too."

Verity turns round. Something white flares in her peripheral vision, but there's nothing. Andy is standing before her, crying. Frank and Jonny are gazing up to where Duggee hovers just out of reach. Jonny jumps a couple of times, waving his arms ineffectually. The balloon jerks and slides upwards on a current. Verity watches it getting smaller and smaller, until the bright sky hurts her eyes.

Andy is still crying. Frank pats his jacket pocket and pulls out his mobile.

"I'll buy you a new balloon," Verity tells Andy, ruffling his hair.

Frank puts his spare hand over his ear.

Beside Verity the carousel starts spinning gently, then faster and faster. The horses swoop up and down. She tries to see the black and silver horse, the one that looks like both the Devil and the angel. Suddenly, she sees another figure walking towards her. It's the red-haired piper. He has the tin whistle to his lips, but she can't hear his notes above the noise of the fair.

He stops before her, and pockets the tin whistle.

"You found your friends then. Is the Flora to your liking?"

"Yes," Verity stammers. "It's very much to my liking."

"You saw the evil. You know it's here. He knows it's here." He gestures to Andy. "Do not seek out the evil. Do not allow it to enter your heart or your mind."

"Is this your boyfriend?" Jonny asks.

Verity flushes. "He bumped into me earlier," she says. "He's just making sure I'm all right."

"That was Caroline," Frank says. "We should start back now. It's nearly twelve o'clock."

"Remember," the piper says, takes out his whistle, and plays a few bars of the Hal an Tow song.

"Who is he?" Frank asks.

"A busker, I think" Verity says, watching his bright head mingle with the many other heads.

"It's her boyfriend," Jonny says.

"I told you, he bumped into me. He was just saying sorry."

But he wasn't. He wasn't at all.

"Come on, troops," Frank says. "We need to go and find Mummy and get off home. I'm sure you're both tired out."

"Verity said we could have ice cream," Jonny reminds Frank, as they tramp across the dusty, scarred fairground.

Verity turns. Andy said he was here. Andy knows. He must be here. Somewhere. She tries to think of any reason to delay their departure – *I've dropped something, I think I've lost my phone, I want to look at the carousel one last time; I'll catch you up* – but she knows the hassle these words would cause.

Frank and the boys are waiting for her a little further on. She dodges a group of shouting lads, a small kid with his fingers in his ears, and tries to look cheerful, rather than desolate, which is how she feels.

"I also said I'd buy you a new balloon, Andy," she says.

"Really, you don't have to," Frank says. "I can –"

"I'd like to," Verity says, and suddenly, as they step out onto the road, she sees the shifting colours of a cluster of balloons. "Let's go and see what they've got. Here," she gives Frank a twenty-pound note. "You and Jonny go and get some ice cream while Andy and I look for a balloon."

She takes Andy's outstretched hand and whisks him over to the balloons. This may be her last time alone with him.

"He's not here now," Andy says simply. "He was watching us, and he's gone."

"Gone where?"

Andy shrugs.

Verity asks the balloon man if he has a replacement Duggee. He swings the shoal round, and Verity catches her breath, expecting the angel to appear behind the balloons, but there is only the road and, over the stone wall, the boating lake. People are walking by the water; some are throwing crusts to ducks. A dog is racing round and round on the grass under the trees. Verity is aware of a balloon being jiggled in front of her. She pays for it, and ties it round Andy's wrist. As they move away, Frank and Jonny come over from the ice cream kiosk.

"I didn't know what you'd like." Frank hands her a cone, with a flake jammed into it.

Verity takes the ice cream, licks the trail of vanilla down the side of the cone. It's sweet, synthetic, and she really doesn't feel like eating it.

Andy is tired. Frank shoves the last of his own cone into his mouth, and picks him up. Verity's hands are sticky from the ice cream. There's probably a pale crust on her lips. She wipes her mouth on the back of her hand. The road back up into town seems too steep and long. Frank has arranged they will meet Caroline opposite the public lavatories he went to with Jonny and Andy. Verity scans the crowds, looking also for the piper. Caroline's waiting on the corner. She is holding bulky carrier bags. One is an awkward shape: it looks like it contains a tray of bedding plants.

"Did you have a good time at the fair?" Caroline asks the boys.

"Andy lost his balloon," Jonny crows.

"Verity bought him a new one," Frank explains.

"Did you see everything you wanted to see, Verity?"

"Yes," Verity tells Caroline. Yes, but I want to see him again.

Verity trails after the others up the hill. It really is all over. They're leaving Flora Day. In ten minutes' time, they'll be squashed into the car, sticky fingers on the upholstery, shopping bags in the boot, balloons jammed up against the roof.

"The twelve o'clock dance is about to start from the Guildhall," Caroline says to Verity.

Verity nods, suddenly exhausted.

"We won't get anywhere near it now," Caroline goes on. "They always show it on the news."

Verity nods again, glances up to the signboard on the right: The Angel Hotel. Her eyes fall down the building to the garlanded porch. Standing between the poles of laurel and bluebells is the angel himself, glowing against the darkened doorway of the pub. Verity stops. Someone bumps into her from behind. The angel raises his hand in recognition. She tries to barge through to him, but a gang of girls with linked arms straggle in her way. The angel moves, turns into the doorway and slides inside.

"Wait!" At last Verity finds her voice. "Who are you?"

She glances across the heads of the people around her, sees Andy's face, over Frank's shoulder. He's beaming, like he truly has seen an angel.

Verity stumbles into the pub. It stinks of beer and sweat. There are people milling everywhere. The music playing on the stereo – *Devil in Disguise* – is hardly audible over the voices.

She looks round wildly, but he's not there.

He *has* to be in here.

He challenged her to follow him. She can't walk out onto the street, leaving him behind. She's buffeted by new arrivals pushing through to the bar. Someone turns up the music. The front window is bright with colours and shapes outside, and a man in white, with tumbling pale hair, striding past, and up the hill.

He must have left by another door. Verity struggles out onto the street. She's crying. He tricked her. He's not there. He's playing a game with her. She takes a few steps. A familiar face, two familiar faces: Frank, with Andy in his arms. Andy's still beaming.

"I'm sorry," Verity stammers. "I felt really ill. I thought I was going to faint. I had to get out of the crowds." She gestures feebly to the pavement, to imply she'd rested a moment against a wall, or on a windowsill.

"You do look a bit done in," Frank says. "Are you all right to walk now? Caroline and Jonny have gone on to the car."

"I'm fine," Verity says.

"Don't cry," Andy says.

"Are you crying?" Frank asks.

"No," she says hastily.

"Angel," Andy says, gazing up at the inn signboard.

~

The bungalow seems even quieter than usual. It's as though the whole of Mullion has gone to the Flora, leaving the village and cliff road deserted.

Verity drops her rucksack in the hall, suddenly realises how tired she is. She should eat – she's only had the ice cream down at the fair – but it's too much effort to find anything. Her feet smart from the dancing and the walking up and down town. For a second she considers driving back into Helston on her own to look for the man, the angel.

That's ridiculous, she thinks, suddenly furious with herself.

She would never find him now. He may not even be there. In any case, the first time she saw him, he was only yards along the cliff at Carrag Luz. She wanders to the front window, looks out. There's a dark wedge of rain over Wolf Rock. The waves have a stiff edge of white. On the cliff path the tamarisk bushes sway: the wind is coming up.

She peels off her sticky clothes, showers, then makes tea and takes it back to the window. While she was in the bathroom the weather has come in; a splatter of drizzle hits the pane. The Land's End peninsula is hazy with rain but, over the bay, the sky is a washed-out blue.

She stares at Carrag Luz. The bluebells below the crag have blurred to mauve. Something about bluebells; she can't remember. But she can remember every word she exchanged with the angel man on the cliff that morning – was it only a week ago? – after the earthquake. The last words he spoke were *there will not be another earthquake*, and there has not been.

She should go back to Helston. She should down to the fair, and up to the Guildhall, searching for him; she should go to Carrag Luz, stand on the top of the crag like he did. She should do something, but she does nothing. She does not think; she does not sleep. She simply waits.

~

Verity stands on a rocky headland.

Below her is a long crescent beach. The sand is pale, looks soft and untouched. Waves cream in, rising and curling with gentle hisses. Beyond the breakers the sea is translucent green, darkened with streaks of seaweed beneath the surface. Eventually the green lightens to a blue-mauve horizon, unbroken by islands or weather systems.

That inky line – how far away? – *hurts Verity's eyes with its intensity.*

Verity looks away from the brightness of sun on the sea, and down to the ground beneath her feet. The headland is rocky, with little grass to soften its jutting edges. She cannot see any way down to the beach from where she stands. Her eyes drift on, on and down, to the white-gold sickle of sand. She imagines she can see the individual grains of sand – tiny chips of silica washed over and over by the waves – pink, white, black, bronze, gold.

There is no-one on the beach. No footprints, no litter, no evidence of any human presence. Stunned for a moment, she realises there is no indication of time anywhere. This could be the twenty-first century; this could be hundreds of years ago; this could be the time before Christ. The thought makes her nauseous and dizzy, as though she had fallen asleep sitting upright. She looks all around for something to ground her in her own time: a telegraph pole, a car, a jet trail in the white-blue sky overhead. There is nothing.

Still dizzy, her eyes move along the beach to the shallow promontory at the far end. It is much lower than where she stands, and seems to be formed from natural steps of rock. A wave breaks against its base, and spray cascades, glinting for an instant, suggesting both lightness and weight.

Suddenly, she sees a movement on this lower spit of rock.

There is a horse, a black horse, on the pale, spiky grass atop the headland. As she watches, the horse steps towards the edge and leaps down to one of the rocky ledges. In seconds he is on the beach.

Verity stays still, mesmerised by his fluid movements.

He starts to race effortlessly along the beach, soft sand spilling up under his hooves. As he nears the apex of the bay, she sees he has no saddle, reins or stirrups. She feels a squeeze of fear. The stallion is still now, long sable nose to the air.

Verity wants to crouch down, make herself as small as possible, but her legs seem unable to bend or move. The horse runs straight into the waves. Water crystals fan out in glittering arcs as he plunges in deeper. The sun is so bright on the sea Verity can hardly see the horse, only a dazzling shimmer of light and water.

At last, the horse changes direction, seems to break free of the sparkling air. He cuts diagonally in to the shore, hauls himself from the water, and shakes the salty droplets from his coat. He churns the sand with his large hooves, shakes himself once more, and canters towards the base of the cliff, his eyes on Verity. She stumbles back in fear, but she knows he cannot climb the sheer cliff face.

A movement in the lee of the promontory. It's a young man with red hair. She recognises him from somewhere, some other time, some other life lived before. He must be the stallion's owner. Adrenaline floods out of Verity, the relief leaving her limbs heavy, uncoordinated.

The man – piper, she thinks, for some reason – reaches up to the horse's long black mane, tries to stop him forging onwards to the cliff. Then flailing hooves, sunlight on black, a cry, dreadful and timeless, from the man – or was it from the horse? The cracks of a huge stallion trampling across a broken human body, as blood pumps into the sand, flooding the glassy shards with crimson.

Verity cries aloud. The horse is directly below her. It raises its head to her, and she sees the primaeval anger in its eyes. Behind it the waves continue to swell and break in arches of green and mauve. The horse places its foot on the bottom of the cliff. Unable to move, Verity watches, as a goat track forms beneath the relentless hooves. She can smell the horse, and she can smell the blood from the dead man below her. The stallion delicately steps onto the top of the headland, only yards from her. She raises her head to its silver eyes, to her death.

Eyes that remind her of someone else.

The beast's head shatters in a kaleidoscope of black flesh, blood, and light on water: always the light, broken and diffused into prisms and crystals.

Always the light.

White light shafts into Verity's room through the half-drawn curtains. She's sweating, caught in the duvet, and her heart is leaping. Her surroundings jerk into focus.

89

She is in bed in Mullion. It's daytime. She is not on a cliff. There is no horse, no dead man. She is alive.

Verity shuffles up in the bed. She can still smell sweat, horseflesh, the sea, blood. No. She can't. It was a dream. She rubs her gritty eyes, checks the time. It's after eleven. On the carpet under her closed window is a pale swathe of sand.

Tim. Jack. She sits up suddenly.

Tim is ill, and she hasn't heard anything from either of them. Worse, she hasn't tried to call them. She slides out of bed, and feels the grit of sand under her feet. Where is her phone. She must have taken it to the Flora. Where did she put it?

As she paces through the house looking for it, she realises she hasn't even been online for days. She hasn't uploaded pictures of the beach and Carrag Luz to Facebook and Instagram. She hasn't even thought to do it.

Her phone isn't in the living room or in the hall. She rifles through her rucksack. It's not there. She must have dropped it in Helston.

Shit.

In the kitchen she opens the fridge to get orange juice. As she reaches in for the carton something slim and dark falls onto the floor. Her mobile. She puts down the juice and picks up the phone. It's cold from being in the fridge. When, why, how did she put it in there?

She plugs it into its lead. The screen flares with a burning white. Then the list of missed messages: mostly Jack, one from Tim, one from Caroline this morning. She dials her voicemail.

Verity, it's Jack. Tim's a bit better...still not right. Says he has things to do the next few days then we'll come.

Look, are you OK? Tim's having kittens about you.

Verity, can you call me back please? This is all kinda weird here. Whenever Tim...this sounds nuts right, but listen, when he says anything or does anything to do with coming to you, he gets ill again. When he decides he'll stay here he's fine. Some weird shit going on. Please ring me. Verity. Tim. I know Jack's been trying to get you. I've been ill. We've had to change our plans. Listen to me. Do not trust anyone. Keep yourself to yourself. Jack and I have to...prepare. There are things we need to do. Then we'll be with you. Just let us know you're all right.

Hi Verity, it's me, Caroline. Hope your legs aren't too stiff. I wondered if you'd seen the news about Flora Day? Some poor guy was murdered in the fairground. It can get rough down there at night...think it was a local bloke...awful business...Anyway, hope all's OK and see you soon.

The phone whistles with static in Verity's ear and she drops it with a clatter. *Some poor guy was murdered.* She hits the icon for the internet and the screen burns her eyes out with white. Something's wrong with it. The night in the fridge.

She gulps her juice, cold and acid in her throat, and dresses quickly. This time she takes the cliff path towards Mullion, away from Carrag Luz. Both cars are parked on the neighbours' strip of tarmac. Verity almost runs past, expecting to hear her name called, or to see Caroline opening the garden gate to intercept and trap her. She pauses at the wire fence, looks down to the second bay. The sea is way, way out. She can see the dark flash of rock pools, and the film of water left by the receding tide.

At the hotel, she turns left and scrambles down the steep path to the beach. Soft sand sprays round her feet. This is nothing like the beach in her dream. There are people here, sitting behind striped windbreaks, or splashing at the shoreline. Two dogs race round each other. Verity cuts across the beach to the far headland, moving fast. Barnacles are clamped to the charcoal-black rocks, and seaweed streamers have unfurled onto the sand. She stops at the entrance to the further bay, feeling queasy, standing where, in a matter of hours, the tide will surge in. She moves on, round the headland, noticing the dark strata that mark the high water mark, and into the second bay.

There are footprints. Verity stops and looks down. The prints appear to come out of the water itself. She walks down to where the waves are creaming in.

Gulls cry overhead. Mullion Island looks hazy, as though its outlines have been painted in watercolour onto wet paper. As the sand gets wetter, the footprints too appear blurred, less human, more like those of a horse or a goat. Verity stops at the water's edge, uneasy. There's no-one in the second bay. She follows the footprints back up the beach. With every yard they become firmer, more definite, more human. Long feet, slender feet, bare feet, leading her across the damp sand to the further side of the cove, to the rocks at the base of the cliff. The prints stop. They simply stop at the rocks. There's a dusting of sand – like that on her bedroom carpet this morning – on the lower ledges. She wonders if the solitary walker had climbed up onto those shiny green-veined black rocks. She raises her face; her eyes travel upwards, up the rocky scree, over the stubbly grass and bluebells, higher and higher, to Carrag Luz looming above her, and, in that moment, she knows who walked across the sand, and how, like the horse in her dream, he ascended the sheer cliff. She shades her eyes, stares up at the wild crag overhead, expecting, wanting, to see a shining figure on its summit.

The booming of the waves startles her. She turns, stumbling in the wet sand. She's alone at the far end of the tidal beach. She feels dizzy, from the height of the cliff above her, and from standing where soon the ocean will flood, and from the knowledge that the angel – her angel – was here on this beach, that he left his prints there in the sand for her to follow. A large wave breaks, and water surges up the beach. The sea is still a long way from the headland, but Verity starts walking quickly back towards the point. The waves are higher, more powerful. The wind stings her cheek with crystals of spume.

She trudges across the larger beach. The dogs are still playing. One of the family groups is packing up the windshield, the rucksacks. Verity walks along the edge of the stream to the scattering of rocks that marks the start of the track. Above her rises the tough shoulder of land, vibrant bluebells, wild garlic and campion. She cans smell the garlic and the sea. She scrambles up the first few steps cut into the cliff side. The climb to the top seems insurmountable. As she climbs, Mullion Island and its skerries appear over the cliff edge. The jagged coastline softens to blue, as it winds on towards the Lizard. Now she can see across the second bay to Carrag Luz. There is no-one on the rocks.

Verity is exhausted when she reaches the top. On her way back along the cliff road she stops again at the wire fence and looks down. In the time it's taken her to climb up the cliff the sea has advanced closer to the headland. She can just discern the jumble of her own footprints by the rocks, though any time now they will be sucked at, drowned by the water. The elongated footprints have gone.

She checks the time when she gets back indoors and flicks on the TV for the news. It's the first item on the local bulletin.

Thirty-two year old man found dead the morning after Helston Flora Day. Shots of the fairground: the Big Wheel. *Found with fatal chest and abdominal injuries beside a fairground carousel. Peter Twiggs, better known as Twig, was a well-known busker and familiar figure at Flora Day. Police are appealing for any information.*

As the report closes, a photograph of the dead man appears on screen. Verity realises she knew all along who had been killed at the Flora. It's the piper, the red-haired man, who shouldered her aside in the street to stop her reaching the angel; who tried to stop the stallion climbing the cliff to where she stood in her dream.

A Porthtowan man has become the first to – Verity snaps off the TV.

"Jack," Tim calls from the kitchen. He can hear the TV in the living room, and knows Jack is in there in a sulky heap, not understanding what is happening. "Jack, come here. I need to talk to you."

"What about?" Jack in the doorway.

"Go and get me one of my Tarot packs. Any one. You choose. I need to show you something."

"Do me a spread?"

"No. Just get a pack. I want you to choose them."

Jack slouches away and returns a moment later with a parcel of dark silk.

"Thanks. Sit opposite me."

Jack slides into the wooden settle by the window. Tim unwraps the cards. It's his favourite set, with intricate Celtic illustrations and jewel-bright backs. He gazes out of the window as she shuffles. The white sky, the uneven chimneys of the Royal Crescent.

"I'm going to close my eyes," he says to Jack and turns back to him. "I'm going to select five cards. I can't see what I'm doing."

"You auditioning for BGT?"

"This is serious. Very serious."

"I'm watching."

Jack's voice sounds oddly distant coming from the place beyond Tim's eyelids. He drops a card quickly onto the table, that old oak table with pen marks and knife lines and all the years of love and happiness and heartache. Another card. Again, and again and again.

"Take the cards. I'll tell you what they are. My eyes are still closed."

He hears a faint scuffle of cards being gathered together.

"The cards are the Moon, the Magician, the Fool, the Empress and the Devil."

"Jeez. You *should* go on BGT."

Tim snaps open his eyes and snatches the five cards from Jack. There's no magic, no trickery in what has happened. He is not in control of the cards, they are in control of him.

"These cards." He lays a finger on the Devil, on the red and black goat face with twisted horns. "These cards have haunted me since Verity went to Mullion. First there were four." He shoves aside the Empress. "And I couldn't work out what they meant. They appeared in my room when I hadn't taken any cards to bed with me. Then this card joined them. The Empress. The fifth point of the pentacle."

"What's this got to do with Verity?"

"The Moon. The Moon represents Verity. The Magician is me. You are the Fool."

"Cheers, mate."

"You know what I've taught you. The Fool is a complex character undergoing changes. He does not remain a Fool."

Jack reaches out as if to touch the fan of cards, then withdraws his fingers.

"What's really going on with Verity? Why were you ill? It wasn't the Indian."

"No, it wasn't. I was ill because I was hoping we could go down and rescue her."

"From what?"

Tim picks up the Devil. "I don't know for sure. Not yet. The Empress has appeared and I think she will protect Verity to some extent. I don't know who she is."

"Protect her from what? Come on, what the fuck is going on? Why can't we ever get hold of her?"

"Exactly. She doesn't answer her phone. Have you looked at her social media? Her Facebook, Instagram?"

"Nothing I've noticed."

"Right. She hasn't been online at all. She's cutting herself off from people, from us. Because of what has happened to her. She has been caught up in some kind of…evil. I sense it, I *know* it."

"There was something," Jack starts.

"What?"

"When I was on the train the other day. I was looking through my pictures and all the ones of Verity had disappeared. Well, not disappeared as such, they were all just this bright white light. I meant to mention it but you were ill and…"

"Show me."

"Sure."

Jack returns a moment later with his mobile.

"I don't get it." He puts it down on the table amongst the scattered cards. There is the picture of him and Verity. He opens the gallery. Verity, Verity with him, Verity with Tim, Verity with a friend. "Well, they weren't there. They were this burning white light."

"Burning white light. That is important. Somehow."

"You're better now. Let's go."

Tim walks down the stairs in his mind, out onto the street to his car. He unlocks the car, settles into the driving seat. Four hours to Cornwall. Suddenly he doubles over the kitchen table as a fiery pain surges through his stomach.

"Tim?" Jack's hand on his shoulder.

"No. We can't." The pain softens. "The evil knows I am watching…waiting. It is calling me. It knows I must come for Verity and it knows that it faces a deadly adversary in me."

"Adversary," Jack repeats.

"Yes. I believe it set its sights on Verity, then discovered me, that I was getting warnings. The cards, the dreams. And now it is challenging me. And I am not ready. You and me, we must stay together, help each other grow strong. I will know when it is time to go."

96

"And Verity?"

Tim shakes his head. "I would be more afraid if it weren't for the Empress. I can only hope Verity can stay safe until we arrive, and we cannot arrive until the challenge has been given and I am fit for it. We stay together, you and me, the Magician and the Fool."

Tim hasn't been entirely honest with Jack. He already has had a premonition of who awaits him. He cannot go unprotected or he will lose his sanity, even his life – and Verity too. Somehow Tim has to arm himself physically and spiritually to bring her home.

"The Magician and the Fool," he says again.

Monday morning, and Verity wakes with the dawn. Moments later she leaves the house and scrambles up to the mossy ledge of Carrag Luz. The tide has just turned, pulling back across the sand in the larger cove, sucking darker streaks of pebbles through the pale gold. The tidal beach is still underwater, the grey-green waves exploding on the headland with a crack of spray.

Hours later and it is still only mid-morning. Verity has taken a cup of tea into the garden. She stands at the edge of the lawn, near where the boys found the rabbit. She can smell the salt and the sand from the beach below. The leaves and flowers glow with a jewelled intensity. There's a click behind her and she spins round.

"I'm sorry to bother you." Caroline sounds puffed. "Frank's got to shoot off to the university for a meeting and I need to go to Helston and Andy's refusing to come. He's being really difficult. I don't suppose you could come and sit with him for a couple of hours, could you? He says he wants to see you. He screams and cries if I tell him he has to come with me, and Frank has to leave in ten minutes. I'd be so grateful. If you're not busy?"

Half an hour later Verity walks round to Caroline's house. Andy is at the kitchen table, drawing. He looks up and beams as Verity comes into the room. She can see his eyes behind his glasses are blotchy from earlier tears.

"I'm so sorry," Caroline tugs her aside and whispers. "You won't believe it, but I've never seen him so upset. As soon as I said you were coming round, he stopped screaming. It will be so much easier when he starts school too. Then I'll only have this one to worry about in the day." She places her hands on her abdomen.

"It's no problem," Verity says. "I'm very fond of Andy."

"There's milk and juice if he wants a drink. You can let him have a chocolate biscuit, but not too many, or he won't eat his lunch. I've got my mobile, and I'll be back by one. Promise. Do you need any shopping?"

Verity shakes her head and sits opposite Andy at the table, where she sat the night she came round for a meal. The mats are heaped in a toppling pile at one end of the table. Andy has spread his pencils and felt tips across a makeshift tablecloth of newspaper. There are coloured lines on the newspaper where his pen has gone over the edge of the paper. He hunches low over his work. Left-handed, Verity notices, like Tim. They both see other things, through windows into other worlds. Andy's hand curves round the pen like a tiny claw. There's ink on his fingers.

"What are you drawing?" Verity asks.

"Guess," Andy says, still hiding his pad.

"Flora Day?" Verity suggests.

Andy shakes his head, then nods.

Verity feels colour in her face.

"The angel?" she asks.

Andy moves his hand, turns his drawing pad round for her to see. There's green grass in the foreground with huge blue flowers she takes to be bluebells. Carrag Luz is angular and black. Andy has not got the crag's outline correct – Verity believes she could draw that silhouette blindfolded – but she knows immediately what it is. Dark blue sea. A huge yellow sun in the top right-hand corner, and a man outlined in black felt tip – to show he is white – leaping from the top of the rock, his golden hair streaming behind him.

"I don't know what colour to use." Andy points at the white man. "I don't like not colouring him."

"There isn't the right colour," Verity says, at last. "You have to leave him like that. You're very good at drawing."

"I've done some more." Andy reaches down to the empty chair beside him and drops two more pages in front of Verity.

Balloons. Lots of balloons. There's a Duggee and a blue-green fish. To the side of the balloons is a white and yellow figure.

The other drawing is just of the man, the angel. Andy's immature hand has made his features like a mask. Verity shivers. In this picture the angel looks sinister, not the beautiful, fine-featured young man she met on the cliff.

"I'm going to make a cup of tea. Would you like some milk?" Verity asks, suddenly wanting to put down the drawings that tell the narrative of her life for the last few days.

"Mmm," Andy says absently. He puts aside his picture of Carrag Luz and takes a fresh sheet of paper.

Verity brings over milk and a chocolate biscuit for Andy, and a tea for herself. She places her mug on the dresser behind her chair.

"What's this one?" she asks.

"This is the last one," Andy says.

"Can I see?"

"When it's finished."

Andy curls low over the page again. Verity feels uncomfortable sitting there watching his hand move in lines and circles. He casts aside the black pen, reaches for a blue one, then turquoise, then yellow.

Verity picks up the Sunday colour supplement that's been discarded on the floor. She flicks through, trying not to watch Andy over the shiny pages.

"Jonny says he's not real," Andy says suddenly. "He can't see him."

"I can," Verity says, letting the magazine slide out of her hands in a rustle of glossy pages.

"You and me," Andy says.

"Who is he?" Verity asks again.

"He's an angel," Andy says.

"Have you always seen him?" Verity asks.

Andy shakes his head vigorously. "Finished," he says, and shoves his drawing across the table.

Verity can smell the ink from the felt tips. The paper, when she touches it, is slightly damp. She turns it the right way up.

Andy has drawn yellow and orange sun-burst lines coming out from the angel's form to suggest a greater, brighter light. He is facing another man, who is pointing a sword with his left hand. In his right he holds a shield. His hair is long and black, and he's wearing a turquoise cloak. Sprouting from his back are huge wings, with frantic blue and turquoise lines, and huge green eyes on them. Like peacock feathers.

Verity feels sick suddenly.

The man – there's something about the man. She runs her eyes over the details. He's left-handed. So is Andy. But so is Tim.

"Tim," she breathes. "This is Tim."

"What?" Andy says.

"This," she points at the man in the picture. "This man here. This is Tim. He's someone I know. You've not met him, but you've drawn him. How? Why? Why Tim?"

"Not Tim," Andy says simply, starts slotting his felt tips into their plastic holder: lemon yellow, through golds to oranges and reds.

"Yes. Tim. He's called Tim." Verity hears her voice rising.

"No, he's not," Andy says, sliding in grass green.

Verity puts the drawing down. She thinks her hands may be shaking.

"What's he called then?" she asks Andy.

Andy shrugs.

~

The day is stagnant, holding its breath. In the afternoon there's a shower of rain, not an angry squall that whips the waves into crests, just a gentle – almost warm – drizzle, as though the clouds above are silently weeping. The raindrops fall softly, silently, with no rattle on the glass, as Verity stands at the window. The Land's End peninsula is in sunlight and, as quietly and as gently as it came, the shower drifts away, leaving only a sheen on leaves and petals, and the scent of damp earth in the air.

Verity turns left onto the cliff path. Behind Carrag Luz the sea is a vibrant cobalt, the clear blue that only comes after the rain. There are a few snails sliding across the track and, in the undergrowth by Carrag Luz, Verity sees a rabbit veering towards the cliff edge. She draws parallel to the great outcrop and hesitates. She can sense a magnetic power, deep and ancient, flowing between the rocks and her feet. She envisages this force as white light, lightning even, searing through the crumbling cliff, through the fault line, cleaving the land in two.

She leaves the rocks behind her. The path plunges down and up again. In the chasm below, the water is green and purple, slapping and sucking round the cliff base. As she rises once more, she sees, over the next headland, the wedge of Mullion Island, and the humped stacks between it and the coastline. She shivers as the watery sunshine fades. Unnerved she stops, turns. There is no-one behind her, just a faint rustling in the undergrowth: another rabbit?

Across the gully she can see Carrag Luz from the south. From this side it resembles more the wild seaward face. She sways a moment, giddy on the edge of the precipice. The drop to the water is steep, sudden; there are black rocks just under the surface.

In moments the path has opened up onto the next headland. Verity finds some steps cut into the cliff, which lead her to the harbour below. As she descends the air becomes warmer, thick with the smell of fish and seaweed. The frail sunlight has gone, hidden behind a cool grey film. When she jumps down the last few steps she is almost on the jetty.

The sea, high and rising, looks oily, viscous. There are boats moored up at the jetty, and a pile of pink and orange floats. Verity starts along the jetty. The harbour wall turns at right angles. She scrambles up onto a higher ledge. She can see over the top of the wall, across the listless strait to the island. Beyond the jetty, a conical stack juts out of the water, stained white and gold with guano and lichen. The sea slaps its base with each half-hearted wave.

She walks along this ledge to the end of the jetty. A man is standing on the very edge with a line cast into the green-brown water. The cliffs south of the harbour are wounded with cracks and caves. Sea bubbles over the last strips of sand, leaving a spittle crust on the dark rocks. Gulls soar overhead; some bounce on the queasy swell. Verity gazes out to sea, past the island to the horizon.

She thinks about Andy's drawings, his portrayal of Tim. By the time Caroline had returned Andy had packed up his pens and paper and taken the pictures to his room. Verity had folded up the newspaper and shoved it in the bin. She hadn't got her mobile to take photos of the drawings, and wanted to ask Andy if she could keep them. Instead, she had to memorise them: the angel, the balloons, the rocks, Tim.

Verity shakes her head.

It's crazy, but that drawing *was* of Tim: the left-handed swordsman dressed in peacock blue. Andy had given him wings of peacock feathers, as though he too were an angel.

Verity turns away from the sea and the solitary fisherman, starts walking back along the ledge. Watery rust stains bleed down the wall from iron rings. A gull lands a couple of yards away, watches her insolently with a prehistoric yellow eye.

The climb back up the cliff is steep, and she is breathless when she arrives at the top. The light has changed again, and the sea below now shimmers silver. She can pick out smudges of green on Mullion Island.

As the cliff path dips towards the deep chasm in the cliff Carrag Luz looms up, tough and monstrous. Verity blinks in a sudden sharp flash of sunlight. As she opens her eyes she sees him, the angel, standing on the very top of the crag, his arms hanging loosely at his sides, his face turned away from her so she sees the hazy gold of his hair. It looks as though he is watching the currents surging into the tidal bay at Polurrian. Verity stops. She wants to cry out to him, but she is afraid her voice will startle him. She slithers down the track, and a scree of small stones skitters under her foot. She cannot stop herself from looking over the edge into the chasm she stared into on her way to the harbour. A wave curls and slithers over the slimy rocks. She looks back to Carrag Luz and, in the instant she was watching the water below, the angel has gone.

"No!" Verity cries and starts running up the uneven path to the rocks. "Wait for me!"

The cliff path winds on ahead past her bungalow and through the fault line. He's not there. He could not have walked out of sight in this time. She stumbles through the grasses – dried now in the sunlight – to Carrag Luz. There are wet footprints on the lower boulders, slender like those she found on the beach. She reaches down, and touches one of the dark images. The rock is vaguely cool, but not wet. She places her foot on the print and hauls herself up to the first ledge. Bracing her shoulder against the rounded boulder beside her, she leans over the edge. He's not on the grassy slope below the rock where she first saw him. The undergrowth looks undisturbed. Waves flood into the tidal beach, breaking listlessly, lazily. Almost all the sand is covered by the water. Foam curls mark the rocks under the surface.

Verity turns her head to look up.

The outline of the giant rock shudders as though she has drunk too much wine on an empty stomach, and she grips the rough stone wildly and stumbles back from the precipice. Then she sees higher footprints scaling the crag. For a crazy second, she considers placing her foot over the angel's mark. Surely, following his path, she could climb Carrag Luz too, and stand on the top of the world surveying the deep blue bowl of the bay. Maybe she could stretch out her arms, and soar off the rocks on a thermal current.

Verity unlatches the garden gate, lethargic with loss.

Andy hurtles down the bank onto her front lawn, arms flapping. His legs slide from under him and he sprawls on the grass.

"Andy, be careful. Does your Mum know you're here?"

Andy staggers up on chubby legs. There are grass stains on his shapeless jeans.

"I'm flying," he says. "I'm going to fly. Like the angel."

"Did you—?" Verity starts.

"He flew away," Andy says. "He saw you and he flew away."

"Where were you?" Verity asks.

"Here."

If Andy had been standing on the lawn outside her front door, he would have seen her on the crag, would have seen the angel on the top, glowing white-gold against the washed-out sky.

"Did you see him fly?" Verity asks Andy.

Are you fucking crazy? she asks herself. *You're asking a four year old boy if he saw an angel fly. But, more than that, you believe the angel can fly.*

Andy screws up his eyes behind his glasses.

"Not really," he says. "He was there, and then…"

"He wasn't."

"He can fly." Andy scrambles back up the bank, walks a few yards up the side of the house. Verity watches him run to the top of the bank and skid down again, arms waving.

"I think flying is much harder than it looks," Verity says. "Come on. Let's get you home before your Mum gets worried."

"I can't fly yet," Andy protests.

"Have another go tomorrow," Verity says. "Perhaps the angel will make your wings grow overnight."

~

Andy screws up his eyes. He's aware of light on his skin, but it does not feel warm like sunshine. The sensation of light shifts subtly to that of being watched.

Carefully, Andy opens his eyes. White light; white and gold. Andy's vision is blurry without his glasses, and all he sees is the colours, the shimmer. He fumbles a chubby fist to where his mother puts his glasses overnight on the cupboard beside his bed. As his hand lands on the spectacles, he feels fingers, cool and strong over his own.

"No."

105

He's not sure if he heard the word, or if he felt it in his head, but he knows instinctively it is the voice of the angel. He opens his mouth to speak, does not know what to say. Vaguely he can see a hump in Jonny's bed. His brother must still be asleep. Andy wants to call out to Jonny, He should wake up and see the angel, see that he is real.

Hot tears run down Andy's face. Without his glasses he cannot see the angel's face.

"You want to fly."

"Yes, please." Andy struggles to sit up, tearing at the jumbled quilt.

"Be quiet, and come now."

Andy feels those strong hands once more, this time lifting him from the bed. The angel carries him to the window. Andy can discern the pale pearl light of dawn. He shivers in his thin pyjamas. The angel slides through the open window – is that how he got in? Andy wonders. Their window is only ever left only a chink: now it is wide open.

"Where are we going to fly to?" Andy asks.

It already feels like flying, being borne aloft in the angel's arms.

"You will fly over the edge of the world."

Andy is silent. He doesn't quite understand, but he doesn't want to admit to the angel, who is so beautiful and clever, that he is confused. Although he can hardly see, Andy feels a gentle zephyr on his skin, smells the thick scent of wild garlic, hears the distant waves rolling onto the rocks below.

"Verity wants to fly too," Andy says.

"One day I will show her," the angel replies.

⌣

Jonny wakes in surprise. The bedroom is freezing.

"Andy," he hisses, and drags his covers onto his shoulders. "Andy."

Andy's quilt is on the floor, discarded, tangled. Andy's bed is empty. The window is open, which is why the room is so cold.

Something moves and he jumps. It's his green and blue fish balloon, bobbing below the ceiling.

Jonny slides his feet to the floor. The house seems very quiet. The bedroom door is shut, but even so he pads out to the hall and looks up and down. It's cold this early in the morning, and the tall lamp left on all night looks wrong in the grey almost-daylight. Jonny goes back into his room, and picks up Andy's duvet to make sure Andy isn't hiding under the bed. As he gathers up the lumpy material, he sees a pile of coloured pages under the bed. Strange, but he hadn't noticed them before. He pulls them out. More of Andy's weird drawings. He glances from the balloons on the paper to the two bobbing quietly side by side in the corner. He shuffles through the drawings. It must be that angel Andy's always going on about. That's the rocks up by Verity's house. And there's an angel leaping from the very top. Jonny feels suddenly queasy. He throws the drawings down, and shoves his feet into a pair of trainers. Standing on his bed he manages to get astride the windowsill. Then he notices Andy's glasses on the bedside cupboard. Andy can't see anything without them. Jonny slides back into the room, scoops up the glasses and, once more, clambers up to the window.

The drop is only a couple of feet and he lands upright. There's something black on the grass. Jonny recoils. It's a blackbird, lying still, neck twisted. He runs across the lawn. There's another blackbird, and a blue tit. Jonny knows the names of a lot of birds because his mother has shown him pictures in her big hard-backed bird book. He stops in the middle of the lawn. There are dead birds all over the grass.

Jonny sprints to the gate and fumbles with the latch.

Another day, another dawn. Verity's bedroom is hazy with the muted light of daybreak. *If only I could see Carrag Luz from here*, she thinks. *I could lie here in bed, and watch the rocks until he comes back.*

She thinks she may have been dreaming about the angel because she can sense him close to her. She feels the inexplicable intimacy of having shared her dream-time with him. She imagines – or does she remember? – the scent of his hair and skin, the taste of his mouth on hers. Unsatisfied she drifts into the living room. The curtains are half drawn. The sea is a crumpled silver like tin foil. As she tugs the curtain back, she can see the mottled bulk of Carrag Luz. There's movement in the grasses below the crag.

The angel straightens. His hair is pale as milk, hanging down the back of his white tunic. Verity gasps and blushes at the memory of her dreams. The angel leaps up the crag, spreads his arms, and spins round to face her. She gazes back at him, unable to move, then suddenly sees it is not her he is watching. A small figure is stumbling blindly through the tufty grasses towards the crag. He trips, falls, on his face, staggers upright again.

Andy.

Verity's hands are shaking as she unlocks the front door. She runs out in her nightdress and slippers. The lawn is broken with dark shapes: blackbirds and starlings, all still, all twisted, in the dewy grass. All dead. As though they – like Andy – tried to fly from the top of the grass bank, but their wings did not unfurl.

Perhaps the angel will make your wings grow overnight.

Verity hears the words, hears her own voice. Nausea stings her throat. The jagged stones of the cliff path punch her feet through her slippers. Her nightdress is slipping off her shoulder. The angel stands on the highest point of the crag, arms spread. Only feet below him Andy is clawing his way up the boulders. Verity remembers the footprints on the rock yesterday, how she so nearly placed her feet over the angel's marks.

"Andy, Andy!"

She spins round at the voice. Jonny's hurtling towards her, arms pounding.

"Jonny, ssh," she says.

"It's Andy," Jonny gasps. He uncurls his hand to reveal Andy's glasses. "He can't see, and he's on the rock."

Verity closes Jonny's hand round the glasses. "Keep those safe," she says, and grabs his spare hand.

Together they run the last few yards to where the grass track forks off towards Carrag Luz.

Tim wakes, tearing at his shoulders with his fingernails. The itching is unbearable. He tugs off his T-shirt and twists around in front of the mirror. There are vivid red scratches over his scapulae, and speckles of blood. Tim steps closer to the mirror, and squints in the pale light. It feels like there's something writhing under his skin, trying to burst forth. Queasily he remembers the dream he had, where he was split open like the landscape after an earthquake. It's not just the itching: his left hand, shoulder and biceps are aching with a hot pain, as though he had been wielding a sword in his sleep.

"How did he...?" Jonny gapes at Andy, who is almost on top of the crag.

"The angel," Verity breathes.

The angel glows with white fire. His hair lifts gently in the breeze like spun sugar. Verity can feel the same energy she felt the day before

109

pulsing from the rocks to her feet. Her toes are wet from the dawn dew where her slippers have torn. She knows there is gooseflesh on her arms, but she's not cold: she's warmed by that white fire.

"What? Andy! Andy!" Jonny cries. "Andy, don't!"

Andy doesn't turn. He's sprawled across the edge of the uppermost rock, his fingers clawing out for handholds. The angel stands above him: remote, stern, glorious. Andy grabs onto the rock. His hand slips and his body slides towards the edge.

"Andy!" Jonny cries. "He's sleepwalking, isn't he?" he screams at Verity.

"No," Verity says. "He's with the angel. He's going to fly with the angel."

"There's no angel."

"I want to fly too," Verity says. She lets go of Jonny's hand and steps through the wet grass towards Carrag Luz.

"Verity, stop! Andy! Come back. There's no-one there! You can't see! Look, I've got your glasses. Andy!"

Verity is distantly aware that someone – Jonny? – is crying behind her, but all she can see is the angel, balanced on the edge of the world. She no longer notices the small boy who shudders to his feet beside the angel, and reaches his arms wide above the silver-blue of the bay.

~

Andy's spectacles are digging into Jonny's hand so much his palm hurts. He's cold, icy cold, and shivering, and when he calls again to his brother his voice is broken and shaking. Ahead of him Verity is wading through the grass, her hands out, reaching for the rocks. Andy's on the top of the crag, high above Jonny's head. His arms are raised, like an aeroplane or a bird. Jonny remembers the dead birds on the lawn.

"Andy!" Jonny barrels past Verity, knocking her sideways.

110

He jumps up the first ledge, slips and crashes down on his knees. He throws out his hands to break his fall, and Andy's glasses shoot out of his grip and tumble down the scrubby grass towards the sea. Tears sting Jonny's eyes. His hands are grazed and his knee is hot with pain.

"Andy, don't move."

"Jonny?" Andy's voice is thin, uncertain.

"I'm coming to get you."

"I'm going to fly with Angel."

"There's no-one there."

"Angel's here."

Jonny reaches onto the next rock. He daren't look down, down the slope of the cliff where the lenses of Andy's glasses wink like broken eyes, and beyond to where waves slap the jagged rocks. If he slips, he'll die. And so will Andy.

"There's no fucking angel," Jonny gasps. The word falls in the morning stillness. Bracing his left side into the crag he stretches his right arm and grabs Andy's ankle. His pyjamas are soaking.

Andy screams.

"Andy, it's OK. It's me, Jonny. Don't move."

"I can't see! Where am I?"

"Don't move," Jonny says again.

"Jonny, Jonny."

Jonny cannot turn to face the land, without losing his grip on Andy. Where's Verity?

"Verity!" he cries. "Verity, help me!"

Someone's calling her name. Verity shudders to consciousness. She's cold, standing in wet grasses. Carrag Luz, grey and forbidding. She sees two small figures: one clinging to the rock, one tottering on the crag.

"Verity!"

"Jonny! Andy!" Verity runs to the rock, scrambles onto the first ledge.

"I can't hold him anymore," Jonny cries. "Help me."

The rock is only inches from Verity's face. Cold breath exhales from its damp skin. Her eyes move up the mottled surface. There are no handholds. She cannot climb to the top. A sudden gust of wind catches her in the face.

"He can't see," Jonny stammers. "I dropped his glasses."

"It's better he can't see," Verity says. She raises her voice. "Andy, listen, it's Verity. Jonny and I are going to get you down, OK?"

From where she stands, she can't see how much space there is on the top of the crag, or how steeply it slopes down into that ravaged face looking out across the Atlantic.

"Andy, listen carefully. Can you sit down exactly where you are?"

"I can't see!" Andy screams.

"I know, I know," Verity says. "Can you just bend your legs and sit down?"

"I can't move."

"Andy, I'll count to three. On three Jonny's going to let go of your leg, but he'll keep his hand right by you, OK? And you just sit down."

"I can't see!"

"One."

"Jonny, don't."

"Two."

"Jonny!"

"Three."

Jonny releases his hold on Andy's leg. Andy wavers, arms windmilling in another gust. Slowly, he lowers himself to the rock.

"Well done, Andy," Verity says. "You're doing so well. We'll have you down in a tick." She turns to Jonny. "I'll pick you up. You grab him gently. We don't want to scare him. Just slide him towards us. We'll have to slide him down the rock and catch him."

"Where's Mummy?" Andy wails.

"We'll get you back to your Mummy in a minute," Verity says. Before Jonny can protest, she hauls him up, surprised at how hefty a six year-old is.

"Andy, hold my hand."

"I can't see."

"Andy, no! Not that way!"

Verity can't see what's happening. She braces herself against the rock. She's shivering with cold and fear. She should have run back and woken Caroline and Frank. But she and Jonny could not leave Andy there, perched like a fledgling.

Why is he up there anyway? How did she and Jonny end up out on the cliff?

Surely Caroline and Frank are awake by now. What the hell can she tell them? All these thoughts tumble through her mind as, at last, Jonny cries out: "That's right, Andy."

"OK, Jonny, I'll hold you steady. You pull him towards us, let him dangle his legs over."

"Jonny!" Andy cries.

Suddenly, there's a massive jerk above Verity. She stumbles back, under this abrupt velocity, turning her ankle over on the rocky shelf. Two small bodies slide past her into the stubbly grass and thorns.

"Andy, Andy," she cries, rolling onto her knees.

Jonny is on his feet. "We rescued you, we rescued you," he sings. "Andy, are you OK?"

"I'm cold," Andy says. "Where am I?"

"You're on the cliff," Jonny says.

"Why?"

"You said you were with the angel," Jonny says.

Something gold and white flashes in Verity's peripheral vision, disperses into pale sunlight.

"We must go," she says, picking up Andy. She glances over her shoulder at Carrag Luz, warming to pink and gold with the rising sun.

"Don't tell them," Jonny mutters at his parents' gate. It is swinging open, from when he raced out – when? Half an hour ago? An hour ago?

"But, Jonny, you're both hurt. Andy's lost his glasses."

"They have a spare pair for him. I know where they keep them."

"I can't lie to your parents," Verity says, pushing open the gate.

"Our bedroom window's open," Jonny says. "We can just climb in, and they'll never know."

He leads the way across the lawn.

"That's weird."

"What?" Verity says. She's cold, tense, afraid. What would have happened to Andy if she hadn't been there? What the hell can she tell Caroline and Frank?

"Where are the dead birds? They've gone."

Dead birds. Verity opens her mouth to speak, closes it again. Whatever she was going to say has gone.

"Look, that's our window." Jonny has dropped his voice to a whisper. "It's open. We can just go in."

They stand in front of the window. Jonny's got his hands on the ledge. He winces from his cut palms. Verity's still holding Andy. He seems to have fallen asleep.

Suddenly, through the window, as though on television, she sees the bedroom door swing wide. Caroline stops in the portal.

"Jonny! Andy!" Her voice is wild. Then she sees the three of them out on the lawn, bloodied with torn clothes.

"Verity, what the hell?" Caroline shouts through the open window.

114

"Can you let us in, Caroline?" Verity says, suddenly exhausted. She turns away and carries Andy to the front door. Jonny stomps beside her.

Caroline draws the bolts back with vicious squeals. Frank is there beside her in boxer shorts and a towelling robe. For a moment Verity just stands there, as Andy is lifted from her arms. She hears the names *Jonny* and *Andy* over and over again.

Caroline bundles the boys into the house.

Frank stands back to let Verity in. She crosses her arms over her chest, aware of her muddy nightdress and how the cold and damp reveal her nipples through the thin material.

"What on earth's been happening?" Frank asks. He throws her a parka from a hook in the hall.

Verity turns her back on him, forces her shaking arms into the jacket. She can hear Jonny's voice, telling his parents "We went to play in Verity's garden "

"Is that true?" Frank asks.

He walks into the kitchen. Verity trails after him. He clangs mugs down on the worktop.

"No," Verity says, sliding down onto one of the dining chairs. "It's not true."

⁓

There's no obvious evidence of what happened at dawn. The rocks are warm under Verity's hands. She sweeps her palm over the knobbly lichen. No doubt forensics would find traces of blood, of skin, of hair, that proved two little boys and a young woman clung to this crag, but she cannot discern anything different. Leaning against the boulder where Andy perched, she looks down to where his glasses fell. There are grasses and leaves, thorns and flowers. She cannot see the flash of sunlight on lenses.

But it wasn't just two little boys and a young woman. The angel was there too. She recalls this in splinters, like fragments of a dream. Or was it all a dream? No, not a dream, because her ankle throbs from where she fell, and her arms and shoulders ache from holding Jonny. She wonders what evidence the forensics people might find to prove an angel stood on this crag.

She hunkers down on the ledge, rests her cheek against the stone. Below her the sea is surging past the headland into the tidal bay. It is about half-tide, incoming. Miserably she remembers her conversation with Frank. He was cold with her, distant, as though it were her fault.

Was it? she asks herself.

She told Frank she was looking out of her front window and saw Andy walking alone towards Carrag Luz. She immediately raced out in her nightdress. Jonny was on the lane, also racing after Andy. Together they coaxed him back. At this moment Caroline came in, with Jonny and Andy trailing after her. Jonny had been crying, his jubilation gone. Andy was beaming, wearing another pair of spectacles, muttering about the angel.

"I told you not to lie to me, Jonny," Caroline said angrily. She turned to Verity, hunched in Frank's parka. "Jonny said they were playing in your garden."

Jonny pulled a desperate face at Verity. She looked away, unable to meet his gaze. After the moments they'd shared on the cliff edge, it seemed so unfair to discredit him, but she had no choice. She had already told Frank.

"Andy was on the cliff," she said again. "I saw him from the window. He was heading for the rocks. I went after him."

Endless questions for her, for Jonny and Andy. How did Andy get out of the window? Who opened the window? Why was he up there?

"Angel," Andy wailed over and over. "He took me. He was going to teach me to fly. Jonny frightened him away. He'll come again."

116

Verity draws her knees under her chin. Caroline and Frank were furious. Furious with Andy for running away – *was he taken?* Caroline kept screaming. Had a child molester opened the window? Furious with Jonny for not waking them. Furious with Verity for – what? Being there? Rescuing Andy? She knows her relationship with the neighbours has changed. They won't let her near the boys again, and Andy is her only link to the angel.

She stands and edges round to the southern side of the crag, and the finely balanced rock. Surely one day soon it will fall. Stray bluebells and garlic are growing on the steep cliff face. At its foot the mauve and green water sucks round the rocks. Some yards out to sea there is an eddying current on the surface. The water beneath these white streaks is deep purple. It could be a submarine chasm, Verity thinks, shivers, and backs away.

It is coming back to her now, like fractured dream fragments. The angel was on the top of Carrag Luz, calling Andy, beckoning him – no, commanding him – to climb to the top. She remembers that. Then there's a blur, just white-gold light, and then Jonny shouting at Andy, and suddenly the angel had gone, and Andy was trembling alone, blind and terrified on the crag.

Jack pounds up the sixty stairs to the attic flat. He's been for a run to try to clear his head but any endorphins he experienced out there are evaporating the closer he gets to the flat door. He was still asleep when Tim left for Cosmos that morning, after an evening's drinking with old friends. Neither the drink nor the run have helped him sift through the fuzz in his head. Verity, fools, magicians, evil forces.

The flat door is wedged open to the landing as Tim often leaves it when he's in. Jack heels off his trainers and kicks them aside to join the pile of junk beside the door: a woven basket, a broken umbrella, a

117

wooden Buddha, a couple of scarves thrown in coils. Tim must be home for lunch.

"Jack? I need to talk to you."

Jack pads along to the kitchen. Tim is sitting at the table with a mug of clear amber tea in front of him. Jack gulps down the last of the water in his running bottle and refills it at the sink. He turns back to Tim, taken aback.

Tim looks different, Tired and tense, but it's something else. Almost as though – no, it's ridiculous – the features of another man were superimposed onto his face. His mouth and chin are different, his eyes more blue than grey.

"You know Verity did that dance at the Flora? The Hal an Tow?"

"Yeah. That's what we were going down for."

"It's a very old dance. A mumming play. It tells the story of an encounter that took place in Helston at the beginning of time."

Jack drinks water. His skin is heating up indoors and he's aware of sweat in unpleasant places.

"Right. OK."

"The encounter was between the Devil and the Archangel Michael." Tim twists and rubs his back.

"What you done to your back?"

"Pain in my shoulders."

"You pulled something?"

"No. Just listen. They fought their battle down there. Michael defeated the Devil, and cast him back into Hell. He sealed the entrance to Hell with a stone. That's where the name Helston comes from."

"Folklore."

"What is folklore? It's the people telling the old stories, the stories that formed our societies, our beliefs, our atavistic fears. You know this. I've taught you this."

Jack can't deny this. Tim has taught him and Verity about the old tales and songs, the ones as old as time itself. Probably at some point he even told them this story about the Devil and the Archangel.

"Since she got involved in the Hal an Tow she's become the focus for something evil. It will destroy her if we don't save her."

"I keep saying to you: let's go." Jack's not sure what he believes now, but one thing he does know: he wants his sister back.

"You're a geologist. Put that aside for a moment. These earthquakes they've been having down there..."

"Tremors."

"Whatever. They have disturbed something that has lain dormant a long, long time. You know how old the rocks are. When they move, the most ancient places in the earth are revealed."

Jack's sweat feels cold and slimy. "You think the tremors disturbed the Archangel's stone?" He can hardly believe his words. What the fuck would the other students think? The lecturers?

"And it's let loose..."

"That's crazy."

"It's not just the earthquakes. The cards. Remember. The five cards." Tim points at Jack. "The Fool. He's about to set forth on a journey but he's not adequately prepared. He may overturn the whole thing unless he prepares himself. As his journey progresses – and he is tested – he changes."

"You mean the journey to Mullion?"

"Of course."

"So, let's go."

"We are not ready. Neither of us. Both of us are needed for this battle. You must save Verity while I..."

"Do what?"

"I am changing too."

119

Jack flinches. For a second, there's a pale silver-gold shimmer around Tim's head. A halo.

~

Verity's mobile is missing again. She doesn't care, doesn't want to find it because it will pulse with messages from Tim and Jack, but she realises that if only she'd had it with her on the cliff, she could have roused Caroline or the Coastguard.

She trails through the house, the charger in her hand, looking in the most unlikely places she can think of: the airing cupboard, the laundry basket, the freezer. Why these places she doesn't know. She can't see it anywhere, can't recall when she last held it.

She drifts into the front room. The light is slanted, angular, over the bay, in slashes of gold and purple. On the horizon are more storm clouds, blurring the very end of the Land's End Peninsula like a damp thumb mark. The tamarisk hedge sighs with a premonition of the approaching squall.

And there is it. Her mobile. On the windowsill. Perhaps she did leave it there. The screen is dead and she sticks the charger into the nearby socket. Glastonbury Tor flashes up – her background photo – then one by one the icons. She waits for it to start cheeping with notifications. Nothing happens. She looks again. Every icon has become a horned death's head. She scribbles her finger over the screen.

Close it down. Turn it off. Try again. This time she doesn't get the Tor. The screen turns to white, glowing, burning her eyes. She looks away, out of the window. The bright screen is reflected in the glass pane. It flashes, once, twice, three times, faster and faster, like wild sheet lightning.

She jabs at the screen and the flashing increases. For a second, she wonders what it will do to her in the end, this constant flashing. She yanks the cable from the socket and presses hard on the off switch.

The white flashes continue so she kicks it under the coffee table, face down. The battery will die soon.

Disconcerted, she returns to the kitchen and opens the fridge. A hard heel of bread, some cheese. The salad looks slimy. She's nearly out of milk. Spar will still be open. She needs a proper meal; she has not been eating properly. Maybe that is why her memory is so vague, why she seems to lose tracts of time.

Like this morning. She knows something happened with the angel and the boys next door, but she can't recall what it was. She remembers fear in their voices, Frank's coldness, and the flare of Caroline's anger. Were they angry at her? She can't remember. She must have fallen at some point because her ankle is painful.

Ten minutes later and she is unlocking the Getz. She puts it into reverse and glances in her mirror. Something pale behind the car. She turns clumsily, jarring her neck. Her foot judders off the clutch and the car stalls. There is nothing. Only her imagination.

She bumps past the Tripconeys' house. Frank's car is missing from the parking strip. Verity feels hollow inside. Whatever happened has changed everything. Andy was in danger. Andy almost died.

Misty rain blurs the windscreen as she drives into Mullion. She finds a parking place close to the Spar. It's only as she pockets her keys that she realises Frank's car is beside hers.

Frank is selecting potatoes off the vegetable racks. Verity hesitates in the shop doorway, watching him reject one, choose another, and slip it into a paper bag. He straightens, glances in her direction.

"Hi Verity."

"Hi," she says, moving into the shop. "I realised I was out of almost everything."

"Did you walk? I can give you a lift back." He's smiling; the coldness has gone from his eyes. Maybe she imagined that as well.

"Thanks, but I brought the car." She picks up tomatoes and a cucumber, takes a couple of potatoes herself. Because Frank is friendly again, she says, "Actually, I wonder if you could help me out."

"Sure, if I can."

"It's my phone. It's doing some really weird things. I'm no good at this sort of stuff. I can't get it to work at all. I wondered if you could come and have a look in the next day or so?"

"Course." Frank puts milk into his basket. "It's probably something simple. Do you need it tonight?"

"No, whenever you can. No rush."

"I'll come round tomorrow."

⁓

Tim's turned the lights off in his room and pulled the blinds down. He still can't escape the light. A pale glow seeps round the edges of the blinds, mingled with the queasy orange of the sodium lamps. He rolls onto his stomach to ease the rawness below his shoulders.

He cannot do what he has to do without Jack. He cannot fight this evil alone and save Verity. Tim smiles crookedly into his pillow, feels a flood of calm acceptance. Now he knows what Verity has unleashed, and what he and Jack must do. Who he must once more become. He reaches round and rubs his hot itching back. He knows what is causing the pain, knows why his sword arm hurts when he wakes, knows who he was once, and who he will become again. At the birth of time, he failed. He will not fail again.

⁓

The lawn is cool under Verity's bare feet. Daisies and dandelions have sprouted up overnight. She crouches down and twists a daisy's wiry stem towards her. She imagines she can see each tiny mauve-lipped

122

petal open itself to the sun, to the light. She watches a ladybird climb a long strand of grass, watches the blade bend under the round red body. The scent of wild garlic drifts over the tamarisk hedge. Verity stands. There's a faint memory of pain, but she can't recall how she hurt herself. She walks on towards the far corner of the garden. There is a faint haze across Carrag Luz, like a gauze veil, which just blurs its contours, softens its colours of charcoal and rust.

She looks up to the sky. She is not sure what the time is. Mid-morning maybe. She is still in her nightdress. A soft breeze blows the fabric close to her skin.

She walks slowly back across the lawn, enjoying the sensation of the grass under her feet. It has grown long and soft with the rain. The sun hangs just over the house roof, a pale, intense disc. She stares at it, feels her eyes ache, and a sudden dizziness, almost nausea. When she drops her gaze to the ground that fierce ring burns behind her lids. She climbs the bank, rather than the stone steps, to the doorstep. At the top she turns once more to the bay. The horizon is hazy, and she cannot discern where the sea and the sky meet. Instead of a rain-sharpened ink line, they simply bleed into each other imperceptibly.

The clang of the gate, the crunch of gravel. Frank stands below her at the foot of the bank.

"I came to look at your phone. If it's convenient…"

"Thanks. Come on in."

She opens the door and pads into the house, aware of Frank following her, aware of his eyes on her flimsy shift, her knotted hair, her grass-stained feet. She grabs a cardigan from the hall chair and bundles it round her chest. A vague memory of Frank handing her a warm coat in his own hall.

"I'm sorry about yesterday," Frank says, closing the front door. "If I was short with you. I was so afraid."

"I understand." Verity cannot talk about the previous day. She cannot remember what happened, except that Andy was in danger, and somehow she brought him home.

"Caroline's taken him to the opticians this morning. To get him another pair of glasses and to see if there's anything else wrong with his eyes. He keeps talking about seeing an angel."

"Angel," Verity repeats.

"We think he must be seeing flashes of light, poor kid."

No, Verity wants to say. He is seeing an angel. I see an angel. His vision is perfect. He sees what is there.

"Anyway, your phone?"

Verity stops in the doorway to the living room. The last time she had her phone she threw it under the table, but will it be there now? Her feet are cold now, and vaguely sticky with grass juice. She pads into the living room, immediately sees the slim dark shape under the table, and the cable trailing from the wall socket. Frank hovers beside her, apparently looking out of the window, as she plugs it in again, her eyes braced for that ferocious light.

"What was the problem?"

"I couldn't get it to do anything. My icons were all death's heads. I thought it was a virus."

In her hand the screen flares to Glastonbury Tor. One by one her icons flare: red, blue, green.

"It's not doing it now. I'm really sorry, Frank."

"It must have been something. Let's see."

Frank takes it from her and sprawls on the sofa, away from the window's bright light.

"Back in a moment." Verity goes into her bedroom and pulls on a sundress. She catches her reflection in the mirror as she adjusts the straps. Dishevelled and strange.

Frank's still tapping when she returns to him. He doesn't even look up from the screen. Verity feels sick, like she has looked too long at the sun. She slides down onto the sofa.

"You all right?" Frank glances at her.

"Fine," she says, and drops her head to a cushion.

More tapping, swiping. A sigh.

"I don't understand it." Frank's voice, distant and thin. "It seems absolutely fine now."

"OK. I'm sorry."

"You sure you're all right?"

Something flashes. Verity jumps alert.

"What was that?"

"What?"

"That flash."

"I didn't see anything."

Verity leans up on her elbow. The bay, through the glass, is blue and lilac, the sky pale and airy. There are no purple thunder clouds, no clatter of rain at the window.

Frank stands. He seems very dark in front of the window. Behind him the bay glows paler and whiter, like Nick Hersch's painting. Frank moves towards her.

"Verity," he says.

"Frank," she says, swallowing, uncertain of what is about to happen.

Suddenly Frank is upon her, his hands in her hair, his mouth on hers.

"Frank," Verity tries to cry, but he's caught her face in one of his hands, is forcing her mouth apart with his tongue.

She tries to push him off, but he's heavy, and she is trapped between him and the sofa. He grabs her wrists to stop her clawing at his face.

125

"Frank! No!" she manages to croak, as he pulls her dress up with one hand.

Frank is muttering something, she can't hear him properly, she can't understand him. His hands and mouth seem to be everywhere at once: her face, her nipples, between her legs. Verity twists away from him, pushes her face into the sofa, breathes the stale scent of faded velvet. There is another flash, and Frank tugs her hair to turn her head back to him.

She cannot see him above her. The room swims in pale white light. The pain of his probing fingers washes away. She closes her eyes. Maybe he has killed her and this is death, what death feels like, soft and milky, gentle as silk. Something silky on her cheeks. Suddenly her hands are no longer trapped. She reaches a tentative hand, opens her eyes. Hair: long, soft, blond hair sweeping her face and throat. Silver eyes, pale skin, cheekbones. The angel.

"Verity," the angel says.

"You're here," she says, winding her hand into his hair. "My angel."

"You knew I would come."

Did she? The angel's hands are cool on her skin, and her flesh jumps at his touch. When he kisses her his mouth tastes of bluebells, the sea, the summer. She feels sticky tears on her cheeks; she cries aloud.

"Oh, Jesus. Verity. I don't know what –"

Frank's face is ravaged, ugly. Her breasts sting and she is raw inside. She's half-naked on the sofa. Frank stumbles to his feet. His jeans are gaping open. His shrivelling penis glints ominously. He shoves it inside the denim.

"Fuck," he says. "I am so sorry. I don't know what that was about. Verity, say something, please."

"What happened?" she says, and her voice sounds strange.

126

Her body hurts as though she has been attacked – raped – but somewhere deep inside she feels the glow of a healing light, remembers the soft hair falling on her face, the joy that brought tears from her eyes.

"Please, Verity. I didn't mean to. I don't know what came over me." Frank drops to his knees beside the sofa, grabs her hand.

"Don't touch me," she says.

He snatches his hand back. "No, of course not. I'm so sorry, so fucking sorry. Please don't say anything to Caroline about this. She's got enough with the boys and the baby, and Andy's not well, he keeps seeing things, and…"

"Just go." Verity swings her legs to the floor, stands shakily.

Frank hauls himself up.

"Can I do anything for you?" he says.

"Yes. Just go."

"What about Caroline?" Frank backs out of the living room.

"What about her?" she asks.

"What are you going to say to her?" Frank glances at his watch. "They'll be back soon. I love Caroline. I've never done anything like this before. I love my boys. Please don't say anything to her. I can't lose my family."

"I want to be alone. *Leave.*" She reaches past him and opens the door.

Sunlight falls onto the lawn. A blue butterfly twirls away over the tamarisk. Frank staggers unsteadily out onto the doorstep. Verity follows his eyes to his own bungalow, the roof just visible over the tangled hedge.

"I don't know what happened," he gabbles again.

"You tricked me."

"No, no, I came to fix your phone. That was all I came round for. I promise. I never tricked you. Don't think that."

"You made me think you were someone else."

"What?" Frank starts away from her towards the steps cut into the grassy bank, squinting in the white-gold sunlight. "Verity, I have to go now. Caroline and Andy will be back. We'll talk later. Somehow."

"I don't want to talk. I just want you to go."

"I am going. But please understand, what happened then, it's not what I'm like. I'm not like that. I just don't know. Don't say anything to Caroline. It would destroy her."

"Frank. I know," Verity says slowly. "I know it wasn't you."

"Thank you, thank you. I'm not an arsehole. I don't want you to think that."

"I don't know what happened," she says.

She doesn't know what she is saying, only that the words make some strange truth.

"Please, can I have your word?"

"What?"

"That you won't tell Caroline."

"No, no. Just go."

"You won't? You won't say anything to anyone?"

"How many times?" Verity cries. "Go away. Leave me."

She pushes him away. He flails for a second, stumbles backwards, his foot turns over on the top step. With a howl he lands on the grass at the bottom of the steps.

"Frank? Shit, I'm sorry. I just wanted you to..."

Verity slides down the bank to him. Frank gasps. He tries to move, cries out in pain.

"Have you hurt your leg?"

"Oh Jesus." Frank reaches out for the steps, and tries to pull himself up. He collapses again on the grass. "My ankle. I think it's broken. Please, can you go and see if Caroline's back?"

Verity straightens, sees them both as though from a distance. A man crumpled in pain at the bottom of the garden steps, and a girl standing over him, with bruises rapidly blooming at her neckline. She runs up the bank and into the house.

The sun is bright, too bright, over the house roof. Frank gazes at the white disc and it seems to judder down the sky. He's sweating, but he feels cold. The pain in his ankle is swelling again. He knows he shouldn't, but he tries to move, and cries out again.

Where is he? He's not in his own garden. This isn't his house. The front door opens. A girl comes out. Verity, that's who it is. She's wearing jeans and a T-shirt. She looks different to when he last saw her. When did he last see her? Moments ago? Hours, days?

"Frank. Can you move your ankle? Do you really think it's broken?"

"I don't know," Frank gasps. She's crouching down next to him. He senses a strange intimacy with her he's not felt before.

"I'll find Caroline." Verity straightens.

"Verity?"

"Just let's forget that."

"That's it. I have forgotten. What am I doing here? I can't remember."

"You...fell down the steps."

"No, here. In your garden. Your house. What am I doing here? Did I bang my head?"

"You came to fix my phone," Verity calls over her shoulder as she runs out of the gate.

Phone. Yes. Frank remembers that much, but he can't recall how he got to the foot of the garden steps. He can't remember leaving the house. Did Verity open the door for him? What did they talk about as he left? Did they laugh? Did they talk about Caroline and the boys?

129

What the hell is wrong with him? It must be the pain. His ankle feels huge and throbbing, strangely disconnected to him.

He lifts his eyes once more to the sun. Like his ankle, it seems to have swollen. It must be three times its size. Frank blinks and shakes his head. No, the sun is the same as it was a few moments ago, high and white, but that is all.

He's aware of something else. It's probing at the edges of his consciousness. He slides a hand into his jeans, and his fingers come away sticky. No, he couldn't have. Not with Verity.

Verity is relieved and afraid to see Caroline's car on the parking strip. A helicopter buzzes overhead, and Verity wonders if the men up there can see Frank twisted on her lawn, if one comments to the other, wondering why he's there, and what has happened to him. She bangs hard on Caroline's front door.

"Verity?" Caroline says.

Memories spin back to her: standing here with a shivering Andy in her arms, her shoes torn and her ankle burning. Strange, she hardly has any pain in her ankle now, whereas Frank…

"It's Frank," she starts.

"Where is Frank?" Caroline interrupts.

"He's at mine. He's…"

"What's he doing at yours?" Caroline asks coldly.

"He came to fix my phone. He's…fallen over in the garden. He can't move. He thinks he's broken his ankle."

"Fallen?"

"Angel," Andy mutters, trotting up to the front door beside his mother.

Verity glances at Andy. "Please come. He needs help. Shall I stay here with Andy?" She does not want to stand on the lawn with Frank and Caroline, knowing what he – the angel – did to her.

130

"No, it's fine," Caroline says. "Andy can come with me."

"Stay with Verity," Andy cries.

"No, Andy, you're coming with me." Caroline says flatly. "Where the hell's my mobile?"

"I'll tell Frank you're coming," Verity says, and turns away from the door, away from Andy's insistent *Angel, Angel.*

In her garden Frank has tried to ease his shoe off. His heel is free, but the shoe is jammed around his arch. His shirt blooms dark with sweat.

"They're home, they're coming," Verity says to him.

"Help me," he says, gestures to his twisted foot. "What's going on?"

"What do you mean?" she says warily, gently tugging at his shoe.

Frank gasps. "I just don't remember...I was doing your phone, and then I was here. Did I hit my head?"

"I'm not sure," Verity improvises.

Frank won't meet her eyes.

There are things she wants to ask him – *Did you rape me? Did you see the angel? What happened?* – but she cannot.

"Frank!"

"Daddy!"

Verity steps back as Caroline hurries across the lawn. Andy hesitates, his face turned to the sun. His eyes are screwed up behind his glasses. Verity watches him, watches his features relax into a smile.

"Angel's here," he says.

"Where?" Verity asks.

Behind her she hears Caroline and Frank muttering, hears words – *slipped on the steps, my head, can't remember.* Caroline leans down awkwardly and moves his discarded shoe.

"Dunno," Andy says, takes a step towards Verity. "You smell like Angel."

"I'm calling an ambulance," Caroline says, taking out her mobile.

Verity stares miserably at Frank. She pushed him out of her house. She made him fall. If he has broken his ankle, it's her fault.

No, he tricked her.

He raped her, made her believe he was the angel. But Andy says the angel has been here, been with her.

Caroline ends her call, comes over to Verity.

"Frank says he met you in the shop yesterday and you asked him to look at your mobile."

"Yes, that's right," Verity says.

"Right." Caroline's eyes seem to absorb anew Verity's dishevelled appearance.

Does she know? Verity wonders. *Does she know what Frank did?*

"If he goes to hospital I can look after Andy so you can go with him. I could pick up Jonny from school…"

"It's OK. I can sort out something for them. I'll call one of the mothers."

"Caroline."

"What is it about you?" Caroline demands. "Ever since you came, everything's gone wrong. Andy's seeing things, the boys creeping out to the rocks, Andy could have died – *Andy could have died* – and now Frank."

"I don't know," Verity says quietly.

"What are you doing to my family?" Caroline shouts. "Am I next?"

~

Verity hesitates in the bedroom doorway. On the bed is a crescent of fabric: the dress she took off before going to fetch Caroline. She walks slowly through the room and picks it up, uneasily both repulsed and aroused. She remembers the soft sweep of long hair on her face, silver eyes, the taste of summer.

132

By the time the ambulance had come, its silent blue strobes eerie in the white light of the cliff top, Caroline had calmed down, but she'd hardly spoken to Verity again. Caroline called the mother of one of Jonny's friends, and asked if she could drop Andy off at her house, and if Jonny could go there after school. When Andy slipped his hand into Verity's, Caroline tugged him away angrily and, while the paramedics got Frank into the back of the ambulance, Andy started crying, wailing that he wanted to stay with Verity and the angel.

"Frank slipped on the steps", Verity told the paramedics. "We were talking at the doorway. He was stepping backwards, and slipped. I hardly realised what had happened, it was so quick. One moment he was here talking to me, then he was on the ground."

One moment he was tearing my clothes from me, forcing himself into me, and then he'd gone, and it was the angel, only the beautiful angel.

Verity shoves her crumpled dress to the back of drawer.

In the living room her phone is still plugged in to the socket. She picks it up, aware of Frank's fingerprints on the screen. Glastonbury Tor. Icons. Messages and a voicemail from Tim, saying he and Jack are coming on Friday. Two days' time.

"No, no!" Verity cries aloud.

She can't leave the angel. Not now he has found her, loved her. She dials Tim's number; it goes to voicemail and she hangs up. Tim sounded different on his message: more determined, more commanding. She does not think she will be able to stop him and Jack coming down.

The phone flashes in her hand: that pulsing blinding white light again.

"Fuck you," she cries and lobs it into the corner behind the TV. There's a crack as it hits the wall, and the light extinguishes.

She grabs clean clothes and runs a bath, unsure of who she's washing from her. She cries, and the tears drip into the cooling water.

"You've got blood on your shirt," Jack says. "What you done to your back?"

"I haven't done it." Tim yanks the cheesecloth shirt out of his jeans and throws it down. "Look."

Jack gasps aloud, nausea rising. Tim's shoulder blades are red and raw from his scratching. Knobbly swellings disfigure his back. Embryo wings.

~

Darkness falls over the cliff, pouring down the sky like a stain. The last light glows on the horizon. Wolf Rock swells and fades, swells and fades, as imperceptibly the sky darkens. Verity's reflection blurs on the window pane. She thinks she sees a movement on the lawn, jumps, and pulls the curtains round herself to blacken the glass. There is nothing. The tamarisk shivers at the edge of the garden. Carrag Luz glows silver.

She has to find out about Frank. She heard Jonny in the garden earlier, and there are lights on in the house. Her heart races as she walks the few yards to the neighbouring house.

"How's Frank?" she asks when Caroline opens the door.

"Not great."

"Is he home?"

"No, and not likely to be for a while."

"Oh Caroline."

"He's got to have surgery on the ankle. He's broken bones. I don't know how long they'll keep him in."

"I'm so sorry."

"What happened? At your house? How did he fall?"

134

Verity closes her eyes. She can feel a migraine pulsing at the edge of her consciousness.

"We were just saying goodbye. He was walking backwards. He misjudged it."

"And you came round straight away?"

"Yes." *After I had gone in to the house and changed my clothes.* "He will be OK, won't he? In the end?"

"We won't know until after the surgery."

"Is there anything I can do to help? With the boys or anything?"

"I don't think so," Caroline says. "I don't want you near my boys or my husband, or me. You've done quite enough. Goodnight."

Verity trails back to her house. The garden is bleached of colour. There are tiny bumps all over the lower lawn: snails. Wind exhales through the tamarisk fronds. Across the bay, the street lamps of Penzance shimmer and Wolf Rock punches its white pulse.

She scuffs her toe along the edge of the step where Frank fell. Guilt flares inside her. Frank is awaiting surgery on his ankle. He won't be home for days. Tim and Jack are coming at the weekend. She won't see Frank again. She wonders whether she could call him at the hospital, or get a message to him. A message of what? Apology? Understanding? Anger? All three and more, so much more, and she will never have the chance to speak to him again.

Caroline won't talk to her. Caroline knows, knows about Frank, and knows about the angel. She won't let Verity near the boys either. Andy is the only person who understands. Verity knows where the boys' bedroom window is. Should she – could she – creep into Caroline's garden and tap on their window? A snail clings to the edge of the step, its antennae unfurling. Its shell sways as it heaves onto the stone. Verity shudders and moves towards the front door.

The hall is warm and airless after the garden. She pushes the door to, her hand hesitating on the keys. If she leaves the door unlocked the

135

angel could come back to her. There is nothing, no-one, to fear on the cliff at night: only the snails and the moths, the rabbits and the other night-time creatures that squeak and churr in the undergrowth. And the angel.

~

Tim is changing. He is growing wings. Tim is growing wings, earthquakes have opened the underground way to Hell, and Verity is in danger from the Devil. Jack has touched Tim's mutilated back, stretched out a tentative finger and brushed the lumps. The touch of them repulsed him. He didn't say *let me take you to A & E*. This goes beyond that.

"Why are you…growing wings? Are you growing wings?"

"I am." Tim slides his arms back into his shirt, gasps as the material catches on the growths. "People have written this. People have predicted this. People have seen this in the stars. His return. My return."

"I need a fucking drink."

"Who am I?"

"I don't know."

"Who am I?" More gently.

Jack looks at Tim, sees once again the features of another man overlaid on his cheekbones and chin, sees the strange bright blue of his eyes, and finally the pale circle of light around his head.

"Michael," Jack stammers at last. "Archangel Michael, the warrior."

~

Caroline eases open the boys' bedroom door. Two humps, both still. Even breathing. She wishes she could bring a sleeping bag in and put

136

it on the floor between their beds and sleep there with them, but then they would know she was afraid.

She pulls the door to once more and pads back to the living room. The TV is on, a film she's not watching. Caroline jabs the remote at the screen onto another channel. Raucous studio laughter, a panel of celebrities, crass comments. She moves the curtain aside and gazes out into the night. She can just see Verity's bungalow over the hedge. The sky seems to be washed with silver light, but Caroline cannot see the moon.

Alone now, she is afraid she will cry, overwhelmed by her doubts, her insecurities, her fears. Since Verity arrived terrible things have happened. Andy is obsessed, muttering all the time about an angel.

Is Verity the angel? What has she done to make Andy adore her? Was it her, was it Verity, who crept into the garden and stole the boys from their beds?

Verity enticed the boys out of bed – no, probably just Andy; he would do anything she asked of him. She took him to the cliff, to Carrag Luz.

What did she do to him there? She threw his glasses away and dangled him over the edge. Did she command him to step, blinded, off the precipice? Did she beguile him with stories of angels? Then Jonny woke, and found Andy gone. He raced out into the garden and saw them on the rocks. When Verity saw him coming, she had to scramble down with Andy, pretend to rescue him.

Caroline sits down abruptly, her stomach heaving. That was it; that was what happened. Jonny was reticent, but he was too afraid to speak the truth. And then Frank.

When she and Andy were at the optician's Frank went round to see Verity. He never told her he was going. He says he saw Verity in Mullion when he went to get the food the previous day. She asked him to go round and look at her mobile.

He didn't tell me, Caroline sobs. He never intended to tell me. He waited until I was out with Andy and then he went round to Verity, the young, beautiful, slender girl next door with the swinging hair and long legs.

She runs her hand over her bump. She's enjoyed her pregnancies, enjoyed the feelings of fertility and birth. Now she stumbles to her feet, goes into the bedroom she shares with Frank. She pulls her clothes tight to her skin, stares angrily at her silhouette, at her tired eyes, her faded fair hair.

Caroline's not stupid.

When Verity came beating on the door this morning – only this morning – she saw it all immediately: the flush across her cheekbones, her tangled hair, her grazed mouth, and other things, sensed rather than seen, things feral, dark and ancient. Contentment, wariness, guilt, shame. Verity had been with a man only moments before.

Can I have Caroline Tripconey's number? Tim texts Ellen.

He hopes she will just reply with the number, not call him back. He doesn't want to talk to anyone but Jack at the moment, but he does need to speak to this woman, Caroline, next door to Verity.

Ten minutes later Ellen replies. *Is everything OK?* She adds after the number.

All fine, Tim writes.

Although the sun has long set, the ultramarine sky glows, as though it were lit from behind. Verity cannot sleep. She gets out of bed, open the curtains again. That same strange lightness in the sky. She pads to the living room, to the front window. She can pick out the humps of the snails of the lawn. A moth clings to the huge pane, though there is no lamplight from within the house. She can sense, beyond the glass, the other creatures of the night stirring, moving, stretching their wings.

She returns to her room, to her bed, lies down. That unearthly light seems to be seeping into the house itself. It touches her face and she feels a coolness, soft as a summer zephyr, on her skin. It kisses her eyelids, and they drop into sleep.

A tapping awakes her, soft, insistent. She glances to the exposed window. Just the dark-light sky over Caroline's bungalow. The tapping comes again, then a quiet squeaking.

The door, she thinks. I left the door unlocked. And now she can hear the front door closing, clicking into place. Someone is in the house. She can hear no footsteps, no breath, but gold light glows around the bedroom door, and she feels no fear.

She closes her eyes. He is in the room with her. A moment later she feels that sweep of hair on her cheek, slim fingers tracing her eyelids.

"Look at me," he says.

She opens her eyes.

"I knew you would come back," she says.

"I knew I would come back."

He drops his mouth to hers, and, far away, she hears a gentle growl of thunder across the bay.

"This morning," she gasps.

"This morning was beautiful, Verity."

"How do you know my name? How did you...this morning. Frank..."

"He was most unfortunate," the angel says, sliding her arms out of her nightdress. "To fall like that."

"I don't understand," Verity starts, but he silences her with kisses, and suddenly the morning seems a long time ago, and no longer important.

~

Jonny wakes, instantly alert. Something is different. It's Andy. Andy is standing at the bedroom window. The sky outside looks funny: silvery blue. Not really like the night.

"Andy," Jonny hisses. "What are you doing?"

"Angel's out there," Andy says, without moving.

"There is no angel." Jonny wishes he sounded more certain. "Anyway, you can't see anything. You haven't got your glasses."

"Don't need them," Andy mumbles. "I can see the light. And I can smell him."

"You're silly," Jonny says, "You make up stuff. Perhaps you're mad."

"Angel likes Verity more than me."

Jonny slides out of bed, goes to stand beside Andy. There must be a big moon somewhere, but he can't see one. There's a faint light coming from Verity's house, like she's left a light on behind a curtain. Is that what Andy's talking about?

"It's not an angel," Jonny says. "It's Verity's light."

"Angel won't come here again. He likes Verity."

They both jump as the bedroom door opens. Their mother is in the doorway.

"What are you doing out of bed?" she asks. "Get back in bed now, both of you. It's the middle of the night. What are you looking at?"

"Nothing," says Jonny, scrambling into his bed.

"Angel," Andy whispers, blundering into the end of Jonny's bed.

His mother steers him to his own bed.

140

"No more talk of angels, Andy." She reaches to the curtains, stares out a moment into the strange night, then pulls the material tight across the glass.

"Angel's out there," Andy says. "He's with Verity."

"And no more talk about Verity either. She'll be going away soon."

I bloody wish she would, Caroline thinks, as she closes the boys' door behind her.

She can't sleep either, and goes into the kitchen to make tea. She imagines the ward where Frank is: the snores, the farts, the movements of wounded, miserable men, the blur of yellow light at the nurses' station, the trundle of wheels on the corridor outside, the stale air. The constant presence of death.

Where did that come from? Caroline slams her mug down on the worktop and hot water splashes her wrist. He's broken his ankle. People don't die from that. Get a grip.

~

"Who are you?" Verity asks. "You know who I am, but I don't know who you are."

The angel gazes down at her, gathers a fistful of her hair, and lets it slide through his pale fingers. "You know who I am, Verity."

"I don't," she stammers, confused.

"What do you call me?"

Verity turns away from him. The night sky through the window is still washed with silver. There's a soft roll of thunder. She knows he is watching her; she knows she must speak. "My angel," she whispers at last.

"Angel," he repeats. "I like that very much."

"It's not your name," she says.

"No," he says, "but that is what some people call me."

"Andy?" Verity is drifting now, heavy-eyed and -limbed, into a strange sleep not induced by tiredness, but by something else: something she cannot control, like anaesthesia.

"Andy knows who I am."

"Andy," Verity says again, her mouth loose, the word shapeless. She can see fragments of a waking dream: the rocks of Carrag Luz in the pale dawn light, a tiny figure tottering on the summit, arms raised for flight. "Andy wants to fly with you."

"I will fly with you now, Verity."

The angel kisses her throat, her eyes, her mouth. She tries to open her lips but they are too heavy to move, and her mind is too clotted with strange words and pictures, and she cannot command her body to do a thing.

"Sleep now," the angel says.

Caroline opens the front door. She has hardly slept, worrying about Frank, worrying about the boys, sending poisonous thoughts through the restless night to Verity's house. When is she going to leave?

Jonny stumbles past her with his school rucksack on his back like a huge snail shell.

"Yuck, gross!" he cries.

Caroline feels a cold touch on the back of her neck. She turns to where Jonny points. The lawn is covered with countless slugs and snails, dead, curled up, oozing yellow fluid, shells crushed into shards.

Caroline cries out, wavers on the step. Jonny crouches on the edge of the lawn, staring at a huge orange slug that is leaking slime into the grass.

"Jonny, don't touch it. Stay on the path," Caroline says. "Andy, come on. Jonny will be late for school. Andy, hold my hand."

142

Andy totters out of the house. He looks different and, for just a second, Caroline can't identify how, then she sees he is not wearing his glasses.

"Andy, where are your glasses? You can't come out without them. Put them on now."

"Urrgh!" Andy cries, pointing at the corpses on the lawn. "Snails."

"Snails?" Caroline asks. "You can see the snails without your glasses?"

"Everywhere," Andy says. "Angel put them there."

~

Verity wakes with a thick throat and a headache. She reaches out an arm to where a normal man, a normal lover, would lie, perhaps on his back, or perhaps sprawled away from her, the quilt bundled round his shoulder. She knows immediately she is alone. The angel will not sleep in a bed, lie on his back staring at the ceiling through the sleepless hours of the dawn.

She sits up, slowly, gently, and the covers fall from her chest. She is wearing nothing. He was there.

Her nightdress is on the floor, inside out, but she doesn't care and tugs it over her head. Through her bedroom door she can see a strange, dappled light on the hall carpet. She hears a frantic tapping. Outside the glass front door, the garden is swirling with butterflies, hundreds, maybe thousands, swarming round the pane. Their wings beat against the glass, leaving tiny coloured cells on the glass. She can see tortoise-shells, whites, blues, browns, admirals, commas, peacocks.

Their insistence is threatening.

She backs away from the front door and into the living room. The wide bay window is darkened by yet more butterflies. The tapping of their wings is like a driving rain, a dry rain, hitting hard on the glass. Verity tugs the curtains across and runs back to her bedroom. She covers her ears with the quilt so she cannot hear the distant beating. Her bedroom window remains clear. After some time – ten minutes, half an hour, she's not sure – she ventures out to the hall.

The glass door is speckled all over with the cells and dust from numerous wings, but there are no butterflies anywhere. She opens the living room curtains. There is one butterfly clinging to the glass. Pale gold, pointed wings like tiny horns: a Brimstone. She reaches out her hand to the dusty glass. The butterfly bobs away across the lawn, over the tamarisk hedge, towards Carrag Luz.

I will fly with you now, Verity.

~

Tim unlocks the door to Cosmos. The high blue sky promises a warm day, but he is wearing a thick jumper to hide the swellings on his back. He hooks the windchimes up outside the door, but turns the key as he returns inside, and keeps the closed sign showing. He takes his mobile out of his jeans pocket and dials the number Ellen texted him.

"Hello," a woman answers quickly, as though she is expecting a call, expecting bad news.

"Caroline Tripconey?" Tim asks.

"Yes." Her voice is terse, stressed, but there's something else.

She has only said two words to Tim, but he knows, in those few seconds, as they connect through the ether, that he has known this woman somewhere, sometime before. He closes his eyes, sees green and gold, sees the earth, crops flourishing, flowers blooming, hears the strength of a powerful heartbeat. The Empress.

"Hello, who is this?" Caroline says.

"I'm sorry," Tim says. "My name's Tim Hurford. I'm Ellen Hurford's brother. Verity's step-father."

A pause. "Yes, I know who you are," Caroline says.

144

Caroline's heart still races with both relief and dread. She thought, when the phone rang, it would be the hospital, to say Frank had deteriorated in the night, had had to have his leg amputated, had died. Her hand still hurts from the boiling water she spilled in the night, that dark time of the soul when thoughts of death tap so insistently at the brain.

"I must talk to you about Verity," Tim Hurford says.

Andy's watching a DVD in the living room. Caroline can hear the cartoon voices, but still, she takes the phone into her bedroom.

"I haven't seen much of her lately," she says.

She wants to tell Tim that Verity has brought evil to her family, that she's filled Andy's head with rubbish about angels and flying, stole Andy from his bedroom and held him, blind, over a precipice, that she seduced Frank, and caused his accident, but the man's voice is familiar, remembered.

"I'm sorry, Tim. I was taking the phone away from my son."

"Jack and I are coming down tomorrow," Tim says. "We're taking her home. I have…concerns about her, and I'd like to know how she's been. I know she did the Hal an Tow with you, but since then, she's been much harder to get hold of."

"Yes, she did the Hal an Tow," Caroline says. "She doesn't do much. She goes to the beach, she moons around in the house, I think. She's been, I don't know, distracted the last few days."

"What do you mean?"

"You'll see for yourself."

"Please Caroline. I need to know now."

"Why?" Caroline asks suddenly. "You know something, don't you? You know what's wrong with her."

"What's she done? Tell me, whatever it is, and then I'll tell you what I know."

145

"Is she on drugs? Crazy? Is she dangerous to my children? Why didn't anyone tell me before?" Caroline's voice is rising, and she kicks the bedroom door shut.

Tim wanders round the shop. He trails his spare hand through a basket of amethyst tumblestones, he gently flicks the paddle of bamboo windchimes so they clunk softly, he straightens silk wrapped tubes of incense.

"She's not on drugs," he says. "I don't know if she's dangerous. I couldn't tell you before because I didn't know then what I know now."

"She is dangerous. I know that already. She's poisoned my family. She abducted my son, tried to throw him over the cliff, she tricked my husband into…into…something happened, and Frank broke his ankle, and now he's in hospital, and it's all because of her."

"Caroline, I'm so very sorry," Tim says.

"She's evil. I can't wait for her to go. What's the matter with her? She seemed all right until Flora Day."

"Since Flora Day, yes," Tim says, almost to himself. "What has she said?"

"Oh, I don't know. My boys are obsessed with her, especially my little one, Andy. She's filled his head with dreams about angels."

"Angels?" Tim shouts. The embryo wings seem to stir beneath his skin. Sharp pain flares across his shoulders. He twists his spare arm to his back. "What kind of angels?"

"I don't know. Stop doing this. Just tell me what's wrong with her. Is she crazy?"

"Not crazy. In terrible danger." Tim sighs. He's not doing this well, not doing it right.

"What danger? What about me? My family?"

"Verity has unleashed a most ancient evil."

"Ancient evil?"

146

"The oldest of all. Tell me what you know about Helston and the Hal an Tow.

"What's that got to do with it?"

"Everything. What does the name Helston mean?"

"Helston? The stone of Hell. St Michael fought the Devil in Helston. He sealed up the doorway to Hell with the stone. It's under the Angel Hotel."

Tim hears Caroline catch her breath at the word angel.

"It's not under the Angel Hotel," Tim says. "It's much closer to you than that."

"It's just a legend. I don't know what angels she's on about."

"The earthquakes you've had. No-one has been able to explain them, have they?

Verity was fine until the last earthquake, I suspect. Those tremors split the stone and opened up the gateway to Hell, and the angel Verity has told your son about has come out of that gateway." Caroline tries to interrupt him, but he carries on. "Has your son seen this angel?"

"Yes," Caroline whispers. "He said it was the angel who took him from his room and led him onto the rocks. He said the angel was going to show him how to fly. He draws pictures of the angel."

"What does he draw?"

"A white figure, gold, with light coming out of him."

"Light. Yes, there will be a lot of that. Have you seen any strange lights?"

"A little last night over the cliff. Andy says he's seen lights at Verity's at night. What is all this? I don't believe any of this. You're telling me my son has seen St Michael?"

"Not St Michael," Tim says. "Not yet."

Caroline's ear is hot from having the phone pressed to her skin, but she is shivery, and feels again that cold touch on the nape of neck.

147

What Tim Hurford has told her is unimaginable, terrifying, yet she believes him because of the remembered pattern of his voice, that knowledge – that ridiculous belief – that she has met him, trusted him, before.

"What are you drawing, Andy?" Her voice is thin, high.

She strides across the kitchen. The cartoon is playing on, ignored, in the living room. Andy is hunched over his drawing pad, left hand curled round a dark blue felt tip. Caroline recoils. On the pad is a white and yellow figure with gold shimmers round his head. The other figure – a girl – has flowing dark brown hair. They are holding hands. Andy is drawing blue wavy lines across their feet, like the sea.

"Who are they?" Caroline demands, but she knows.

"Angel and Verity," Andy says. "Angel likes Verity."

Caroline snatches the pad, and rips off the top sheet. Andy wails. She tears the paper to shreds, lets the pieces flutter to the floor. Andy's still howling.

"Don't ever say that," Caroline says. "Don't ever say their names. Don't draw them."

She grabs a handful of Andy's pens and jabs them randomly into the packet, colours jarring against each other. Andy reaches out and she knocks his hand aside. When she's filled the long plastic pocket she swipes it, and the drawing pad, off the table, and forces them into the kitchen bin. Andy cries on and on.

Caroline slides into the chair opposite Andy, and takes his hands. He tries to snatch them away, but her grip is firm.

"Andy, you don't understand. Verity and the…angel." She gulps the word. "They're bad people. I know they're bad. You must never speak to them again, or go near them. Do you understand? Andy? Do you understand? This is really important."

"Angel's nice. Verity's nice. Angel came here. He took me out of bed."

148

"No, no!" Caroline cries. "No, Andy. It was Verity, wasn't it? Not him. Not him."

"It was him," Andy shrieks. "We were going to fly. He promised. Jonny and Verity spoilt it. It was the angel. He took me. He took me."

"What does he look like?" Caroline whispers.

Andy smiles. "He's big and white and yellow. He has lots of yellow hair. He has a nice face. He can fly. He flies off the rocks. He likes me but he likes Verity more." Andy's smile flattens and he looks sad.

"You don't want him to like you," Caroline stammers. "When he…when he woke you up that morning, he wasn't going to take you flying, he was going to hurt you. If Jonny hadn't…" Her brain is full of unfinished thoughts and sentences.

She stands, and tugs Andy to his feet. With Andy trailing beside her she checks every window in the house. She locks and bolts the front and back doors, knowing, as the satisfying clang rings in her ears, that it is probably a false protection.

"Frank, Frank," she mutters, and tears start in her eyes.

Frank has left her and the boys, alone on the cliff, where the devil walks unchecked. No, no, that's ridiculous. There is no such thing. Something moves in Caroline's peripheral vision, and she swings round. Nothing. Through the front window pale sunlight splashes the front lawn. Caroline moves closer to the glass and looks out. The grass is clean, a soft green-gold. The slugs and snails, the broken shells and the slime, have all gone. She turns round to where Andy is curled up on the sofa, disconsolately twiddling a toy car round and round. Caroline hesitates. She wants to speak to Tim again, indeed she craves the steadiness of his voice, but she doesn't want Andy to overhear her conversation. She's torn. She doesn't want to leave Andy for even a moment, but she cannot speak to Tim in front of him.

"Do you want to watch another DVD?" she asks, and crosses to the pile of coloured boxes, takes one out, waves it at Andy.

"No," Andy says.

"What about this one?" Caroline offers another.

"No," Andy wails. "Want to draw. Want to the draw Angel. Want to see Angel."

Caroline throws down the DVD. "Andy, I told you. You mustn't talk about the angel. You mustn't see him. Or Verity. They're bad people. They'll hurt you. They hurt Daddy."

"Angel didn't hurt Daddy."

"He did," Caroline improvises. "It's because of the angel that Daddy isn't here now. Daddy's hurt because of the angel."

Andy mutters something she can't hear. Did the angel – the devil – hurt Frank, or was it Verity? Are they one and the same? Andy throws the toy car to the floor. The landline rings, sudden, shrill. Caroline dives onto the receiver without checking the number display.

"Tim," she says.

"It's me."

"Frank. Hi. How are you?" She finds it almost impossible to speak the simple words.

"Who's Tim?"

"Tim?"

"You said *Tim* when you answered. Who's Tim?"

"Oh…someone who rang a few moments ago. He was going to ring back."

"What about?"

"He's…one of the fathers from school."

"Do I know him?"

"Frank, what is this?" Caroline shouts. "I don't think you're in a position to give me the third degree, not after what you did yesterday."

"What the…?" Frank lowers his voice. "What the hell are you on about? What have I done? I went to fix her phone. I told you."

"Oh yeah, and the rest. I'm not stupid, whatever you and she may think." There's nothing more to it than that. No devils, no angels, just a beautiful young girl next door who seduced her husband. Nothing supernatural, paranormal. Only natural and normal. Too natural, too normal.

Frank doesn't speak for a moment, and Caroline hears the whistle of bad mobile reception, and something clanging.

"I just wanted to tell you I'm going to theatre very shortly," Frank says at last.

"Right, good luck," Caroline says. "I'll bring the boys up later."

"You don't have to," Frank says. "If you don't want to come, it doesn't matter. I have to go now."

He hangs up without saying goodbye. Caroline holds the buzzing receiver in her hand. It sounds like a huge bluebottle between her ears. She jabs a finger to silence it.

Her mobile rings in her pocket.

"Frank?"

"Caroline, it's Tim. How are things?"

"Tim. Oh. I don't know."

"You have to stay focussed. There is a great danger out there, and you can channel into it. I know it, I feel it. I've known you before. Do you know what I'm saying? Do you understand?"

"Yes, yes," she cries. "When you called before, your voice, it was like someone I'd always known, but I didn't know I knew him."

"You must keep your children away from Verity," Tim says. "It is good your husband is in hospital. He will be safe there."

"He's having surgery in a moment," Caroline says. "He just called me."

"Are you going to visit him afterwards?"

"Well, yes I was, but he hung up on me." Caroline knows she sounds petulant.

"Go and see him. Take your children. You must see him, and you must repair whatever damage has occurred."

"It's her fault! Your Verity! It's all her fault. She got Frank to go round there and...and..." Caroline moves down the hall, out of Andy's earshot. "She seduced him. She screwed my husband. I'm seven months pregnant, and she screwed my husband."

"I'm really sorry," Tim says. "But it's not what you think it is. She didn't know what she was doing. Neither did he. You're all being taken over, one by one. Your son, you said...Is there anywhere you could take your children? Relatives? Friends? Somewhere safe?"

"No, they're staying with me."

"OK."

Caroline walks down the hall towards her room. Her reflection in the mirror startles her.

"I'm waiting for something," she says at last. "But I don't know what. Things make me jump. I feel something is going to happen."

"Something is going to happen. Something you cannot imagine. It will happen tomorrow when Jack and I arrive."

"What can you two do?"

"Jack can save Verity. They're twins. They have a bond."

"And you?"

Tim is silent.

Beyond the bedroom window a blackbird swoops across the lawn. Caroline jumps. She imagines the shadow of a horned creature falling across the grass, the silver and purple mask of the devil, with slitted silver eyes boring into her own. Or does she imagine the beautiful, blond man of Andy's drawings? Which is she more afraid of? She cannot answer.

"The devil...the angel...What will he look like to me?" she whispers.

"I don't know."

"My older son, Jonny. I don't think he can see him at all."

"He doesn't believe in him."

"That's good," Caroline interrupts. "He's safer."

She sinks down on the bed. Only moments ago, when Frank was on the phone, she had dismissed everything Tim had said. She had blamed Verity for seducing Frank, nothing more, nothing less. But there is so much more. She cannot ask Tim all the questions she needs answers to; she simply goes with what he says, accepting, understanding.

"So…Jack?" Caroline asks. "How can he save Verity?" And why, she adds silently, would he want to? Why would anyone want to save that bitch?

"He loves her. He's the closest person to her. They shared the womb."

"And what about you? What are you going to do?"

"I shall fight the devil once more, and this time I must win. I may not survive, not in this body anyhow, but I must banish him for ever."

Caroline does not speak.

"You read the Tarot, yes?" Tim asks.

"I used to. Not for years."

She is already reaching to the bottom drawer of her bedside cabinet. Behind the jewellery boxes, the hair ribbons, the safety pins and mismatched buttons is a small oblong pack, wrapped in a simple white cloth. Frank never goes in here; he doesn't know it's there. He wouldn't like it.

"Do you have the cards there?"

"They're here on the bed." She wedges the phone under her ear and sifts through the pack. The cards are cool on her skin. Vivid images slide between her hands.

"Take five cards from the pack. Don't look. Just take them."

Caroline pulls five cards at random, lays them face down on the quilt.

"Turn them over. Don't tell me what they are. I know. The Magician, the Fool, the Moon, the Devil, and the Empress."

"How do you know?"

"They're the only cards I turn up now. They represent five people."

"Who?" But she is counting names in her head. She knows.

"Me, Jack, Verity…"

"The Devil himself."

"And you, Caroline. You are the Empress."

Caroline stares at the cards. The black horned Devil grins back at her. Red anger blazes in his eyes. Behind his head is a flaring sun. The Moon depicts a young woman with tumbling dark hair holding aloft a silver crescent to the night sky. Caroline gazes at her face, and her features soften into Verity's.

The Fool wears a scarlet tunic. Fair hair streams behind him as he runs. To what? From what? The Fool is embarking on a journey, she recalls. As he travels and learns he transforms into the Hanged Man, with new perceptions of the world.

Wheat sheaves surround the Empress on her garlanded throne. Her hair is threaded with flowers and she rests a hand on her swollen abdomen. Caroline's hand creeps to her own bump and finally she studies the Magician, a shrouded figure, barely distinguishable from the starry sky behind him. High above is the same crescent the Moon held up. The Magician's cowl falls open around his face. Caroline sees clear blue-grey eyes, long black hair, a sculpted jawline. This is Tim, this is the Archangel.

"You need some rest, Caroline," Tim says. "And then you must take your boys to see their father. I cannot tell you who will survive tomorrow's storm. You must go. Do you hear me?"

"Yes," she says quietly.

154

She feels ridiculously tired. She can hardly hold the receiver to her ear any more. Tim's voice is soaring away from her. Her vision prickles with stardust. She must lie down before she faints. She is hardly aware of Tim saying goodbye, and lets the phone slide from her hand. As she drops her head to the pillow, the last thing she sees is the Devil's grin, and from far, far away, she hears the drum, the whistles, the chants of the Hal an Tow.

Andy is aware of something. He's not sure what it is; it's not something he can see or hear, it's more like a vibration in the air. His mother has disappeared, her voice fading further as she walked away from him, and now he can't hear her at all. Something is wrong with her. She doesn't understand. She tore up his drawing. She yelled at him. She dragged him round the house locking the doors and windows. She said Angel hurt Daddy. Andy knows that's not true, and he knows Verity knows that too. If only he could find Verity. She could explain everything.

Andy slides off the sofa and pads into the kitchen. A soft cool breeze is blowing. Andy stops in surprise. The back door is wide open. But his mother closed it; she turned the key, tugged again and again on the handle, slid the heavy bolt across. Perhaps she is in the garden. That's why he can't hear her voice any more. Andy steps towards the door. The light outside is bright. He reaches up to his glasses, and takes them off. It's still bright. He puts them on again. Sometimes he can see without his glasses, like this morning with the snails on the front lawn. As he pauses in the doorway, he feels warm sunlight seeping into his skin. He looks to left and right. His mother is not here. Across the garden he can see the hidden gap to the tunnel into Verity's garden. If he could just slither through, under the tangled plants, he could find Verity. Yes. Verity will know what to do.

Verity stands on the grassy bank outside her front door, staring across the bay.

The sea rises and falls gently. On the horizon to the left of Wolf Rock a tanker slides onwards to the Channel. Sometimes a gull swoops over the tamarisk. She can smell bluebells and wild garlic. The sun lightens Carrag Luz to a warm gold-grey.

"Verity. Verity!"

She jumps at the voice.

Andy comes stumbling around the side of the bungalow. There's a smear of blood on his face.

"Andy," Verity runs over to him. "What are you doing here? Have you hurt yourself?"

Andy bats the side of his face nonchalantly.

"Verity, come and tell Mummy."

Verity hesitates.

"Tell Mummy he didn't do it."

"Who didn't do what, Andy?" she asks as evenly as she can.

"Angel didn't hurt Daddy. Mummy says Angel hurt Daddy, but Angel won't hurt Daddy."

Verity exhales, turns back to the sea. The tanker has disappeared behind Carrag Luz's giant mossy shoulder.

"No, he didn't hurt your Daddy. Your Daddy fell. Look, just here." She indicates the steps. "That's where he fell. The angel wasn't even here."

"I know, I know," Andy cries. "Tell Mummy. She says he's bad, but he's not bad."

"I think your Mummy has a lot to think about," Verity starts, "with your Daddy in hospital, and the baby. She didn't mean any of it."

"She did, she did." Andy's starting to cry. "Tell her."

Verity gazes helplessly at Andy.

"Where is she now?" she asks suddenly. Surely Caroline wouldn't have willingly let Andy come crawling through that tunnel alone?

"I don't know."

"What d'you mean?"

"She was there, she was talking, and then she went away."

Verity shivers. The sunlight doesn't seem so warm now. She can feel her arms prickling. The sea swells with a new vigour. The horizon no longer looks so clear; when she scans for Wolf Rock's tower, she can only see a grey haze.

"We must find her," she says, almost to herself. "Come on, I'll take you home."

"You must tell her."

"Yes, OK," Verity says. She reaches out for Andy's hand. The blood on his face seems to be a scratch, probably from a thorn or a sharp twig in the tunnel.

"I'm not crawling through a tunnel," Verity says. "We'll go this way."

The wind gasps through the tamarisk as Verity unlatches the gate. She knows Caroline won't want to see her, but she must return Andy to his mother; otherwise Caroline will accuse her of abducting him. She fastens the gate behind her.

Andy has trotted down the lane to the left.

"Wrong way, Andy." Verity jogs up behind him. He's standing in the middle of the track gazing up at Carrag Luz.

"That's where we were flying." He points to the crag.

"Andy, Andy! Stay right there. You leave my boy alone."

Verity turns. Caroline is struggling down the track, waving her arms.

"Caroline, be careful," Verity says.

"Stay away from me."

Verity stands back in the bluebells. Their scent wafts up from where her shoes have crushed them.

"Andy, come here. What happened to your face? Has she done this? Has she hurt you?"

"He didn't do it," Andy cries. "Verity says he didn't do it."

Caroline lifts her head to meet Verity's eyes over Andy's head.

"Yes, he did," she says, and Verity looks away.

"He didn't!" Andy yells, twisting out of his mother's grip. "Angel didn't hurt Daddy. Tell her, Verity, tell her. You said you would, you promised."

Verity opens her mouth. She doesn't know what to say. She cannot untangle the emotions in Caroline's face. Hatred yes, but others too: jealousy and fear.

"What have you done to my boy?" Caroline shouts.

"Mummy, don't."

"What have you done to him? He's cut his face. Where were you taking him?" Caroline follows Andy's gaze to Carrag Luz.

"Angel!" Andy cries, waving his little arms.

Verity looks too, and there he is on the top of the crag, her angel, her lover, white against the blue-mauve sky. The wind lifts his long hair, as he watches the group below him.

"Angel," Verity whispers.

She's aware of Caroline shouting again, but she can't hear what she's saying. She can hear Andy saying *Angel* over and over again. She sees him totter down the lane. She sees his mother stumble after him, almost tripping on an uneven stone, and grab him awkwardly, then hoist him kicking and wailing against her bump.

"Angel," Verity whispers again.

The angel turns away from her to face the sea. He raises his arms and, in a heartbeat, soars off the crag. There's a sudden flash like lightning and he's gone.

"Angel!" Verity and Andy cry.

"There is no angel," Caroline shouts, and her voice carries along the cliff.

"Mummy, he was there." Andy kicks so hard Caroline lowers him to the ground. "He was there. He's gone."

"He's gone," Verity repeats. "But he will come back. Tonight. He will come back to me."

Caroline grabs Andy with one hand, crosses herself with the other.

"I cannot see him," she says. "But I know who he is. He's no angel."

"You don't know anything, Caroline."

"Yes, I do." Caroline backs away up the lane, dragging Andy with her. "I know what you did with my husband."

"He tricked me."

"You evil bitch. You stay away from me and my family. I know who he is, and what you're doing with him. You're evil, sick. Come on, Andy. Home now."

Verity watches Caroline tug Andy towards their gate. Once Andy looks back to her, his mouth open with words she cannot hear over his mother's anger. Raindrops fall, soft and plump on her bare arms, and on the ground, releasing the scent of loam and bluebells.

⁓

Tim closes up Cosmos at lunchtime to walk into town.

His part-time assistant, Daniel, is working in the afternoon and Tim has a hypnotherapy client, but until then his time is his own. He's about to turn left down Brock Street, but he pauses and turns right instead, walks slowly towards the Royal Crescent.

Pale sunlight turns the creamy stone to gold. Tourists wander round the giant arc, lifting cameras to their eyes. On the lawn below the Crescent, people are walking, dogs are running. Tim stands still a moment and watches the scene. At the far end of the lawn the uneven jumble of Marlborough Buildings straggles up the hill: roofs staggered like a staircase to the sky, complicated windows, ornate balconies. It's a beautiful place, this city of his. Beautiful, and dark too. He'll never really know every vein that runs through it, however long he lives here. And he may never see it again.

He may never see any of it again.

He is leaving tomorrow and he may not return. He may never stand here at the end of the Crescent, watching the picnickers on the lawn below, he may never walk again into town, may never again stand on the kerb at the corner of George Street swearing at the relentless traffic grinding past, may never hear the Abbey clock chime the hour. Tim finds tears in his eyes, turns his back on the Crescent and strides quickly into town. The stumps on his shoulders itch. Soon his skin will break.

After he's been to the bank he hesitates. He wants to walk once more round the city, wants to say goodbye to roads, buildings, views. No, he must return to Cosmos. His client is due in an hour's time. He cannot tell her he may never see her again. Daniel's coming in any time now: he may even have opened up by the time Tim gets back. He cannot say anything to Daniel either. He has to pretend everything is all right, that he's just going to Cornwall to bring Verity home. Bring Verity home. It's so much more than that, and yet nothing more.

When he gets back to Cosmos, Daniel has opened up. He has a new blue streak in his hair, wears a matching eye liner. Pan pipes are playing on the stereo. Tim nods a quick hello, leaves Daniel to advise a customer about dream catchers and medicine wheels, and shuts himself in the back room.

He's just got time to phone Verity. His shoulders sting again as he dials her mobile.

~

Jack stares at the pictures of Verity on his mobile. They are there, just as they always were, but it's though he has put weird filters on them all. Some are stretched long and wraithlike, like chloroform dreams, some are pixelated, some have sprays of white and gold across them. One flashes at him and, in the pulses, his eyes see his sister's face as a death's head. He slams the phone down on the table. He's alone in the flat and he's afraid.

He has tried to deny his growing fear, but he and Tim are going to Cornwall tomorrow and Jack has no idea what is going to happen; he simply knows something will. He has suspended his disbelief to a point, but believing the Devil has erupted from a geological fault line is a step too far.

But what has happened to his pictures of Verity? Why is it only happening to her image? And why does he feel he has completely lost the magical blood-link to his twin? She seems more like stranger than his closest relative.

~

Verity's mobile rings from beside her on the window seat. She's sure it wasn't there a moment ago. *Tim*, it says on the display. She reaches out for it to silence the call with red; somehow hits green instead.

Tim never expected Verity to answer. She doesn't speak, but he knows she is there.

"Verity, hi, how are you?" He tries to keep his voice neutral, cannot let her know the torrent of feelings – fear, relief, love – that swirl in his heart.

"I'm fine," she says.

"We'll be down tomorrow evening." He waits for her to speak. He wonders if the connection's gone.

"I'm happy here," she says at last. "I don't want to go back to Bath."

"I know," Tim says. "But you know you have to. It was never for ever, you know that."

"But everything's different now. I can't just go."

"What do you mean – different?" Tim asks carefully.

"Just different. I can't go back. I have to stay here. I'll have to find somewhere to live here. I have to be here."

"Verity, you can't. Your home is here. I'm here. Your friends are here."

"But I have to be here. I don't expect you to understand, but I just do."

"What's his name?" Tim interrupts her.

"Whose name?"

Tim rubs his shoulder. "I know you have met someone," he says. "That's why you say you have to stay there. Tell me his name."

"I don't know what you're talking about. Look, I'm not coming back…"

"His name!" Tim shouts, glances towards the door. He can just hear the pan pipes from the shop.

"It doesn't matter."

"It does matter. It matters very much. You don't know his name, do you? He's never told you what people call him. He's very beautiful, isn't he, this man of yours? Golden hair."

"You been smoking dope again?"

"Ask him his name, Verity. Ask him what everyone else calls him."

"It doesn't matter what other people call him. He's my angel. I love him. I have to be with him."

"He's not an angel, Verity. Not anymore."

"You've been talking to that cow Caroline, haven't you? What's she been saying about me?"

"Yes, I have spoken to Caroline," Tim says. "She needs to know to protect her children."

"From me, I suppose. I saw her this morning, shouting the odds at me on the cliff. She thinks I'm a baby snatcher or something. Just because Andy likes me more than he likes her. Andy knows the angel too. He likes the angel, and the old bitch hates it."

"You really have no idea what you're saying. Caroline's very knowledgeable, very perceptive. She knows what's going on too. She knows all about your angel. Verity, please, believe me, you must not see him anymore. I will explain when I see you tomorrow. Just stay in the house, lock the doors and windows, don't let anyone in." Tim's words sound ridiculous. As if locked doors would stop the Devil himself.

Daniel knocks on the door, opens it a fraction.

"Excuse me, Tim. Julie's here now for her hypnotherapy."

"OK, thanks. I'll be out in a sec." Tim waits for the door to close again. "I have to go now. Please don't see or speak to anyone until Jack and I get to you tomorrow evening. Promise me."

"Don't come. I don't want you to come."

The line buzzes; she has gone.

⁓

Clotted towers of dark clouds are massing on the horizon. A single laser of sunlight beams onto Verity's lawn. Over the tamarisk the sea is whipping into peaks. She stands at the bay window, watching the sharp point of the Land's End peninsula blur into a dark mauve smudge. The sunbeam has gone, extinguished like a lamp. Verity turns away from the glass, grabs her jacket and flings open the front door. The temperature has dropped. She shivers, and gulps the air, tasting rain and salt and iron. A gull wheels overhead. She does not see any flash, but a low growling resonates over the bay, on and on, rolling from cliff to cliff. She steps out onto the upper lawn. The clouds over the sea are nearer, swollen. Rain falls, hard on her face, like grit. She slithers down the bank, and through the gate.

The rain is falling faster now. This time Verity sees the lightning as it crackles from cloud to cloud. She stumbles through the wet grasses to Carrag Luz, as thunder booms again. The giant boulders are slimy with the rainfall. She hauls herself on to the first ledge, cranes her neck back, hoping, expecting, to see that glowing white figure silhouetted against the dark sky. There is no-one. Verity opens her mouth, laughing, drinking the rain on her tongue as around her the sky explodes in sudden white light.

Caroline jumps at the flash of lightning. Rain rattles down the window. She snatches the phone and dials Frank's ward. It rings on and on.

At last, a woman barks, "Trauma. Staff nurse."

"It's Caroline Tripconey. Frank Tripconey's wife. He was having surgery on his ankle today. I wondered if he was back from theatre yet."

"Tripconey," the nurse repeats. "Bay three. Yes, he's back now. Everything went well."

"Thank you," Caroline says, remembers Tim's words about seeing Frank. "Can we come and see him yet? We're coming from Mullion, and the weather's getting worse. I'd rather bring the boys now than tonight."

"Yes, that'll be fine." the nurse says curtly. "Goodbye."

Back now. Everything went well. Caroline rolls those few words round her head.

Frank is all right.

Thunder. Closer now.

She doesn't want to drive to Truro and back in this storm, but Tim said she and the boys must see Frank. More than anything she does not want to be abroad after nightfall. Quickly she rings Jonny's school and explains to the secretary that she will collect Jonny in fifteen minutes to take him and Andy to see their father in hospital.

Verity slides off the wet rocks and onto the grass. She is both afraid and exhilarated by the storm, by the massive purple anvils on the horizon, the sudden thin beams of bright sunlight that spear the surface of the ocean. Her thin jacket is drenched, sticking coldly to her arms. Her hair hangs in heavy twists over her shoulders. She stops at her gate, shrugs, walks on, past Caroline's bungalow, towards the path down to the beach.

Caroline straps Andy into his car seat. Her hood blows back, and cold rain stings her face. She glances up at her bungalow, wishing again that she did not have to go any further than the school to collect Jonny. Lightning flickers once more. Caroline gets into the car and fires the ignition. The dashboard lights up as she turns on the headlamps. Her wipers cut a swathe through the streaming windscreen. Andy is muttering to himself in the back. She thinks she hears the word – that terrible word – *angel* – and she half-turns in her seat to silence him, then closes her mouth, engages reverse and judders out of the parking space

As they bump along the stony cliff road, she turns the wipers up to top speed. Still she sees bright flashes in her peripheral vision, but the comforting roar of the engine hides the growl of thunder. Caroline wipes the inner windscreen with her cloth. At the end of the lane, where the track becomes the tarmacked road, is a slight figure, hunched against the rain and wind.

"It's Verity," Andy cries from the back. "Stop!"

Caroline glances at the girl drifting at the top of the beach path. Verity's clothes are soaked, and she has no hood or hat. She does not seem to know which way she should be walking.

"Mummy!" Andy wails as Caroline accelerates up the hill.

The headlamps. That is what Verity notices above all else.

She thinks it's Caroline's car: it's the right colour and size, and she thinks she sees Caroline at the wheel, peering through the wet misted glass, but the lights are what she focuses on. Two bright gold eyes staring straight at her for a moment; then the car swings away, and roars up the road, and she is left standing in the icy rain. Puddles are forming in the uneven beach path. Verity takes a step or two down the slope. She's startled by a huge flash overhead and a matching crack of thunder. She shakes her head and rain flies from her hair. She had not realised the storm was so close. She starts running back along the cliff road towards her house. The air still reverberates from the last strike. Carrag Luz seems a long, long way away. Rain cascades around her with a new energy. By the time she reaches her gate her eyes are swimming and she finds the latch by touch alone.

Through Helston. Through the storm. Unconsciously Caroline floors the accelerator. In the rear mirror she can see the thick dark clouds gaining on her. She's turned her wipers down to intermittent; now they squeak on the glass and she turns them off. The eastern sky is pale and clear. A driver coming the other way puts on his headlights as he passes Caroline.

166

"Why are they all doing that?" Jonny's voice from the back.

"Doing what?" Caroline asks, glancing in her mirror.

Behind the boys' heads, the back window is murky with gunmetal clouds. A hard spray of rain hits the car. Caroline jumps, fumbles for her wipers again.

"The other cars," Jonny says. "They all put their lights on when they go by us."

"They're heading into the storm," Caroline says, trying to sound even, calm.

A bright blue sports car comes roaring towards them. With a white flash its headlamps and spotlights come on as it passes Caroline.

"See, it happened again," Jonny says. "Why are they doing it?"

"It's just the storm," Caroline reiterates. "They can see I have my lights on, so they think they should put theirs on."

The car climbs onto the high ground between Helston and Falmouth. Two cars pass them; each flicks on its lights. Caroline brakes abruptly for a speed camera then puts her foot down again, watching the accelerator rise to sixty, seventy.

"Why are we going so fast?" Jonny asks nervously.

"I'm sorry," Caroline says, lifting her foot. "I want to get to Daddy before the storm."

Heavier rain rattles down the windscreen. Lightning flashes overhead. Caroline's heartrate jumps. The storm has caught them. She swerves round the roundabouts, and plunges into the trees.

"They're still doing it," Jonny says, craning forward to see the oncoming cars. "Every car. They don't have lights on, then they put them on. Is there something wrong with our car?"

"Car's fine," Caroline says, sweeping her eyes over the gauges.

The wind has come up with the storm, and the trees sway against the darkening sky. Under the tunnel of trees beside the river it is even darker. Caroline jumps as an approaching car turns on its headlamps.

"But..." Jonny starts.

"Just leave it, Jonny," Caroline snaps. "It's really hard driving in this weather. Please be quiet."

She exhales as they come out the other side of the trees. The rain clatters harder and harder. Lightning flashes in Caroline's rear view mirror. I've brought the storm, she thinks. I tried to outrun it, but I've brought it with me instead. She guns up the slope. The wooded road to Truro closes in. She wants to be through there before the lightning comes any closer. She keeps her eyes on the left hand carriageway; she does not look in her mirror, or at the oncoming traffic with its sinister salute of headlamps. In the back seat the boys are quiet, but she can sense their unease. Her head aches; her throat is dry. Through the final bend, and the trees fall back once more. The grunt of the wipers on top speed fails to clear the rainwater, and the side windows are blurry. She opens her window and cold rain blasts into the car. The boys cry out in the back. Caroline forces the car on, up to Arch Hill roundabout.

A car horn, long and loud.

"Shit!" cries Caroline, braking, stalling half-on the roundabout.

An estate car swings across her bows, flashing its main beam on and off. Caroline fumbles with handbrake and ignition, and lurches onto the road for the hospital. It seems the dark sky is sinking down onto the car. Caroline feels the race of panic in her chest again. The cars on the opposite carriageway are inching forwards towards Truro city centre. Flick, flick, flick go the headlamps, one after another after another.

The hospital car park is washed with rain. Tall fir trees at its perimeter sway roughly in the gale. Caroline takes her ticket from the dispenser; the barrier rises and she shunts through. She trawls round the car-park; at last finds a space under a dripping tree. As she opens her door, it is flung from her hand, almost into the neighbouring car. She tugs on her hood, and opens the back door to get the boys out.

It is dark as twilight. The amber lamps are on, turning the puddles into iodine stains. Caroline locks the car, grabs each of the boys and tugs them across the wet tarmac to the entrance. The rain turns to hail: hard icy crystals beating on their faces and hands, bouncing off the ground.

"Looks at the lights," Andy cries. "Lights everywhere."

He is gazing up at the massive edifice. Lights have been turned on in every window. She can see figures moving, containers on window-sills. Her boots are leaking already, and her socks are wet and clammy. Hail stings her eyes and thunder booms overhead. The giant electric doors hiss open and they stumble through. The lobby is crowded with people standing, hardly moving, staring with glassy eyes through the rain-washed doors. The air is thick, foetid, with people and sweat and food, but there's a darker smell beneath those that makes Caroline gasp and gag for a second.

"Zombies," Jonny laughs.

"What?" Caroline asks.

"They're zombies. Standing like that." Jonny lets go of Caroline's hand, staggers a few steps with outstretched zombie arms.

Yes, Caroline thinks, he's right. Zombies. Waiting. Waiting placidly for something. Don't be stupid. They're waiting for the hail to stop: that's all.

"How do you know about zombies?" she snaps at Jonny, as the glazed crowd parts silently and the three of them pass through into the interior.

~

Tim leaves Cosmos after the hypnotherapy session. He's angry with himself. He has let down his client. She has been coming to him for help with her anxiety, and today he was too anxious himself to be any help to her. As she handed him the money at the end of the session, he folded her fingers round the notes, told her to keep it. His shoulders are hurting, itching and throbbing. In the shower he turns to examine himself in the foggy mirror. The twin humps are bigger, bonier. As he runs his hand over the wet skin, he fancies he can sense movement beneath: the knitting of fibres, the multiplication of cells, the growth of new limbs.

He's walking to his bedroom, wearing only a pair of jeans, when he hears the flat door open. He stands where he is. He wants Jack to see.

"Bloody hell, Tim. You should get a doctor to see that. It's not…normal."

"They'll go. After the confrontation."

Or I won't be here to know, he adds silently.

"Let's go tonight."

"I'm not ready."

"And you will be in twenty-four hours? What difference does it make. Come on. I'll drive. You've sorted the insurance, haven't you?"

Tim scratches his left shoulder. The skin is taut and slimy. He checks his palm: blood.

"What's going to happen to them?" Jack asks. "Is that why you say you're not ready?"

"Partly. But I feel it in here." His head. "And here." His heart. "It's tomorrow. Tomorrow is the day. I have been right all along."

"But I could go now and get her back and there would be no confrontation, except with me and her."

"You can't do this without me. If you go alone, Verity will die, and so will you, I thought you believed me."

"I do…some of the time. And then I think: fuck me, this is crazy."

170

"These stumps. They are going to become wings. I will become the Archangel Michael. But only for a very short time. That is why we wait until nearer the end."

"The end?"

"The end. Or a new dawn."

Frank's bed is in the corner under a high window. While he laughs with the boys Caroline watches the relentless tattoo of first hail, and then more rain, on the glass. The sky is purple-black with storm clouds. Inside the ward the electric light seems even harder and brighter. Caroline feels she can't breathe. Frank hasn't said anything about Verity or about the accident; neither has she. It doesn't matter now. Caroline eases out of her plastic visitors' chair, and stands beneath the window.

"Awful, isn't it?" Frank says. "I expect you want to be off now."

Caroline shrugs. Yes, she does, she wants to be home in Mullion with the boys, and the doors and windows locked; she also wants to stay here in the safety of the hospital until it's all over. Whatever it is.

"It's the rush hour now. Why don't you all go to the canteen here and get something to eat? Wait for the rain to pass."

Caroline checks her watch automatically. "I don't know," she says.

"Oh please," Jonny says. "I'm starving. Are you starving, Andy?"

"Yes, starving," Andy agrees.

Caroline cranes her neck. She cannot see any lightening of the sky, but it will keep them here for a little longer, put off the moment of hurrying across the flooded car-park, and back to their lonely home on the cliff.

"Go on," Jonny wheedles.

"All right," Caroline relents. "Let's go."

Frank hugs each of the boys. Caroline bends down to kiss him on the cheek, but he takes her face in his hand, finds her mouth with his.

"I love you," he says, as they draw apart.

"Yuck, gross." Jonny makes vomiting noises.

Caroline smiles uncertainly at Frank. Will I see you again? she asks silently. Will you see any of us again?

She grabs the boys by the hands and leads them out of the ward. She does not look back to Frank, or to the oblong of pewter sky above his bed.

The canteen is on the ground floor. Plate glass windows stream with rainwater. The smell of institutional food makes Caroline gag. She buys fish and chips for Jonny, chips and beans for Andy when he appears unable to make up his mind what he wants.

"What are you eating?" Jonny asks.

Caroline takes a pre-packed sandwich from the cold cabinet, orders a cup of tea. As she stands in the queue to pay, she feels a vibration in the air. She blinks. The air from the cold cabinet seems colder, voices and clangs seem louder. She takes her change, keeps her head down, and leads the boys to find a table.

"Here, by the window," Jonny says.

Caroline would prefer to be in the centre of the room, away from the dark glass, the rain, and whatever may be moving in the bushes outside, but it is tea time, and the canteen is busy. It is the only spare table. She places the overcrowded tray on the sticky, crumby surface. Jonny gobbles chips. Andy messes with his food, eats a few chips, a mouthful of beans, discards his fork. Caroline simply sits with her cooling tea in front of her. Everything is more acute: her vision, her hearing, her sense of smell. She thinks she may retch from the smell of food and damp people. She can see the colours of diners' eyes far across the room; her head pounds with the conversations around her.

"You're not eating," Andy whines, shoving beans round his plate.

"Sorry," she says and tears the wrapper from her sandwich. Sharp cheese and salad scents hit her nose. She gulps a mouthful of tea.

172

"Are you ill?" Jonny asks, squirting tomato ketchup from a sachet.

"No." Caroline looks up, around the room, at the heads bent over cups and plates.

Suddenly she sees other things: ghostly colours blurring heads and faces. Auras in different hues. She jerks round to face the boys but she sees nothing around their heads. She reaches up to her hair, but she cannot sense any warmth or light there. There is no spectral halo in her reflection in the glass. She takes a bite of sandwich before the boys can say anything else about her not eating. She chews and chews, unable to swallow.

When she turns back to the dining hall, she instantly sees a dark murky yellow light around an old man's head. She recoils, almost chokes on her sandwich.

"He will die," she says.

"What? Who?" Fear in Jonny's eyes.

"Oh, er, nothing."

"Who will die? Daddy? Daddy's going to…"

"No," Caroline almost shouts. "Daddy's had his operation. He's fine. He'll be home soon."

She looks at the old man again, talking to his wife, lifting his cup.

"I want to see Daddy," Andy says.

"We've seen Daddy. I want to get home now."

"Can't we see him again?"

"No. He's probably eating his tea. We wouldn't be allowed in."

"Let's see if we are," Jonny says.

"We're going home."

Caroline is not going up to that ward again. She is not going to see what colour aura shimmers above Frank. The elderly man gets up, walks stiffly out of the canteen with his wife. When will it happen? Caroline wonders. Tonight? Tomorrow? Next week? She sees other dirty yellow auras, in different tones.

173

"Are you two ready?"

"What's the matter, Mummy?"

"I'm fine, Jonny. I'm tired and worried and the journey will be horrible in this storm. Let's go. Finished, Andy?"

Andy is gazing out of the window, at the darkened foliage and heavy sky.

"What you looking at, Andy?" Jonny asks.

"Looking for Angel."

Caroline stands abruptly, knocks herself on the table. Cutlery and voices jangle in her head.

"Come on. We're leaving."

As she weaves between the tables she holds her hands tightly in front of her abdomen, afraid of touching, breaking, the auras around her. On the corridor outside she stares and stares at the boys' heads, but still she cannot discern anything there. She takes hold of Andy's hand. Jonny refuses her grasp. As they hurry along the corridor, she averts her eyes from the patients on trolleys and in wheelchairs. The air is thick with auras of death. She can smell it: sweet, cloying at the back of the throat.

The giant doors hiss open, and colder air blasts her cheeks. Suddenly Caroline's sight and hearing return to normal. The stink of death has gone, washed away in the rain that still pours down, forming pools in the car park. She does not see any coloured haloes above the people at the pay point. She looks all around her. It is just a car park in the rain, with people in wet coats stumbling through the puddles towards the hospital.

It's after six o'clock. The rush hour traffic has gone. The roads are awash with rainwater, and the cars travel slowly. As Caroline turns right at Arch Hill, she sees approaching thunder clouds mounting over the treetops. This time she is driving right into the storm. Great arcs of water spray up on either side of the car ahead, and Caroline brakes just before she hits the flood. She's jumpy – really jumpy – waiting for the first flash of lightning. It comes on the wooded, creek-side road, lighting the trees from behind and above, transforming them instantaneously into shivering silhouettes.

"Angel would like that," Andy says suddenly.

"If you get hit by lightning you get picked up in the air and burnt and dropped down again," Jonny says. "You could land miles away."

The car ahead peels off for Falmouth. Caroline glances in her mirror, sees the two behind follow him. The route to Helston stretches out: darkened, empty. Suddenly hers is the only car on the road. The sky bursts with blue lightning again. Bright green sparks skitter along an electrical cable overhead. Caroline hits a patch of water, almost skids, eases her foot off the gas. Sweat prickles her face and neck as she visualises the tumbled wreck of her car, upside-down, burnt-out, her children trapped inside. She almost sobs with relief when she sees the lights of Helston through the streaky windscreen.

"Twenty minutes and we'll be home," she says, and her voice sounds thick in the stale car, over the drone of the engine.

"Andy's asleep," Jonny says.

"Why don't you have a nap too?" Caroline asks him.

"Not tired," Jonny sniffs.

Caroline checks her mirror. There is no-one behind her. Around the bend ahead she can see the glow from red rear lights. She speeds up to tuck in behind the car in front but, as she sweeps round the bend, the red glow disappears and there is only the empty road ahead.

"Ten minutes," she mutters to herself. "Ten minutes and we'll be home."

Trees close in thickly, their leafy crowns obliterating the darkening sky. There are still flickers, but they're further away, and she cannot hear any answering thunder. She slows right down for the bends at

Bochym. Water is running off the wooded hillside, pooling across the carriageway in an oily black flood.

"There's a man."

Caroline jumps at Andy's voice.

"Where?"

"There."

The car judders up the hill. Caroline snatches at the gear lever, and the car squeals.

"Where?" she says again.

"Over there."

"There's no-one," Jonny says. "Put your specs on."

"They are on."

"I can't see anyone," Caroline says, her voice quivering.

Suddenly the sky flashes with sheets of lightning.

"It's Angel!" Andy shouts. "There, Mummy, by the trees. Angel. Stop, Mummy."

Caroline's feet tremble on clutch and gas. Thunder crashes overhead, and a squall of rain hits the screen. She forces the car on up the hill, her eyes on the mirror. With a shriek the tyres hit muddy grass.

"What you doing?" yells Jonny.

"Sorry, sorry, boys." Caroline feels the burn of diarrhoea in her bowel.

"Angel was there," Andy says.

"There wasn't anyone," Jonny says. "There's no angel."

"There is! Mummy, tell him."

"There's no angel," Caroline says.

"Should have gone to Specsavers," Jonny hoots.

"You said he hurt Daddy, but he didn't."

"Andy, shut up."

176

The car's choking, as though there's dirt in the fuel. Caroline turns the wipers up to fast. She checks the petrol gauge. The needle is spinning back and forth: empty, full, full, empty.

"Have we broken down?" asks Jonny.

Caroline doesn't answer. She just can't speak. Onwards, onwards, she wills the car, inch by spluttering inch, to the crest of the hill. The fuel line clears, but the petrol gauge is still frantic. Caroline accelerates. Rain water sprays up from her tyres. She knows she's going too fast again. She bumps over a pot hole. At last, the road sign for the Mullion junction. She swings right towards the coast and the lightning.

It only takes a few moments, but it feels like forever. Caroline pulls onto her parking strip, flicks off her lights and wipers, kills the engine. She rests her head on the wheel, tears in her eyes, as the rain drums on the car roof and windows.

"Are we getting out?" Jonny demands.

"Yes, yes," Caroline whispers.

Her door is almost wrenched from her grasp. The wind roars across the bay. There are lights on in Verity's front room. Caroline shudders, opens the back door for the boys to get out. She's about to say *you two go on, and I'll lock up* then remembers she cannot let them out of her sight.

She gathers her bag and keys, opens the gate. The boys run through into the dark wet garden. Caroline slams the gate behind her. It bounces on the catch and swings open. She steps back to reach for it, still watching the boys. A flash of light in her peripheral vision, but it's not lightning. It stays there. She turns quickly. Her car headlamps are on. But I turned them off, I know I did, she thinks. I sat in the dark, and Jonny had to rouse me.

She hesitates. The boys are on the doorstep. Jonny's jigging up and down. Andy's gazing upwards, letting the rain mottle the lenses of his glasses. Caroline fumbles for the key with her cold fingers. As soon as the front door is open, she shoves the boys inside, turns on the light. She should feel safer with lights on, but she doesn't, and her car lamps are still on, out there on the cliff road.

"Stay here, right here, behind the door," she says, throwing her bag into the hall. "I have to go back to the car for a moment. I'm going to lock you in. I'll only be a minute."

She locks the door, checks the handle, and slithers down the wet gravel path to the gate, suddenly terrified she will fall, leaving the boys trapped indoors and alone. The gate has blown right back in the wind, leaving a yawning gap onto the cliff. Caroline keeps her head down, wrenches open the driver's door, and reaches in to turn off the lights. As she finds the switch, she half expects it to be in the off position, or to find that, whatever she does, she cannot kill the lights, but they die silently, and now she stands in the dark. Slowly she turns to face the cliff edge, sensing the presence of someone, something, in the shadows.

The tamarisk is waving wildly. Ocean, clouds and sky blur into a thick blue-black darkness. She can just see the pale outline of Carrag Luz on the cliff edge. As the wind pauses to inhale for another gust she hears the crash of waves far below, and imagines she can taste the salt on her lips.

"Angel," she says quietly. She feels the word with her mouth and tongue, rather than hears it. "Angel," she says again, louder this time. "You're no angel. I know who you are."

She waits, but nothing happens; no-one appears. She breathes deeply: cold air into her lungs. The pain in her bowel has gone; her heartrate is dropping. She realises her fear is ebbing.

"I'm not afraid of you," she says. "You will leave my children alone."

And now she can taste the spray on her lips. She can smell the ocean and the rain and the sodden, crushed bluebells and garlic. She can hear the rustles of tiny creatures burrowing in the undergrowth. She can see Carrag Luz clearly; the rocks are glittering with crystals and veins. She inhales deeply, swallowing the rain and the wind, and the power of the night.

~

Caroline realises she knew all along Tim would call her.

It's late now, almost eleven. The boys are in bed. She checks on them every fifteen minutes. They both seem to be sleeping, despite the storm outside. She's still dressed and wearing her soggy boots. She will not go to bed. She's not even tired, not tonight. She will stay awake, all night, watching, waiting.

"Tim?"

"Caroline."

"It's been…"

"What?"

"Awful. Frightening."

"Are you all right?" he asks. "Are the children safe?"

"Yes, yes, they're in bed."

"Are you in bed?"

"No. I'm staying up. I can't sleep. I need to know…whatever. The weather is terrible. We've had storms all afternoon. I had to drive the boys to Truro to see Frank, and I was so frightened, and the boys picked up on it too. Things kept happening."

"What things?"

"I could see auras round people in the hospital. I knew who was going to die. The journey was terrifying. I was driving badly, too fast, I just wanted to get there, and on the way back Andy said he saw the…angel." Caroline whispers the word.

"Did you see him?"

179

"No, but I know he was there. It was in the trees, on a dark road, in the storm. Andy saw him in the lightning flash. Jonny said there was no-one."

"He still doesn't believe in him."

"No."

"That's good. It will protect him. Don't let him believe. Not in anything."

"I couldn't wait to get home, but I was afraid of what I'd find here."

"What did you find?"

"Just darkness. Then, after I'd locked up the car, the headlights came on again by themselves. I went back to turn them off and then something came over me, and I felt myself becoming stronger. For a few moments, I felt I was absorbing power from the land, the earth. It's gone now. When are you coming down?"

"Tomorrow. It will be tomorrow."

"What can I do?" Caroline asks. "I can feel it. I can feel it in the storm and in the air and in the earth, but I don't know what it is. I can't see what Andy sees."

"You don't want to."

"But if I can't see it, how can I do protect the boys?"

"Have you got lights on in the house?" Tim asks suddenly.

"Only a couple. The boys are in bed."

"Turn them off. He craves light. He seeks it. Turn them off."

Caroline's hand is already on the switch. She bumps into the sofa in the dark, jumps. The rain seems louder now. There's a wail of wind.

"It seems wrong," she says.

"Keep the lights off. Whatever you do, don't let the boys put a light on. He will see it. It will attract him to them."

Caroline pads along to the boys' room, but there's no sliver of light under the door.

"I thought he wanted Verity."

"He does, but Andy has got his attention. Andy flatters him, Andy wants to see him."

Caroline walks back to the living room and lifts the curtain aside. She can just see a corner of Verity's bungalow.

"Verity has lights on," she says to Tim. "I can't see the whole house, but it looks like she has a lot of lights on."

"She's calling him," Tim says.

~

Verity unlocks the door to the studio and jumps back in surprise. The light is already on. She knows it was off before, that it hasn't been left on for days. Nothing seems changed in the studio. There's the faint smell of stale air and pigment. She lets the door drift shut again. Now every light is on. She can do no more to keep out the dark and the storm.

She returns to the living room. She's shut the curtains, disturbed by the room's mirror image in the glass. She slides between the curtain and the window pane. At first all she sees is her own face – pale, strained – and the slice of room reflected behind her. Rain on the glass. Something blowing around in the garden. The tamarisk tossing this way and that. Beyond the ravaged fronds she sees the streaky lights of Penzance and three pulses of the lighthouse there. A moment later Wolf Rock swells and dies on the horizon.

"Caroline," Tim says. "You must go outside and…"

"I can't leave the boys."

"You must go outside and make a circle of protection around your home. Can you do that?"

"I can't leave the boys."

"Do you have rocks, stones, crystals, anything like that?"

"Yes. But I…"

"OK, do you know how to cast a circle?"

"Yes," Caroline says. It's been a long time, years and years. Memories of casting a circle round her favourite hidey hole to keep her brother away, rings of protection around dying pets.

"Are you sure?"

"Yes," she says more firmly.

"If Verity has all the lights on you may not have much time. You need to gather your stones, as many as you can carry. Place them round your house, especially at doors and windows."

The wind shrieks through the letterbox and Caroline shivers.

"And…"

"No." She knows what Tim's asking. She can read the unfurling string of words in his mind.

"Please Caroline. When you've protected you own house, please protect Verity for me."

"I can't. I can't leave the boys and go next door. Not tonight."

"The boys will be safe once you've cast your own circle," Tim says. "I can't force you, but please would you do it for me?"

"I'm afraid," she says.

"When you were on the cliff earlier you said your fear was subsiding. When you're out there in your elements, in the weather, on the land, you can be strong. Who are you, Caroline? I know now who you are. Do you know yourself?"

Elements; weather; land. Birth and children.

"The Empress."

"Yes," Tim whispers. "The Empress. Mary Moses, the Earth Mother, the Goddess."

Caroline ends the call. She's shivering and cold. Over the wind she thinks she hears thunder. She stumbles into her coat, twists off her suede boots and puts on wellies. In the dark she blunders into the coat

182

rack, jars her head on a hook. She muffles a cry of pain. Her hand reaches for a torch, a Maglite with a thin beam. She shoves it in her pocket. She cannot go out into the storm without the security of a light. But what danger does that light attract?

She opens the hall cupboard for her wicker baskets. Strong ones to hold the weight of stones. She runs her hand over the rocks and crystals, feels their cold roughness and smoothness on her palm. One rugged piece feels like ice shards. Amethyst for the boys' window. She places it at the bottom of a basket, snatches other stones and rocks. She recognises the feel of some of them, identifies them in her head: quartz, obsidian, granite, serpentine, haematite, malachite. The mantra soothes her. When the stones are packed, she steals to the boys' room. Gentle breathing.

At the front door she hesitates. The night is hostile. At last, she opens the door. The garden heaves and flaps with foliage. Squally rain stings her face. She closes the door as softly as she can, and reaches into one of her baskets for a stone. It's serpentine; she can sense the whorls with her fingers. She bends clumsily in her boots and lays the stone at the front door.

"Serpentine, serpentine," Caroline repeats the word, until it has no meaning, only sound.

The wind seems more distant; she can hear its power, but it no longer flays the skin on her face. She trails her fingers over the serpentine. It is dry: warm and dry. She stumbles to her feet, reaches into her basket again. As she lays black obsidian, she's aware of tiny green flickers in the undergrowth. The eyes of little creatures, mice and shrews, hiding under the wet leaves, watching her. They are no threat, no malevolent imps; they are her companions of the night. She lets her hood fall back, faces the sky. Rain shafts down onto her, but her skin remains dry. As she lowers her gaze, she feels a faint shifting in the foliage and grasses, as colours seep through the shadows. She does not need the Maglite in her coat pocket: her vision is growing moment by moment.

At the boys' bedroom window, she places the jagged amethyst crag. She balances it on the windows sill, as close to their sleeping heads as she can be.

"Amethyst, protect my boys," she whispers and, in this new strange light, she sees a glowing purple-white aura around the crystal. She holds out her hand to it, and her skin crackles with its energy.

In her peripheral vision she sees the flare of lights from the bungalow next door. She does not have much time. Through her boots the ground is moving, but she feels no fear. The grass at her feet pales and she can see ghostly images below. Worms crawling, roots twisting, seeds swelling. The earth exhales again and, far, far below, she watches the very infrastructure, the tectonic plates, shifting. She imagines there are roots attached to the soles of her feet, holding her fast to the earth, to the centre of power. She can sense the life blood of the planet surging through her limbs.

"I am not afraid of you," she says, and her voice is deeper, stronger, the earth speaking. "Angel or Devil."

Lightning flickers over the tamarisk hedge; the thunder's distant retort reverberates along the coast. Though she is dry and warm, almost glowing, the storm is approaching swiftly. The boys will wake, find her gone.

She works quickly. The names of the stones are like a benediction. She no longer feels she is moving on the surface of the earth; she is part of it, as one. Beneath the thunder and the wind, she hears tiny chirrups and burrs as the night creatures huddle in the foliage. A snail's shell sparkles like quartz crystal. She breathes the aroma of soil and leaves and rain, until the elements themselves burrow into her soul.

"The circle is complete." Caroline stands at the doorstep, by the first serpentine. She bends, trails her hand over its warm, dry surface.

She has only one stone left: a rough hunk of iron ore, the colour of clotted blood. She holds it a moment, feels the beat of its heart. She leaves the basket on the lawn and slithers down the wet path to the gate. It slams shut behind her, a barrier between her and the boys. Rainwater is running through the furrows and dips of the cliff road, and now she feels it on her skin. Waves boom below. She stumbles over the fault line; below the surface is a deep slash in the earth, leading to black nothingness. Panic swells in her chest, as she steps over the chasm under the transparent topsoil. Carrag Luz is white, monstrous, against the ragged sky. Caroline averts her eyes from the glowing rocks, puts her hand on Verity's gate. She hears something on the cliff road behind her: a yowl, a cry. She turns and an icy squall smacks her face. Under her coat she's cold. She stands there a moment, too afraid to move either into Verity's garden or back over the fault line to her own house.

I have to do it, she says silently. I have to do it for Tim. She kicks open Verity's gate and leaves it swinging in the wind. Her night vision has gone. Her fingers close on the cool slim Maglite in her pocket, but there is so much light coming from Verity's house she does not pull it out.

The stone steps to the front door are slippery, and she almost falls. She hears tortured noises in the undergrowth. She can no longer see into the ground; indeed, she does not want to know what may be buried where she now stands. She drops the red-brown iron onto Verity's doorstep and staggers down the stone steps once more.

On the cliff path she reaches for the torch in her pocket. Her fingers shake as she twists it onto the thinnest beam. Shielding the light with her other hand, she staggers through her gate and, at once, the earth opens up its secrets. She watches roots unfurling like bony fingers; she sees the veins in the leaves, the pollen on stamens. Warmth pulses through her body. She opens the front door and falls through into the darkened hall. When she peels off her coat the fabric is dry. Her hair is dry, her face is dry. She tugs off her wellies. Her heart rate has calmed. She pads long the dark passage to the boys' room and inches open the door. They are still asleep. Through the flimsy curtains Caroline can see a mauve glow.

"Amethyst, protect my boys," she says again.

She leaves their door open a chink and goes to the hall to phone Tim.

"I've done it," she says quietly. "I've made the circle."

"And Verity?" Tim asks.

"I did what I could," Caroline says. She finds she can't remember details, just an overpowering terror in the garden next door: strange noises, eyes – not the benevolent eyes of mice – upon her back, throwing the rock down on Verity's doorstep.

"Thank you."

"And now what?" Caroline asks. "What will happen tonight?"

"Had she still got her lights on?"

"Yes. Every light I should think."

"He will come tonight," Tim says.

"Will he come here?"

"You are protected."

Caroline visualises the circle of stones, the amethyst's energy, the moving earth beneath her feet.

"Yes," she says at last. "We are protected."

"Even so, do not open the doors or windows," Tim says. "Not for anything, anyone. Whatever you hear or see. Do you understand?"

"Yes," she says again, uncertainly. "He will come here then?"

⌒

Verity stands at the giant window. The curtain strokes the back of her neck. Rain washes down the glass in swathes, distorting the pale outline of Carrag Luz. Wolf Rock is an indistinct wavering blink in the indigo distance. Suddenly a jagged fork of lightning spears through the sky into the garden. Verity jumps back from the glass. The lights expire, and she is left in the darkness, with the rain cracking against the black window. Thunder roars and, over that terrible noise, Verity hears another, a howl of pain, of anger and, for a second, her heartbeat shudders, and she stumbles backwards through the gap in the curtains into the darkened living room.

Then another sound. Crashing at the back door.

~

The boys are awake, afraid. Andy's crying. Caroline's sitting on his bed, cuddling him.

"I want the light on," he says.

"The lights don't work," Caroline lies. "The electricity has gone off."

In the pocket of her cardigan, she has the Maglite. She won't use it unless she has to, but it must be safer than putting on the main lights.

"When did the lights go out?" Jonny asks.

"While you were asleep," Caroline says.

She slides off Andy's bed and pads to the window. She can still see the pale violet light from the amethyst through the curtain. Very carefully she moves aside the material and stares out into the night. Light glows from Verity's house. She still has all the lights on. Calling him.

It happens so quickly. Forked lightning splits the sky; thunder crashes; Verity's lights go out. Caroline gasps, yanks the curtains. It could be a power cut – that does happen in storms – but she knows it is not. Verity has called him, and he has come.

"Jonny," Caroline whispers shakily. "Come over into Andy's bed. Let's all get in and cuddle up together."

Thunder still booms outside and Caroline imagines she hears something else: a cry – human yet inhuman – that makes her shiver. She pulls Andy's quilt over their three cramped bodies and waits.

~

Verity blunders though the room, knocking herself on the sofa, on the door jamb. In the hall, she almost trips on something – a shoe? – that's lying in her path. Light flows from the kitchen. She can taste the cold of the rain and the wind. She cannot see the angel, but she knows he is there, knows it is his light she can see. It's not a golden warmth, not tonight, it's a cold blue-white glare, and Verity shivers at this change.

He's standing in the open doorway. His pale hair sparkles with the rain or electricity or something else. Behind him the rain slashes down, glittering shards, onto the paving slabs. The cold air brings up goose-flesh on Verity's skin. She opens her mouth to speak.

"What are you doing to me?" the angel asks. His silver eyes are flinty hard, his voice cold as the night.

"I don't understand."

"You are trying to keep me out."

"No, never. I've been waiting for you."

"Your pitiful attempts have no power to destroy me."

"What do you mean? I don't understand."

"I think you do."

Verity reaches out to him. "Please come here. I've been looking for you."

He snatches her hand, and she feels the bones grating.

"You're hurting me."

He swings her round, pushes her out of the back door. She's only wearing socks on her feet. The flagstones are cold, wet, and slimy. He drags her round the side of the house, and the wind smacks her in the face.

"Angel."

"Why have you put that there?" He points at the front door.

"I haven't done anything. I can't see anything," Verity sobs, tugging streaming hair from her face.

Blue light shimmers around the angel. He stares at her implacably.

"You wanted to hurt me, Verity. Didn't you?"

"No, no."

"You wanted to ruin me."

"I didn't."

Suddenly Verity sees it. At the top of the steps there's a rock before her front door.

"That? That rock?" she asks. "Is that it? I didn't put it there."

She wrenches free from his grasp, and slithers to the rock. It's dark red and the rain releases a scent of blood that catches in her throat. She picks up the rock and hurls it into the flower bed.

"If you didn't, who did?" the angel demands.

"I don't know. It's gone now. Please can we go inside?" Her voice falters.

She's afraid of the angel, his intensity, his anger. She doesn't understand him. He's looking at her with hatred, contempt, yet still, under her sodden clothes, she feels her body warming, aching, for him to touch her, fuse into her. She looks away in confusion, into the night.

"If not you, it was her. That woman. She has long tried to keep me from you, Verity." He leaps down the bank.

"Where are you going?" Verity cries, as he vaults over the gate.

His light has gone, and she is standing in darkness. Her socks are soaked through, and her feet ache with cold. Her face stings with the rain, and there is blood on her hand, cut by that ugly hateful rock.

She splashes back along the side of the house. The back door is still open, a hollow mouth leading into a deeper darkness. She staggers inside, and slams the door. Her hand hesitates on the key. She wants to lock the door, she wants to keep the angel out, but she's desolate without him. She moves away from the door, her wet socks slapping on the floor. She fumbles her way to the hall. Lightning shimmers though the black streaky panes of the door, but she cannot see the light of the angel in her garden.

"Angel's coming," Andy says, turning his face towards the window.

"There's no angel." Caroline's voice wavers and breaks.

"He's coming." Andy struggles against his mother's bump.

"Stop it," she says, gripping him to her chest.

"Yeah, just stop it, Andy."

"Don't, Jonny."

"You told him to stop it."

"He's here, he's here. He's come to take me flying. Oh!" Andy howls, covers his ears with his hands.

"What is it, Andy?" Caroline demands. Her eyes are on the window, on that pale amethyst glow.

"Angel's angry," Andy whispers.

"Shut up," says Jonny. "You're nuts."

"Sssh," Caroline hisses.

Under the wind and the rain, she hears it again, that cry she heard before – human, yet inhuman. She dare not move from the bed, she cannot pull back the curtain; she must never see what is out there.

Andy cries again, and clamps his hands to his ears.

"What can you hear?" she asks.

"Angel," Andy mutters. "He can't find me. Angel, I'm here. Mummy, let me go to Angel."

"No," Caroline roars. Jonny jumps at the depth and power of her voice.

"Angel!" Andy waves at the window. "Here I am."

Caroline grabs his arms. She cannot see anything through the curtain, but she knows, she knows. It, he, is out there, on the other side of the thin pane of wet glass. That howl again, anguished, furious. Andy cries.

"He's there. Can't you see him?"

"No," hisses Caroline.

"There's no-one." Jonny moves to get up.

"Don't!" Caroline grabs his shoulder, drags him back down.

"I was going to look out."

"Never look out," Caroline manages to say. "Never, ever."

"But there's…"

"Jonny, stop it. Get under the covers."

Caroline's sweating and shivering. Her breath is ragged. She tries to inhale deeply, calmly, coughs and chokes instead.

"Why can't you see him?" Andy wails. "Can you hear him? He's angry."

The next howl is so loud Caroline jumps with Andy. It comes from outside the window.

"What's the matter?" Jonny asks.

"Nothing," says Caroline.

Andy's reaching out his stubby hand towards the window. Caroline smacks it back down. She can't see it, but she can hear it, and its cry is terrifying, ancient, the despair of a fallen angel.

"He's going, he's going," Andy sobs. "He's hurt."

Caroline stares at the pale glow outside which, for a moment burns with a deeper intensity, like a purple flame.

"Thank you, amethyst," she whispers silently.

Verity's hands shake as she peels off her wet clothes in her darkened bedroom. She's tried the light switches and nothing comes on. She doesn't know if there's a torch anywhere. Her socks catch on her heels and, in the dark, she overbalances, falling awkwardly onto the bed. Her jeans are heavy and clumsy with rainwater; the wet denim chafes her skin as she tugs them off. Her hair is knotted and clammy on her neck. She lies naked on her bed, cold skin chilling further, waiting. The wind still roars round the house, the rain rattles on the roof and down the windows. She seems unable to remember what it was like without this constant noise. She closes her eyes.

She cannot have slept. Her skin is still cold and clammy when the flash blazes behind her closed eyelids. She starts back to consciousness and the room burns with light: white-blue light, and, at its centre the angel. Verity struggles to sit up, her mouth open in a cry of fear and desire. The angel seems to have grown taller, broader. With one hand he pushes her back.

"You know what she has done."

"I haven't seen her." Verity tries to heap the bedclothes round her body, afraid, vulnerable, in her nakedness.

"I went for her child and she has kept him from me."

"How?" Verity whispers.

"You do not usually hide yourself from me." The angel tears away the quilt she holds in front of her.

"You're frightening me."

"You want me. You always have. She tried to keep me from you. She will pay for that. I went to take him but she has stopped me. You must come with me now. You can remove the contamination so I can take the boy. Get up."

"The boy? Andy? Where will you take him?"

"Where his mother will never see him again. Move. You must clear the way for me."

Andy, Andy. Verity sees his chubby face, his blinking eyes large behind the glasses.

"No."

"What?"

"I said no. You will not take Andy anywhere. You will not hurt him. He hasn't done anything."

"You would defy me?"

"Yes."

"Someone will pay for tonight."

"Not Andy," Verity whispers.

The angel twists her face up. Pain jars her neck. His nails have grown into talons. One scores into the flesh under her chin.

"Then it will be you."

"Mummy, what's happening?" Jonny asks.

Andy's crying again. Caroline hesitates. Tim said if Jonny didn't believe in anything it would protect him. She cannot tell him.

"It's the storm," she begins. Her mouth is so dry. She can't remember when she last drank anything. "There's some funny electrical stuff going on, and I find it frightening."

"But Andy…he hears stuff, and you do too. I can't. What is it?"

"Just the electrical stuff. Not everyone can hear it. I'm glad you can't hear it. It's loud."

"It's Angel," Andy howls. "He's with Verity. He wanted me and he couldn't find me."

"What's he on about?" Jonny demands. "Who is this stupid angel?"

"It's nothing." Caroline says.

"I want the toilet," Andy snuffles.

He's with Verity, Caroline thinks. Andy says so. He's not here. Not anymore.

193

"OK, we'll all go," she says. "Remember, we can't turn on the lights. It's dangerous to do that."

She slides off the bed, gets unsteadily to her feet. There's only the sound of the rain and the wind. Carefully she opens the door. The hallway is dark. She takes out the Maglite and twists it onto a thin beam. Shadows waver on the walls as the three of them walk shakily down the passage.

"I must keep faith", Caroline mutters under her breath. "I must keep faith with the stones and their strength. My strength."

~

He's gone.

He's gone.

Verity curls into a ball, shaking. The dark is oddly soothing. She sobs and sobs. He's hurt her, her angel. He forced himself into her over and over again. When she cried out, he raped her harder. He bit her breasts with teeth that drew blood. He tore her face with his nails, those long white claws, then he thrust them inside her, and she howled with pain.

"I could kill you now," he said. "But I have wasted enough of my time here tonight."

And then he was gone, and his harsh light was gone, and she was alone, wounded, bleeding, in the dark, with only the wail of the wind and the relentless crack of the rain.

She rolls onto her knees. Her thighs are sticky with blood. There's blood on one hand too, and she can taste it on her lips. She hauls on the bed, stands upright, shaking with shock and with cold. Clothes, she needs clothes. Her wet clothes are still on the floor. Somehow, she opens the cupboard and reaches in. Her fingers find a dress. It's loose, soft. It won't hurt her skin. She tugs it on, finds shoes, hobbles to the front door. Somewhere out there is the stone that kept the angel away. She'll never find it, not now.

She slides down the bank beside the steps, adrift in pain and terror. She can hear the crashing waves below. She can't see the ground under her feet. It's like walking through the night sky. Her hand lands on the gate. The rain is icy and her dress is too thin. She's shivering. The cliff path has become a black stream. She walks, simply by putting one foot in front of the other. Past her car on her right. Not far now, until the next gate.

Caroline's house is in darkness. Verity flops across the gate, gasping. When she looks up again, she sees strange glowing lights, little will o' the wisps, on the lawn. She tries to focus. They are coming from stones. Her eyes follow the trail. Caroline has laid a circle of stones round her house. That was what kept the Angel from Andy.

"Caroline," Verity cries, as she drags herself up the path to the door. "Caroline!"

"Caroline!"

Caroline jumps. She's in her own bed now, with the boys on either side of her. It's Verity's voice, crying her name over and over, beating on the front door.

"Verity!" Andy cries.

"What's she doing here?" Jonny asks. He's really frightened, Caroline knows, more by what he doesn't know than by what he does.

"Mummy, it's Verity," Andy says, struggling to free himself from the quilt and his mother's arms.

"No," Caroline says.

"Caroline! Please let me in! Please!"

"Mummy, open the door!"

"No, Andy."

"Why not?" Jonny demands.

"We can't. It might not be her."

"It is. She's frightened too," Jonny says. "Let her in."

"Caroline!" Verity's banging and banging on the door.

Caroline wants to put her hands over her ears, hide under a pillow. Tim said she must not answer the door to anyone tonight. It might not be Verity. It isn't Verity. It's him again.

"Verity! Where's Angel?" Andy cries.

Caroline snatches her phone from beside the bed. It flickers with a feeble signal. Her fingers shake on the keys.

"Tim, it's me."

"Yes?"

"Please help."

"Who's that?" Jonny prods her arm.

"Verity's outside, well, it might be her. I don't know. I know what you said. How can I tell if it's her?"

"It is Verity," says Jonny. "Why won't you let her in?"

"The boys are awake," Caroline says. "I can't do this."

"Angel," Andy says.

"Who is it?" Jonny shouts.

"Put me on speaker."

She can't remember what to press. She hits mute by mistake. At last Tim's strong voice comes into the bedroom.

"Jonny, Andy. My name's Tim."

"It's him, Mummy," Andy shrieks. "He's going to hurt Angel."

"Can you both lie down for me?" says Tim. "Caroline, are the boys lying down?"

"Lie down," Caroline says heavily.

"Caroline, please!" Verity's voice is thinner, weaker.

"Who is this guy?" Jonny flounces down on the bed.

"They're lying down now."

"OK, boys. It's been a long night and you're both really tired. You need to sleep. I'm going to count backwards from ten, and you'll fall asleep."

"I'm not…" Jonny starts, but his mouth goes slack.

"Jonny?" Caroline shakes Jonny. "Andy?"

"Are they asleep now?"

"Yes," says Caroline.

"They'll sleep until you want them to wake. You think Verity's outside?"

"I don't know. It might be. It might be him." Caroline stops speaking, listens to the wind and the rain. There is no more calling, no more banging. "I think it was her," she says. "I think she was hurt. I should have let her in."

⌣

Pain. Quiet. Light. Verity is aware of these before she opens her eyes. Her body stings and aches. Now she is awake, blinking around her. She's in the living room, on the sofa. She's wearing a wet, cold dress. Her feet are bare. Outside in the garden the tamarisks are still. There is no wind, no rain, just a faint mist on the horizon, over pale grey sea. There is no sun, but the lights are on in the room. She turns her head. The hall light is on as well. All the lights are on.

Caroline hasn't slept. She sat awake all night, listening to the boys' breathing, as the storm finally spent itself, as the thick darkness paled to grey dawn. She stretches her cramped legs, and feels a kick in her womb. It surprises her, as her unborn child was also lulled to sleep by Tim. Caroline flutters a hand over her abdomen. Without disturbing Jonny, she tiptoes to the window, and pulls back the curtain. The garden is awash. Grass and leaves shine with rainwater. If she opened the window, she would smell the fragrance of wet soil.

197

The phone rings. Still, the boys sleep.

"Caroline, are you all right?"

"Yes, yes," Caroline says. "The boys are still asleep."

"We'll be with you before dark."

"When will the boys wake up?"

"I can call later and wake them for you. Whatever you do, do not break that circle. Do not leave the house. You must all stay indoors, inside your circle, until I get to you. Will you do that?"

"Of course," Caroline says.

Verity is so cold she can hardly feel her feet. She sits up stiffly, and her head swims. She thinks she might be sick. She stares through the window at the sodden garden. A rock. She remembers a rock. Somewhere in the wet soil there is a rock the colour of blood. She stands, and a thin ray of sunlight breaks through the film of clouds. Carrag Luz glitters. Verity stumbles, almost loses her balance. She pads quietly towards the hall, snapping off the light. The switch clicks loudly in the quiet house.

She does not go into her bedroom.

Instead, she walks into the kitchen. A muddy shoe lies in the middle of the room, kicked on its side. For a moment she is confused, then she sees its partner by the back door. She must have wrenched them off when she came back in. Back in from where? She can't remember that much. Slowly, she goes through all the rooms, turning off the lights. Then there is only her bedroom. She baulks at the door. She doesn't want to go in. Something happened in there last night. She slides her hand along the wall, and clicks the light switch. Very carefully she steps inside.

There are clothes on the floor. The cupboard doors are open. The bed is a tumbled heap of covers, stained brown-red with blood. She catches bile in her throat. Now she remembers. She remembers who came here and what he did; she remembers her flight along the cliff to Caroline's, but she does not remember returning, retracing her steps along the wet stony path, opening the kitchen door, throwing off her shoes. She does not remember the moment when the rain stopped, when the wind quietened.

Tim hangs up from Caroline. The humps on his shoulders are huge now. It feels like bone is about to tear through his bleeding skin. He grits his teeth, rather than rub his back again.

By nightfall everything will be over, one way or the other. Tim steadies his breathing. He is afraid. Afraid for Verity, for Jack, for Caroline and her family. And afraid for himself, and the terrible responsibility that is his to bear. He can sense the Archangel's spirit: nearer, stronger.

He pauses in the living room doorway. Something is amiss. White-gold light pulsing. It's coming from his laptop that he'd left in there. He runs into the room, averts his eyes from the burning screen. He can feel hot anger through the airwaves. He reaches out to slam the lid shut. The flashing stops. It doesn't need to continue. Tim has seen it; Tim knows what it is. An acknowledgement that he is coming. An acknowledgement of the battle that will take place tonight. A gauntlet thrown down from Lucifer to Michael. Time has come full circle.

Caroline doesn't want to speak to Frank, to have to lie to him again. She texts him, hoping he still has battery and signal on the ward, and says they won't be able to come and visit this evening because

199

something's wrong with the car. Too late she realises she knows what his response will be.

Use mine, he texts back. *What's wrong with yours?*

Caroline swears. She can't tell him the truth: that she can't use any car, that she and the boys can't leave the house because she has protected them with a circle of stones against the Devil who walks the cliffs. She almost laughs aloud, and thinks ruefully that she is glad Frank is many miles away in hospital. If he had been here last night they would not all have survived: she knows that.

Not sure what problem is, she writes back, and the beeping sounds like some distorted Morse code shooting off into the ether. *Yesterday's drive was very stressful*. Still she doesn't hit send. *Jonny not well and off school*, she adds. She should have just said that at the beginning.

What's wrong with Jonny?

Stomach bug, Caroline texts.

She knows Frank doesn't believe any of it. Well, he might believe the bit about last night's drive, but he doesn't believe there's anything wrong with her car, and he doesn't believe Jonny is ill.

Caroline looks in on the boys. They're still asleep in her bed. They've slept for nearly twelve hours. They must wake soon. They will need food and water. There's a warm wet patch beneath Andy's bottom. She goes to the kitchen and makes sandwiches for them to eat when they wake, soothed by the slicing and cutting, the smell of bread. Then she rings Tim.

"Can you wake the boys now?" she asks. "They need to eat and drink."

"Sure," Tim says. "Have you seen Verity? I can't get hold of her."

"Nothing," Caroline says. "I'm sure it was her here last night."

"You couldn't take the chance," Tim says. "Imagine if it were a trick. Imagine what you'd have let into your home. There would be no protection on earth that could have saved you then."

Caroline shudders, and takes the phone into the bedroom. Andy's dribbling in his sleep; the room smells of urine.

"Do you want me to try to erase some of last night from their memories?" Tim asks.

"Can you erase the angel…him…from Andy completely?"

"No chance. He's far too powerful."

Caroline considers, "Nothen," she says. "I can't face having to go over everything again later."

"Before I do this, remember not to break that circle. Not for anything. Andy's the weak link. Remember that too."

"I will." Caroline clicks on speakerphone.

"Jonny, Andy, it's Tim again. You've both had a long, long sleep, and it's time to wake up now. When you wake up you'll feel strong and refreshed. I'm going to count from one to five, and when I get to five, you'll both open your eyes and wake up."

Tim counts slowly, and Caroline watches the boys' faces, as they drift back to consciousness. Andy splutters on saliva. She turns off the speakerphone.

"They're awake now."

"OK, you go and look after them for a bit. I'll call you when we leave."

"Are you still on the phone?" Jonny asks. "You were on the phone when I went to sleep."

"Not all this time," Caroline says. "It's nearly lunchtime."

"Lunchtime?" wails Jonny. "What about school?"

"You've not been very well. That's why you stayed asleep."

"I feel fine." Jonny slides his feet to the floor. "Why are we here? Why aren't we in our room? Urrgh Andy, you've wee-ed everywhere."

"You were both a bit poorly," Caroline says. "I've made you some lunch. Come along and let's eat."

"I'm starving," Jonny says, then, "Can I go to school this afternoon?"

"Not today," Caroline says, shepherding them to the bathroom.

"But it's PE. I like PE."

"Sorry, Jonny, but you're not up to bouncing around."

"Not fair," Jonny grumbles. "Get on with it, Andy. I'm busting."

Caroline sits the boys at the kitchen table, and places the sandwiches in front of them. She fills glasses of water and puts the kettle on for herself.

"Can't we have Pepsi?" Jonny asks.

"Have water," she says. "You were asleep for so long you'll need a good drink."

Jonny mutters something she can't hear. Andy still has a pink flush on one cheek from where he was lying. They don't seem to have suffered from their long hypnosis.

"If I can't go to school this afternoon, what can I do?" Jonny asks. "Are we going to get dressed?"

"Dressed? Of course." Caroline hasn't even noticed the boys are still in their night clothes. Andy will be leaving damp smudges on the chair. "We'll sort out some clothes when you've eaten."

"Can we go on the computer?"

"It's not working after the storm last night," Caroline improvises.

She can't say the electricity is still off – Jonny has seen her boil the kettle for tea – but she knows the computer is a bad idea. It's a channel of communication. She knows Tim would tell her not to let them use it.

⁓

Tim has thrown together a few things into a holdall. If he succeeds tonight, he'll need clean clothes, a razor, a toothbrush. He laughs at the absurdity of it. He's about to fight the Devil for the sake of

Mankind, and he's worrying about packing a toothbrush. And if he fails? If Verity and Jack survive, they will have lost the only father they've known. He wonders if he should call Ellen, but he can't find the words he needs for her.

~

Caroline walks into her bedroom as though she's wading through water. The boys are in their room, washed and dressed. Jonny's still grumbling about not going to school, not playing on the computer. Caroline tugs the wet bedding off. The bending and stretching exhausts her. The boys are safe. She lies down on the dry half of the mattress for a few moments. Just to rest her eyes.

Jonny sits on his bed swinging his legs, watching Andy.

Andy has coloured pencils and a pad but he's not drawing: he's just staring at the window. After they were dressed, their mother opened the curtains at one side of the window, letting in only a slice of daylight. Jonny reaches out and yanks the curtains back, and sunlight shafts into the room. Andy blinks and looks away from the window.

"Andy," Jonny begins. "Do you remember last night?"

"Angel was here," Andy says. "He was hurt. He went."

"No, no," Jonny hisses. "I mean Verity. She was here in the night. She was banging on the door. Mummy wouldn't let her in."

Jonny can't quite remember at what point his mother took them to her bedroom, but he knows they were there when Verity was banging on the door and crying.

"Yes," Andy says. "Verity."

"She was crying. She was frightened," Jonny say. He glances out of the window towards Verity's house. "I think we should go round and see her. See if she is OK."

"We can't!" Andy cries, dropping a pencil onto the floor.

"Why not?"

"Mummy said we had to stay here."

"But Verity might be hurt. We won't be long. We can get out of the window."

Distractedly Jonny remembers scrambling out of the bedroom window, racing along the cliff path to find Andy flailing on top of the rocks. He and Verity had to get Andy down. Stop it, he thinks. It will be OK if we go together.

"If we both go, it'll be all right," he says to Andy.

Andy looks out of the window again, and then at Jonny. He shoves his pad and pencils on the floor. Jonny fiddles with the window, and eases it open very quietly. It hits something with a clunk.

"What was that?" Andy asks.

"Dunno." Jonny leans out.

On the wet grass is a chunk of greeny-black rock. Jonny slides out of the window and picks up the rock and turns it over. It's that purple spiky one that lives in the hall with the other stones. Its name begins with A. It must have been on the windowsill. When he opened the window, it must have fallen off and landed upside down. Jonny shrugs and shoves the stone to the side, against the wall, so Andy won't land on it.

"What are you doing?" Andy shoves his glasses up his nose and starts scrambling out of the window.

"Sssh. Nothing," Jonny says. No point in getting Andy worried about how the stone got there.

Andy lands with a soft thud on the wet ground. When he staggers to his feet there is mud on his knees and hands. Jonny pulls the window almost closed, then grabs Andy's hand and sprints across the lawn to the secret tunnel to Verity's garden. The overhanging leaves drip cold water on the back of his neck as he wriggles through. His hand lands on something both hard and squelchy and he bites back a cry as the snail recoils into its shell. He can hear Andy breathing behind him, whimpering at something – the snail? the dripping rainwater? the spiky twigs?– and then through the leaves in front of him he can see the wet green of Verity's lawn.

~

"Are you ready?" Tim asks Jack.

His stepson is pale, fair hair unkempt. He still does not understand the magnitude of what he must do this night. Tim prays to whoever may be listening that, when the moment comes, Jack will know.

"I'm ready."

Tim opens his arms and holds Jack close to him. He flinches as Jack's hand catches one of the knobbly wings.

"I love you, Jack," he says. "You and Verity. You're everything, you two."

Tears in his eyes, and not from the pain of his back.

~

Verity showers, washing the blood from her skin. There are bruises on her arms and chest, purple blooms like stigmata. The cuts from his talons sting in the water and she winces. It does not matter how much she scrubs her flayed skin, she will never be cleansed.

~

Jonny tugs Andy to Verity's front door. He doesn't feel so brave now. He turns round, but the garden is quiet, except for a gentle dripping of rain from leaf to leaf. He bangs on Verity's door.

"Verity!" he calls, glancing behind him again. "Are you OK?"

Andy's gazing round, blinking, looking over to the rocks, then up to the sky, where the misty clouds are parting to reveal a pale sun.

"Verity!" Jonny cries again, cupping his hands round his eyes to look into the house.

What if she doesn't come to the door? What if she's hurt? Or dead? Something moves in his stomach. She might be dead. How will he know? What can he do? He'll have to confess to his mother that they came round.

"Verity!" Andy grabs Jonny's sleeve.

Verity is standing at the big window, gesturing at them. Jonny and Andy run over to her.

"Go home," she shouts, pointing at the gate. "Go away. Don't come back."

"Are you hurt?" Jonny can see red marks on her face, and darker ones above the neck of her jumper. "What's happened?"

"Nothing," Verity says through the glass. "Just go back home. Stay with your Mummy. Don't come here again, any of you. Please."

"But…" Jonny starts.

"Please Jonny."

"You're crying," Andy says, reaching his hand up to the glass.

"I'm not." Verity jumps back.

Jonny can see the glint on her cheeks and is about to contradict her, then shrugs. Verity's not dead. She's well enough to shout at them. They've done what they came to do. They might as well go home now before their mother comes to check on them and finds the room empty, the window ajar.

"Come on," he says, and tugs his Andy away from the window.

He looks back once, and sees Verity watching then, a hand to her face as though she's wiping away tears. At the entrance to the tunnel, he gestures for Andy to go first. Andy crouches down.

"Urrrgh! No! I'm not going in there."

"What?" Jonny snaps.

206

Andy is backing out of the tunnel on all fours. Jonny squats down. He's aware they have been away from home for some time. They need to get back quickly. A huge slug is in the middle of the entrance. It's long, thick, pale brown with an orange underbelly. Jonny baulks and steps backwards. There's no way they can crawl through the tunnel without squashing it, touching it. He remembers the lawn of dead slugs, the fluid that leaked from them.

"OK, OK, we'll go the other way," he says.

As he slithers to a halt by the gate, he looks back over to the living room window. He thinks he sees a movement there, as though Verity was finally walking away from the glass. He hesitates a moment. Something's definitely wrong with her, but he can't say anything to his mother without telling her they scrambled out of the bedroom window and came round here alone without her permission, and he can't do that. He fumbles with the latch and shoves Andy through.

The cliff road is slippery from the storm. Most of the rain has dried into thick mud. The bluebells at the roadside have been battered down to a bruised pulp. In a moment they are at their own gate. Jonny peers over the hedge. He can't see their mother at any of the front windows. They should be able to sprint over to their bedroom and get in without too much difficulty. He glances at their dirty clothes. That'll be a problem, but they can worry about that once they're indoors again. He pulls Andy to the gate and starts to lift that latch.

"Angel!" Andy cries, jumping up and down to see over the gate.

Something squirms in Jonny's gut. "What you on about?"

"Angel's here! He's waiting for us."

"Where?" Jonny can't see anything in their garden, but Andy's gaze is fixed and he knows his brother can see something – someone – he cannot.

"Over there! Look!" Andy points. "He's by our window."

Jonny pushes Andy back onto the cliff road. Whatever or whoever is in the garden he doesn't want to know. Things are happening he doesn't understand. Just get away, he thinks. Keep walking.

"Where are we going?" Andy howls as Jonny hauls him along by the jumper. "Why can't we go to Angel? He'll let me fly."

"We're going this way," Jonny says, walking faster and faster, dragging Andy towards the hotel at the end of the track.

"You're hurting me. Stop!" Andy shrieks.

"Shut up. Someone'll hear you."

Jonny loosens his hold but doesn't let go. They're standing by the broken wire fence on the edge of the cliff. It looks even tattier than the last time Jonny saw it. One section has completely fallen down, then the grassy cliff face slopes down steeply to the rocks below, and the pale sand of the tidal beach at the very bottom.

Jonny glances both ways along the cliff road. There's no-one around. He can't hear the crunch of an approaching car on the uneven surface. The bungalow opposite looks empty: the windows blank, no car on the parking strip.

"Look!" Andy cries, pointing in the direction they have come. "He's coming. Angel's coming for us."

The road is still empty. Jonny cannot see anyone. He feels very sick.

"Quick, let's hide here." He squeezes through the gap in the fence, pulling Andy after him.

"But…"

"We're playing hide and seek, aren't we?" Jonny whispers. "If you shout, he'll find us at once. That's not much of a game."

Jonny huddles Andy to him. The springy cliff grass is damp and slippery. He can feel his heels giving way. It's very steep down this grassy face, then there are the black rocks at the bottom of the cliff. He can hear the waves curling in and breaking far out on the sand.

His eyes are just below the level of the cliff road. He waits and watches, with his hand over Andy's mouth, for the sound of footsteps coming nearer, then stopping just inches from his head, but there is nothing. He relaxes the muscles he's been tensing and, as he does so, he slides on the wet grass, and tumbles down the slope. At some point he lets go of Andy, but he hears him screaming, as well as his own cries. Blue sea and sky, gold sand, green grass and black rock all spin in a crazy pattern as he rolls down and down, and then suddenly he is still, wedged against a tussock just above the rock line. Andy slides down beside him. He reaches out and grabs him to stop him falling over the edge onto rocks. The only sounds are the insistent lapping of the waves, his own breathing and Andy's sobs.

"Are you OK?" Jonny asks.

He doesn't think he's injured himself, but when he looks up the grassy slope, they've just tumbled down the climb up looks impossible. It takes him a moment to realise why Andy looks different: he's lost his glasses.

"Where's Angel?" Andy cries. "You said he'd find us."

"Wait here," Jonny says.

He crawls on all fours a little further down. There are crunchy handfuls of seaweed in the grass, and a few shells. Jonny shudders. The sea must come all the way up here sometimes. He's reached the end of the grass. This is where the rocks begin. They are bigger, more jumbled, than he first imagined. Even if he and Andy could scramble down to the sand they'd have to walk round the headland to the main beach, then up the cliff path to the hotel, and then along their road. Their mother would know they'd gone. She probably knows anyway, Jonny thinks, and feels tears in his eyes. He only suggested they should go to see Verity because she seemed so afraid in the night, but she didn't want them, and now here they are almost at the bottom of the cliff because Andy started on about that bloody angel, and something about the tone of his voice and the look in his eyes frightened Jonny so much he didn't know what to do.

"Where are you, Jonny? Don't leave me!"

"I'm not," Jonny calls back. "I'm looking to see if we can get down this way."

The boulders are covered in seaweed and barnacles. Jonny suspects even if his Daddy were standing on the sand the boulders would reach well over his head. There's no way he and Andy can get down that way, especially as Andy can't see.

"Angel!" Andy screams.

Jonny turns. Andy is pointing towards the headland that separates the two beaches. He can't possibly see anything there without his glasses. Jonny crawls back to Andy.

"Up here," he says. "We can't get down that way."

He starts crawling up the cliff face. The wet grass is wiry and hurts his hands as he tugs himself up. He doesn't want to look up at the spindly scribble that is the fence, or down to the rocks, but he must check Andy is coming.

"Don't, Jonny! Angel will come for us."

"He can't," Jonny says. "There's no way up from the beach."

Andy grabs Jonny's ankle and pulls himself up on it. Jonny almost loses his grip.

"Stop that! We'll both fall." Jonny sees a flash in the grass. Andy's glasses. They're not broken. "Here, Andy."

"Angel's coming."

"No he's not," Jonny gasps. "Put your specs on. Don't look back."

He's almost at the top now. He can see the flattened swathe of grass where he first slid down. He grabs a chunk of rock that protrudes from the cliff. Only now does he turn round. Andy's still scrabbling towards him. He reaches down and grabs Andy's hand. It's bleeding, he notices. Or maybe it's his hand that's bleeding. Or both their hands.

"There he is!" Andy jabs his finger down the grassy cliff. "He's coming up after us."

~

Caroline wakes with a start, disorientated. She reaches out for her alarm clock. Under an hour has gone by. Surely if Tim had called, the phone would have woken her? She's dehydrated and nauseous. She swings her legs to the ground, finds her slippers with her toes. The boys' bedroom door is closed, as she left it. They're quiet in there. Too quiet. She shoves the door open. The room is empty. Andy's colouring things are on the floor. The window trembles slightly on its latch and Caroline can see, from where she stands, that the amethyst is no longer on the sill. The circle has been broken and the boys have gone.

She's gasping by the time she gets to Verity's gate. Her legs tremble as she staggers up the steps to the front door. Absently she notices the iron ore has disappeared.

"Verity, are the boys here? They're missing! Verity!" She bangs on the door, remembering how Verity ran to her for help in the night, and she ignored her.

A moment later Verity appears in the hall, moving slowly, awkwardly, as though dazed.

"Jonny, Andy," Caroline gabbles, as Verity opens the door. "Are they here?"

"They were," Verity says. "I sent them home. I told them to stay with you. It's not safe for them here. With me."

"They're not at home!"

"They went to their tunnel," Verity says, "but then I saw them in the garden again, going to the gate."

"They're on the cliff!" Caroline turns to Carrag Luz. It's pale and shimmery in the sunlight. She can't see anyone there.

"I'll come with you," Verity says.

"They'll be on the rocks," Caroline sobs.

"Come on." Verity takes her arm, steers her quickly down the steps and through the gate. "Shall we split up? I'll go to the rock, you go…" Verity gestures up past her car.

"No, we'll stay together. They won't have gone that way. They're on the rocks."

Verity runs past Caroline, through the long grasses to Carrag Luz. Caroline hobbles after her, ungainly and clumsy in her damp slippers. She watches Verity scramble onto the rocks, lean over, look down to the cove, along the curve of the cliff. Suddenly she jumps down, almost falling, and runs back, colliding with Caroline.

"Where are they?" Caroline cries, staggering.

"They're OK," Verity says. "They're on the road. They're going back to your house. Quickly!"

Caroline gasps after Verity, up the muddy stony road, and over the fault line. Jonny and Andy are stumbling towards them.

"Mummy!" Jonny cries.

Andy's peering back the way they've come. Caroline's about to run to them; Verity grabs her arm.

"What?" Caroline catches her breath.

She can't see anything, but she follows Andy's gaze, and her insides shrivel like a slug under salt crystals.

"He's there," Verity says. "Behind them."

Caroline breaks free and lurches towards the boys. Jonny drags Andy towards her.

"Jonny, Andy," Caroline's saying over and over.

"Jonny wouldn't let Angel play with us," Andy says.

Caroline straightens, a child on either side. Beneath her feet she can feel the earth stirring, exhaling. She glances down at the stones. She cannot see through the earth's skin, as she could in the night, but she does feel its power surging up her aching legs and straight to her heart.

"Angel. Look, Mummy." Andy points towards Verity.

"Caroline, take them home," Verity says. She's not looking at Caroline, but at someone else, someone Caroline cannot see, but she can feel.

"Home. Now." Caroline shoves the boys through the gate. She must get them inside, and re-cast the circle, before her courage fails her.

"Verity."

He's shimmering in the sunlight: white and gold. His hair lifts gently in the breeze, and Verity remembers what it felt like falling onto her face. She remembers the taste of bluebells and summer. She remembers the exquisite stab of desire. And still he stands there, not moving, watching her.

"You are wounded," he says and reaches out to her face.

And now she remembers the pain, and the blood, and the talons, and who this beautiful creature really is.

She steps closer to Caroline's gate. She dare not look behind her to see if Caroline and the boys are safe indoors.

"You will not have Andy," she says at last.

The boys are in the house. Caroline pushed them roughly through the front door, then ran, breathless and aching to their window. The words she muttered to the amethyst were hurried, but she still can sense the earth's power rushing up to meet her. With the crystal replaced on the boys' windowsill, she hobbles back to the front door.

Verity is standing by her gate, guarding it. She's looking away from Caroline into eyes Caroline cannot see.

Caroline picks up the serpentine she dislodged as she ran out of the front door. She lays it at the doorstep again, whispering the words of protection. The circle is complete once more. She stands and glances back to her gate. Verity is there, arms widespread, protecting her and the boys. As Caroline swallows tears, Verity vanishes.

She simply disappears.

~

The time has come.

It has come so quickly. Jack roars out of St James Square behind the wheel of Tim's car. Beside him, Tim watches the dirt-stained Bath stone slide by, the familiar terraces, the traffic lights. It's happening too fast. He has not had time to say goodbye to the city. He shifts in his seat, trying to ease the pain in his shoulders. It doesn't have to be goodbye.

He wasn't able to speak to Caroline before they left the flat. He tried both her home and mobile phones; both rang out unanswered. Perhaps she's asleep, he thought, but he didn't believe his own words.

His phone is in his lap. He dials her home number once more.

"Hello? Tim?" There's a raw edge to her voice, a hysteria, a terror, that wasn't there before.

"Caroline, I've been so worried. I tried to call you. Are you safe?"

"He's here. The boys got out. Stupid kids, they broke the circle. They went to Verity's, and something happened. I don't know. They haven't told me. Verity helped me find them, but she's disappeared. He's taken her."

"What?" Tim says.

Jack looks sharply at him, squirts water onto the windscreen. The wipers squeak, smearing damp grime across the glass. The sky ahead is dark; heavy mauve clouds are stacking to the south-west. The storm surging towards them.

"He was there with her on the cliff. We all were. The boys had…I don't know. They'd run away from Verity's. Verity could see him with them. She kept him from us. We got back in the house. I made the circle again, and I looked to where she was, on the path, by my gate, and I know he was there with her, and she suddenly vanished."

"What's happened?" Jack asks. "Is Verity OK?"

"I don't know," Tim says to him. "Sorry, Caroline, I was just telling Jack."

"She disappeared before my eyes," Caroline says. "She didn't move or anything. She was there and then she wasn't. Where is she? Has he killed her?"

Tim feels the stickiness of blood on his shirt. His wings stir beneath the broken skin. Ancient knowledge stirs in his mind. "No. He hasn't. She'll come back. Jack will bring her back."

"Back from where?" Jack demands.

"Caroline, I'm going to go now. I need to talk to Jack."

"What's happened to her?" Jack asks tensely.

"He's taken her."

"Taken her where?"

"Caroline says she just vanished before her eyes."

Jack hurtles round the roundabout, past the twin columns of the university drive. They have left everything behind now.

"You will have to follow her," Tim continues.

"Follow her where?"

"Where he has taken her. That is your journey, your quest."

"Where?"

"Into Hell."

215

"Mummy, what's happening?"

Caroline looks at Jonny, He's pale, twitchy, frightened. His eyes roam the room looking for someone he can't see. Like Andy, his face, hands and clothes are muddy. He's torn the knee of his jeans. Caroline still doesn't know what happened to them on the cliff, because Tim phoned as soon as she locked the front door, and part of her doesn't want to know.

"I don't really know," she says at last.

"Who is the Angel? You said there isn't one, but there is. Andy saw him this morning. He said he was coming after us. I couldn't see him, but I said we should hide from him. Was that right?"

Caroline doesn't speak. If she acknowledges anything Jonny will believe it. He must not do that. But isn't he starting to believe anyway?

"Was it right?" Jonny demands.

"I was very frightened when I saw you'd both gone," Caroline says. "You must never leave the house alone. I've told you that."

"I said we should see Verity." Jonny says. "She was here last night. You heard her. She was frightened too. I wanted to see her."

Caroline turns away so Jonny won't see her tears.

"Where's Verity now?" Jonny asks. "Can she come here with us?"

"She's flying," Andy says. "Angel took her flying."

~

Jack flicks on his headlamps and wipers. Rain cracks on the windscreen. To the south-west the sky is dark and threatening; in his peripheral vision he sees a flicker.

"The storm's coming up," he says. "You said Caroline said the weather had been awful." Just talk about the weather, traffic, road conditions. Normal things.

"Yes," Tim says. "But it's nothing to do with weather systems."

They cannot hear the thunder over the car engine, but a few moments later a giant jagged fork of lightning earths into the field beside the road.

"Jesus, that's close," Jack says.

"He's taunting us," Tim explains. "The lightning. It's his sign. Light, lightning, Lucifer. People think the Devil is dark and ugly, but he's not. He's glowing with pure light. He's beautiful. The most beautiful creature there has ever been."

"You've seen him?"

"I don't recall him, but I know he is. It's in here somewhere, somewhere in my – Michael's – memory. No wonder Verity couldn't resist him."

Jack doesn't say anything. He does not want to think of Verity being unable to resist anyone, least of all the Devil. It makes his stomach slide.

"Go through Cheddar," Tim says suddenly.

"Why?"

"I don't know. I think it's the safest route. I can't say. Just do it. We're being watched, stalked, and I am getting a powerful image of Cheddar gorge."

Jack hesitates, then swings the wheel. Uneven narrow roads crisscross the landscape towards the gorge. He knows these lanes well but, for the first time, he dreads those monstrous cliffs soaring over the tiny car, dreads being funnelled through that twisting road with no escape.

Clouds have blurred the entire sky. The rain falls faster, thicker, silver and heavy as mercury. Jack swallows a hard ball of fear. He knows the road; he knows the gorge. There should be nothing to fear, yet his eyes keep darting to the rear view mirror, expecting to see the something, whatever it may be, that Tim can sense.

The road is bumpy and each time the car bounces over a pothole Jack winces. He feels he can't control the steering properly, that the car is running away with him. He slows down deliberately.

"There's no traffic," he says. "Where is everyone? It's Friday afternoon. It's Cheddar Gorge. Where the hell are they?"

Something red in the road. Jack brakes. It's a road sign: *road ahead closed.* He exhales. That's why there's no traffic. Nothing more than a road closure.

Goats. Black goats with almond-shaped amber eyes. They stand on spindly legs in the wiry grass on either side of the road, not chewing, but watching. Beyond the road sign he can see another goat in the carriageway, still, facing him. The tarmac is shiny, running with rain-water.

"We can't go that way after all."

"No, go on," Tim says.

"We can't."

"Just take it slowly. It's probably only a bit of flooding or something. I'll move that sign."

Tim opens the door. Rain splashes into the car. He strides over to the road sign and picks it up. His peacock shirt is dark with water. Lightning flashes. Jack lets in the clutch and moves forward. In the mirror he watches Tim replace the road sign. It lands on the tarmac with a clang. Jack shivers. Tim gets back in the car. He's soaked. He smells of rain and metal. The solitary goat moves aside and Jack drives on, doesn't speak.

A few humps of limestone thrusting though the wet grasses. The land rises, then suddenly those terrible, ragged cliffs, silver-black with water. Jack cannot stop ducking his head to look at the upper pinnacles. In a flash of lightning, he fancies he sees malevolent faces in the rock, dark eyes in the crevices. Thunder growls round the gorge.

"Why's the road closed?" Jack says, just to hear his own voice over the thunder.

"I don't know." Tim sounds distracted.

The massive buttress of Horseshoe Bend. The road runs with rain and mud. Jack's going too fast. As he swerves round the bend the tyres squeal.

"Watch it!" Tim shouts.

Jack screams to a halt. On the blind side of the bend is a rockfall. The front of the car is only inches from a large rough slab of limestone. Boulders are tumbled across the tarmac. Jack turns off the ignition. The wipers stop in mid-stroke. Rain thuds on the glass, on the roof, turning the cliffs to a streaky curtain. This time Jack gets out. A stream runs across the road. He looks up at the cliffs. Nothing seems to be falling now. The foliage is a deep wet green, splattered by the rain. Jack splashes back to the car. It looks eerie: silent, still, with its headlamps on like the eyes of the goats.

"You got it wrong, then."

"Not necessarily. Who knows what would have happened on another road? And the twists and turns, this running water here, they will all confuse him."

Jack's T-shirt has stuck to his torso in a cold wet swathe. He shivers.

"We can clear it," Tim says. "Just enough to get through. It won't take us long."

"We haven't got gloves or anything. It's pissing down, there's lightning."

"We have to," Tim says. "We have to keep moving. We can't just sit here."

"We can go another way."

"We can't. There's something behind us. We have to go on."

Jack remembers the ominous metallic clunk of the road sign hitting the wet tarmac. Sealing the gorge once more. No way back.

Tim unbuttons his shirt.

"What the hell are you doing?" Jack asks.

"Take off your T-shirt. We're going to get soaked."

Tim gasps as his shirt catches on his stumps. Jack averts his eyes from the mottled humps, marked with a rusty stain of watery blood. Tim gets out into the storm. Jack can hardly see him through the streaming rain on the windscreen. Tim can't clear the road alone. Jack pulls off his wet T-shirt.

He feels vulnerable in the gorge. Small, cold, afraid and half naked. Tim is rolling a large rock to the side of the road. Jack glances up at the cliffs. He feels dizzy. He wonders if he banged his head momentarily in the emergency stop. He's queasy and unsteady. The cliffs appear to be sliding closer and closer to him. More lightning, and an immediate resounding roar of thunder. Jack looks back at the car. It too looks small and vulnerable. Something moves behind it. It's one of the goats. It comes almost up to the car, and gazes at Jack. Jack turns away, even more unsettled, and bends down to the rockfall. The only sounds are the relentless rain, the hollow thunder, and his own heartbeat, dull and painful in his ears.

He straightens again at more movement in his peripheral vision. The car is surrounded by goats. They do not touch it; they simply stand there, watching him, silent and threatening. And then something else. A tall, slender woman steps out of the curve of the bend.

"Mum!"

"Don't," Tim shouts.

"Mum!" Jack cries again. It is her, his mother, Rosie. Elegant and beautiful as she was before the cancer invaded her body. "It's me, Jack! I'm here." He's sobbing, tears mixing with snot and rainwater.

His mother doesn't seem to hear. She's gliding through the goats, lightly resting her hands on some of the dark heads.

"Don't look at her. Just move these fucking rocks."

"Mum!" Jack's cry is desolate.

"Jack. Don't. She's helping us how she can. She can't communicate."

"She's my fucking mother."

Jack stumbles forward into lightning, so bright it blinds him for an instant. When he can see once more, he and Tim are alone in the gorge.

"Mum," he mutters through his tears. He knows what, who, he saw.

Together he and Tim drag the last of the debris to the side of the road. Jack keeps his head down, looking at the mercurial water beneath his feet.

Tim's gazing down at his hands. He has torn his left palm, and blood rushes out and drips down into the water on the road. As the gorge fills with blue-white lightning once more, Tim lifts his wounded hand to the elements.

"Jack, with my blood I give you the sign of the saint you will become."

He draws his hand down and across Jack's chest. His blood forms a dark red cross.

When Jack turns back to the car, the goats have gone. He strains his eyes for a glimpse of his mother but she has gone. His chest stings and he knows it's more than blood Tim has marked him with.

~

Caroline feels trapped. She's at the living room window, scanning for any movement over the tamarisk. Her legs feel tense, like she's ready

221

to run. She can almost taste the adrenaline. And yet she cannot leave the house.

"What are you looking at?" Jonny asks.

Caroline turns round. The boys are on the hearthrug, half-heartedly fiddling with Frank's train set. They don't know how to construct a circuit properly, and Andy's shoving Mallard up and down on the carpet.

"Stop that, Andy. You'll get fluff in the wheels," Caroline says.

Perhaps the train set wasn't such a good idea. Jonny has slotted some sections of track into an incomplete oval, and is trying to slide goods wagons together. Andy has dumped Mallard on its side, and is fiddling in the box of scenery: Caroline sees the green hump of a tunnel, a station platform, a bridge.

"Nothing," she says. "I'm just looking out."

"Can you see them flying?" Andy asks.

"Don't be silly, Andy," Caroline says.

The earth is calling her to step outside her house, place her feet on the grassy, stony ground, to feel that ancient energy crackle up her legs, filling her body with strength. She balls her fists in anger. She's seen a few hikers pass by on the cliff path; someone running – a bobbing baseball cap through the green tamarisk fronds; she's heard a dog bark and, once, a car rumbling along the track, stopping just short of her house. Each time she wanted to run out, through the gate, and ask *have you seen a young girl with long hair?* but she knows what the answers will be, she can already see the puzzled faces as they take in her dishevelled appearance, sense the power of her anguish and smell her terror.

⁓

Tim flexes his injured hand. The palm is stiff with blood and dirt. He and Jack wiped their hands as best they could with a rag held into the rain. Under his shirt are his embryo wings; under Jack's wet T shirt is the cross of St George. They are both changing, metamorphosing into legend.

"You saw her too."

"I felt her," Tim says. "Perhaps that's why I had this certainty we should take that road, that if there was a problem she would help us."

"I wanted to talk to her."

"I know. I'm sorry."

"Have you seen her before?" Jack asks.

The rain beats down. The motorway traffic is slow, warned by flashing speed limits. Jack's wipers are on fast, but they struggle to clear the spray from the giant lorries in the inside lane. The storm has quietened, but shrouds of mist are thickening over the carriageway. Some of the cars ahead have fog lamps on.

"Tim?"

"I should ring Caroline again," he says at last.

He slides his hand over the pocket of his jeans. Nothing. No reassuring oblong form. He tries his other pocket. He reaches down into the footwell. When did he last have it? When he spoke to Caroline as they were leaving Bath. When she told him Verity had been taken. He'd dumped the phone in his lap, rather than put it in his pocket.

"What's the matter?" Jack asks.

"I've lost my fucking phone."

"Mine's in the glove box. Ring yourself."

Tim takes Jack's phone out and dials his own number. Nothing rings in the car.

"Fuck, fuck, fuck." Tim puts Jack's phone away in the glove box.

It must have happened when he got out at Cheddar to move the notice, or to clear the road. He was so cold and wet and tense he never noticed.

"You're angry. I will talk to you about her, about what you saw. But not today. Not tonight."

If we live after sundown.

Jack moves into the inner lane for Taunton services. The petrol gauge is almost on empty. They stumble across the car-park to the main complex, shivering in their damp clothes. The building is blurred by the fog; just a vague dark shape looms through the miasma. Inside people are milling in a confused group, looking up and pointing. Tim looks where they indicate. The travel news screens are flashing, pulsing with painful white light. *No bloody use. Why haven't they fixed them? What the hell? That's shit.*

"Jack." Tim gestures at the flashing screens. "He's here."

In the Gents Tim washes his muddy, bleeding hands. The water starts the blood flow once more, and rusty spirals swirl down the plughole. He closes his eyes. The smell of motorway liquid soap and urine, the staccato roar of hand driers, feet tramping across the wet tiles, men's voices. Memories of so many journeys, but never one like this.

When they come out of the Gents the screens are still flashing.

"I'm going to get some water. You go on." Jack hands over the keys.

The mist outside is so white it hurts Tim's eyes. He can hear the relentless weary rumble of the motorway traffic only a few yards away. In the car, he reaches over to insert the key and turns on the radio, finds a local station.

A few moments later Jack comes back carrying several bottles of water and chocolate bars.

Jack drives onto the garage forecourt and fills up with petrol. Tim waits in the car, the radio silenced. His hand throbs. He makes a fist and winces. He'll need that arm and hand later.

"Let me drive?" he asks when Jack comes back.

"You can't with that hand," Jack says. "And you need to be the eyes."

The radio adverts end. It's the four o'clock news.

"Have you got Caroline's number anywhere?" Jack asks as they slide from the approach road into the inner lane.

"No," Tim says. "I could call Ellen and get it again, but she doesn't know about any of this."

"It was her idea to send Verity there in the first place," Jack says.

"No-one made this happen. No-one could have stopped it."

There are still amber flashing speed restrictions. They can only see a couple of cars ahead. All round them it's white, thick as cream. Tim feels his chest tighten. They're in the middle lane, moving slowly. On the left a lorry curling up waves of spray; on the right a guy in a sports car, with a girl asleep in the passenger seat. Tim feels queasy, trapped. The music on the radio seems to have developed a threatening bass beat. Tim can feel his blood jump in his throat to match it. Stop it, stop it, relax.

At Exeter the M5 blends into the A30. They peel away westwards on the dual carriageway. It's a straight run now to Truro. Bruce Springsteen on the radio. Off the motorway Tim's breathing has eased, and the tense grasp of fear in his chest has subsided. Suddenly Springsteen cuts off.

Some news just in, announces the radio presenter. Tim jumps alert, turns up the volume. *A petrol tanker has jack-knifed and caught fire on the westbound A30, west of Whiddon Down. Fire crews, ambulance and police are at the scene. It's thought two other cars are also involved. There are long delays and motorists are advised to find alternative routes.*

"We'll have to go over Dartmoor," Tim says.

"In this weather?"

"We can't stay on the A30 and get caught up in that. We could lose hours."

225

"I don't like this."

Neither do I, Tim thinks. Dartmoor in the fog: lonely, austere, white and grey.

Are you there, Rosie?

It's gone four o'clock and Caroline hasn't heard anything from Tim. Something's not right. She knows that with the part of her that sees beneath the earth, that feels the ancient force of the land.

The boys have abandoned the train set. She's put the rolling stock into boxes, disconnected the segments of track. Jonny sulked when she said they couldn't watch TV or use the computer. She won't let them go to their bedroom. At the moment they're eating biscuits and drinking milk in the kitchen. She can hear their voices. Andy hasn't said anything about the angel for some time now. Surely that's a good sign.

Caroline dials Tim's mobile. It rings out and out. He doesn't answer. She cuts off, takes her mobile and texts him. *Where are you? When will you be here?* A minute goes by, then another. With the mobile in her hand, she goes into the kitchen. She should do something to occupy the boys, but she can't think what to do. Five minutes have gone by. No text. They must be in an area with no signal, she thinks. Of course, that would be it. Tim will get the text when the signal returns. She dials his mobile again; it rings on and on.

"Who you ringing?" Jonny asks.

"No-one," she says.

"Not him!" Andy cries. "He's going to hurt Angel."

Caroline cuts off the relentless ringing. She can't think of any other way to contact Tim.

As they pass Moretonhampstead, the visibility worsens. Tim's turned the radio off. He opens the window: anything to give the feeling of moving air. He can't breathe in the confines of the car. When he holds his hand out, the atmosphere is cold and clotted; it stings his scarred palm.

The wipers squeak through the fine drizzle that speckles the windscreen. Tim wants to get out, stand in front of the car, and gather armfuls of the clammy, frothy fog and claw it out of Jack's way.

"There's no traffic," Jack says. His voice is loud over the monotony of the engine and the squeaky wipers. A sheep darts out across the road, all horns and eyes. Jack brakes.

"No," Tim says, and drinks from his water bottle.

"There was a car behind but it's just disappeared. I didn't see any side roads. Did you?"

"No," Tim says again.

"Where's everyone else on this diversion? And no-one's come the other way for ages."

"No," Tim says a third time.

"Don't you have any comment?" Jack demands. "Don't you have any answers? I thought you had them all."

"No-one has all the answers."

Headlamps and bright spotlights through the gloom. Four eyes. It's another car coming towards them.

"That's better," Jack exhales. "I thought we were all alone."

All alone would be all right, Tim thinks. If only we were all alone. He doesn't say it. Jack's watching the dwindling tail lights of the other car in his rear mirror. Soon they are gulped into the fog. Tim wishes he hadn't insisted on Dartmoor. Even if they'd ended up in a stationary queue of traffic waiting to creep past the burning tanker, they would have been protected by the other motorists. What was he thinking of? They are exposed, vulnerable, on the high ground, sheathed in fog. He closes his eyes. He has only his inner vision to rely on.

~

Caroline checks her mobile. It's been in her pocket all the time, and she hasn't felt it vibrate or ring, or cheep with a new text. The screen remains blank. She rings Tim one more time, but she knows there'll be no answer.

Andy's watching her. His eyes are suddenly cold behind his glasses. When she drops the phone on the table, he lunges for it. She scoops it up before he can send it smashing to the ground.

"He's going to hurt Angel!" Andy shrieks.

"Yes," Caroline says. "He is. He's going to destroy your angel and you'll never see him again."

Andy howls again.

"Why won't you tell me what's going on?" Jonny cries.

"I'm sorry, Jonny," Caroline says, "I will...after."

"Mummy, he's going to kill him."

"Who's going to kill who?" demands Jonny. He's in tears now, with frustration and confusion and fear.

Caroline reaches for him, tries to put her arm round him, but he shrugs her off and walks away to the fridge for more milk.

"Jonny," she starts, then leaves it. She's not telling him the truth, and he knows it.

And something has happened to Tim. He wouldn't ignore her. He must have a signal by now. He hasn't called her because he can't. He's in trouble. What kind of trouble? Has he been hurt, killed? What if he doesn't arrive?

Caroline leaves Andy in the kitchen and goes into the front room. When she stands by the window she can see the sun – a pale hazy coin – and imagines it sliding imperceptibly, then faster and faster, to the far horizon.

Tim said he would be here by nightfall, but what if he's not? What will happen tonight? And where is Verity?

She gazes at the sea. The horizon is blurred with mauve clouds. More rain coming. More storms. She's cold suddenly. Queasy. She must sit down. She gropes for the sofa arm, slides down. Her vision darkens, leaving only a tiny disc of light, like a kaleidoscope. Is this a near-death experience? Is she dying? She thinks she calls out for the boys, but she can't hear her voice. The circle of light shifts. There's something red there. It's a car, moving slowly through a misty landscape. Caroline can't guess where it is. Around the edges of her eyes she senses a movement in the blackness, a hostility, a destruction.

"Tim," she cries, and the blackness wrenches free from her visual field and swamps the tiny red car, and all she can see is the black, and all she can feel is terror.

"Mummy?"

Caroline opens her eyes. It's Jonny. As she tries to answer him, the living room light flashes on and off, on and off.

~

Jack struggles to concentrate. All he can think of is his mother in Cheddar Gorge. Did he really see her or was she a vision, a hallucination? Tim will not talk about it, and Jack doesn't even know where to begin. He feels disorientated; he's just seen into the heart of forever. And then he wonders: has Verity seen her too?

A thin film of air separates them from the moor and whatever hides there. Jack glances at Tim. Tim looks sickly: pallid and sweaty. He has

229

half-shut his window, but still the chill probes into the car. Jack is cold and turns up the heater.

"Jack," Tim says suddenly. "She's trying to send me a signal."

"Mum?"

"Caroline. She's warning me. Look out."

"What the hell is it?"

There's a dark depth in the fog, twisting, moving. Through the open window Jack feels the rush of displaced air. Instinctively he shrinks in his seat. Tim's saying something but he can't hear him over the beat of hundreds of wings.

"What are they?"

"I think they're crows," Tim says, shooting the window up, before the birds stab their beaks through the gap.

Jack can't see through the windscreen for the beating blue-black wings. Claws screech on the glass and on the roof. Jack brakes and the car slithers to an unsteady stop. The birds are two, three deep. Vicious beaks crack on the glass. Jack thumps his window to try to dislodge the crows, but they ignore his fist, and tug at the window seals. Reptilian eyes regard him coldly. Like velociraptors, they'll open the doors, he thinks, they'll open the doors and drag us out and…

Suddenly, the birds soar up in a dark tornado, deserting the car, blurring once more into the grey-white sky. Something nudges Jack's door. He cries out. A short, tough pony exhales on the scratched window, covering it with mist. It nudges the door again. Already Jack can see more ponies emerging form their mist, hooves clipping on the tarmac.

"They're here too," Tim says quietly.

Jack turns. The car is surrounded by ponies: black, brown and cream. The car rocks as they nudge it with their heavy noses.

"The birds…they were sent to stop us moving," Tim says.

Jack clicks out of his seatbelt,

"No, no, don't go out! They might…"

"Kill me?" Jack asks uncertainly.

"They might not be what they seem."

"They'll have us over," Jack says, as the car lifts and sighs.

The windows are steamed up with the horses' hot breath. One throws back its head, opens its mouth as though laughing. Jack flinches at the howl. It's unearthly, from another time. All he can see are the stocky bodies, the disproportionately big goblin heads, malevolent eyes, steaming breath. He imagines he can smell the horseflesh, feel the bristly manes and tails. The car heaves again.

"Have they got their fucking feet under us?" Jack cries.

His aggression floods from him, leaving a creeping terror that these crazed horses will turn the car upside down. He and Tim will either be crushed in the damaged car or they'll struggle out of the windows only to die under the heavy hooves. It will all be for nothing.

"We'll have to get out," Tim says. "We must find a way of distracting them away from the car."

"But you said…"

"Yeah, but they won't leave us alone. What was that?" Tim says, his hand on his seatbelt release.

Jack can only hear the snorting of the horses, the clicks of their hooves, the creaking of the car as it rocks even more wildly.

"Again," Tim says.

The car settles. The horses turn, one by one, towards the sound that Jack can now hear: it's the clear voice of a tin whistle, a tune that he feels he knows, but cannot place, a tune that seems as old as time and Hell, a tune that brings sudden tears to his eyes. The figure of a man darkens through the fog. A young man with copper hair, wearing a bright woven shirt. He walks out of the mist as though wading out of the sea, the whistle to his mouth.

"Who's he?" Jack asks.

"I don't know."

"He's not from this world, is he?" Jack asks quietly.

"No," Tim says. "I don't know who he is, but he's a friend."

The piper weaves through the horses, closer towards the car. The horses stand quiet, motionless as he passes.

"He's coming to us," Jack chokes.

The piper stops by Tim's window. Tim's hands have fallen loose on his knees; his eyes are closed.

"What does he want?"

Tim does not answer. The piper meets Jack's gaze for a second, then turns away from the car. As he walks away, the horses follow him, trotting obediently, whickering softly. The voice of the tin whistle fades note by note, as the piper and the horses vanish into the mist. Jack strains his ears for the melody, but it has gone, and he finds he cannot recall a single bar in his head.

"Tim." He shakes Tim, and Tim opens his eyes. "What was that?"

"He spoke to me."

"He couldn't have. He was playing the whistle." Again, Jack tries to hear again that tune, that ancient beautiful tune, but there is nothing.

"He spoke to me with his mind. He is a friend. He knows who we are, who we are to be. He saw Verity, when he was in this world. He has not long crossed over. He told me his name."

"What is his name?"

"I can't say it. He said if we need help, we can call him by his name, and he will help us."

Jack twists the ignition key; his feet are shaky and the car stalls. He inhales slowly, lets the breath out, and tries again. He's cold, freezing cold. As the car shudders forwards, he turns up the heater to maximum. His chest smarts where Tim anointed him with the cross of St George.

The mist lightens, stretched like white paint thinned with water. The dark stocky ponies are grazing at the road side. Some look up as the car accelerates past them, some keep their heads down, their eyes averted. Jack scans the emerging moorland for the piper, but he cannot see him, and he knows, in his heart, there is no-one there.

~

Caroline and the boys are curled up on the sofa. The living room light flashes on and off, on and off. It's hurting her eyes. It must be doing something to her brain. She can't think clearly. She's getting a migraine. The TV snaps into life. Its screen glows white.

"Mummy, what is it?" Jonny howls. "And don't say it's nothing."

"I don't know," she says, hunting under cushions for the remote. "I don't know what it is."

"I do," Andy says. "It's Angel. He's upset."

"Why's he upset?" Caroline shouts. "He's got Verity."

"Who's got Verity?" Jonny asks. "I'm frightened."

"So am I," Caroline says.

The TV screen is now a mass of colour. Images are running down it like coloured oil. Overhead the light still pulses. The pictures move faster, faster. Caroline can't register them. She sees flowers, something that looks like a fairground, all coloured light and stripes, waves crashing on rocks, horses. Horses. Something jolts in her brain, like she should understand the meaning of the horses, but she can't. She jabs the remote at the screen but nothing changes.

"Angel's outside," Andy says, pointing to the front window. "In the garden. He doesn't like you."

Caroline whips her gaze to where he points. Shadows are falling across the lawn. The leaves on the bushes lift gently in the breeze. There is no-one out there, but she can feel the gooseflesh rise on her skin, she can feel eyes on her that she cannot see.

"Out of here," she says, yanking the curtain along its rail.

In the new darkness, the screen and the flashing light are even brighter. Caroline reaches behind the TV and pulls the plug out of the wall. Her hand stings as though she's had an electric shock, but the screen dies to black with a boom. She pushes the boys into the kitchen. The light in the kitchen is flashing.

"I can't see," Andy cries, taking off his glasses and rubbing his eyes. "It's hurting me. Why is Angel hurting me?"

"I told you he was a nasty person," Caroline says, and her voice shakes and comes out thin. "I told you he'd taken Verity. He wants to take you."

"Take me flying?" Andy looks up blindly.

"No," Caroline says, without thinking of her words, only knowing she must say them. "No, he wants to take you away from me and Daddy and Jonny for ever, and you'll never see us again."

"Won't we see Verity again?" Jonny demands. "What's that noise?"

It's a low metallic jangling coming from the kitchen getting louder and louder, discordant, tortured. The whole room is screaming with it. There's a crash, and Caroline only has time to see a drawer jump out of the unit, and to push the boys down to the floor before knives and forks fly towards her. She stumbles to the floor, clumsy and gasping.

"Under the table," she says to the boys, and they crawl beneath it.

She jams herself between the legs. Metal whistles through the air. A steak knife lands like an arrow in the ground just inches from her hand.

We can't stay here, she thinks. We have to get out somehow. We have to get to the car. Go somewhere. The church maybe. Sanctuary.

"Andy," she says. "Is Angel in the house?"

"No," Andy says uncertainly. "He can't come in."

234

Caroline travels the circle in her mind, sees and silently blesses each stone. We'll have to break the circle, she thinks. We have to get to the car.

She can hear a tinkly rattling. It sounds like glass vibrating.

"Cover your faces," she says, pulling the boys to her chest as the door blasts off the wall cupboard and glasses and mugs come crashing down. She screws up her eyes, buries her face against Jonny's head. Jagged shards land in her lap. A sliver catches her raised arm, and she feels the sting of blood.

"Mummy, what are you going to do?" Jonny mumbles, his face in his hands.

"We're going to get out," Caroline says. "We'll get in the car."

Should I be saying this aloud? she wonders. But the Devil can hear the words in her head.

It is quieter now. Caroline glances at her arm, sees the jagged trail of blood.

"Are you hurt?" she asks.

"No," they say together.

"OK, we'll get out from this table and go to the front door. Andy, when we get there I want you to see if Angel's in the garden. Can you do that?"

Andy nods.

"And be really careful. The floor is covered with glass and stuff."

Should I clear it up first? Leave the boys under the table until it's safe? No, there's not time, she decides. She crawls out from under the table, wincing at the pain of glass fragments under her hands.

"Wait there," she says.

She stands, dizziness making her faint. She grabs the edge of the table, leans forwards, breathes. Her vision is speckled, or is that just the flashing light over her head? She swallows the impulse to retch, tears two cushions free from the dining chairs and drops them on the broken glass and china.

First Jonny, then Andy, crawls out of the makeshift cave.

"Careful, careful, and mind the knives," Caroline says, wondering if the fallen knives will suddenly prise themselves free from the floor and fly into the boys. She picks up a sharp kitchen knife, pushes it inside her sock. What good a weapon will do she has no idea, but its cold line on her skin strengthens her.

She cannot look at the destruction in the kitchen, at the pile of coloured shards. Something bangs down the corridor – in her bedroom? Whatever it is, she is not going to find out. The corridor lights flash. When she closes her eyes, she can still see the bright pulses. Like a headache, she wonders if they'll ever leave her.

"We'll get the car keys from the hall," she says. "When we get to the door, Andy, you look out."

The floor crunches under their feet.

"Are you sure he's not in the house?" Caroline asks.

"No," Andy says more confidently.

"You said there was no angel," Jonny says. "Now you say there is, and he's done all this."

Caroline taps Jonny's arm to stop him.

"You said you'd tell me. Daddy would tell me."

"I will tell you, I promise," she says. "Just not now. You'll understand when I tell you." She grabs her car keys from the hooks, then, as an afterthought, takes the keys for Frank's car as well. "Quiet, now, Jonny. Andy, have a good look, and see if he's outside."

Andy leans against the lower part of the door. His breath fogs up the glass.

"Andy?"

"Angel's not there."

Caroline unlocks the front door.

236

Into Cornwall and the fog has disappeared, burnt off by the pale low sunlight. Jack wishes he had sunglasses to hand.

"Caroline's in trouble," Tim says.

"What?" Jack asks.

"She's afraid. She and her children. He is pursuing them."

"How can you know that?"

"She can speak straight to me. She has the sight. She is telling me she is in danger. She is the Empress."

"Is that why the road is clear?" Jack asks. "He is busy with them, leaving us alone?"

"Possibly. But I think he's calling us on now. He's calling us to the battleground. Where he and I met once before."

"Do you know where?"

"It's somewhere near Mullion. I don't know it, no, but I will when I see it. I think I've seen it already at other times. I can't tell you how exactly. Just that I know I have seen this place. In dreams maybe or visions. I can't remember afterwards. I'm just left sometimes with a feeling that I've seen a glimpse of something, a glimpse of my destiny."

The car keys cut into Caroline's hand, because Andy is holding her so tightly. Jonny has her other hand. She tugs them towards the gate. As they run she notices abstractly how silent the garden is.

There are no birds or insects; she cannot hear voices or cars or strimmers from over the hedges. The air is stagnant, thick. Over the tamarisk she sees more dark clouds massing on the horizon. The flash of sunlight on glass far, far across the bay makes her blink.

"Where are we going?" Jonny asks.

"I don't know," Caroline mutters.

The Peugeot is only feet away. Soon they will be safe. She struggles out of Andy's curled fingers, and drops the two sets of car keys. One lands in a muddy puddle left in a rut.

"Shit," she mutters, bending awkwardly for one set.

Andy plunges his hands in the dirty water and pulls out the others.

"Give me those, Andy," Caroline says.

He moves towards the fault line and Verity's house.

"Andy!" Caroline shouts.

"Andy, you get back!" Jonny shouts and sprints after Andy.

Caroline unlocks the Peugeot. Jonny drags Andy back to the car, and hands over the keys to his father's Golf. Andy's face is creased like he's about to cry.

"Get in," Caroline says quickly, holding open the back door.

She wants to bundle them in, slam the door and roar away without wasting time to strap them into their seat belts, but she does not dare. Her fingers are fumbly, and her back aches with leaning over, and all the running and bending she's been doing.

At last the boys are safe, and she eases herself in behind the wheel. She glances in the mirror, expecting to see something dreadful. Only the boys, Andy twisting round in his seat to peer out of the back window. Caroline turns the ignition key. Nothing happens. The engine doesn't even cough or turn over. No lights flare on the dashboard. Nothing. She checks the key has moved. She turns it back, inserts it again, jiggles the gear stick, pumps the pedals. Still nothing.

"Where are we going?" Jonny asks again.

"Angel's coming," Andy says tensely.

"Where is he?" Caroline jerks her head round, and cracks her neck. The pain flares down to her shoulder.

"I don't know," Andy says. "But he's coming."

Caroline tries one more time.

"Is the car broken?" Jonny asks, kicking the back of Caroline's seat.

238

Caroline yanks out the key, wipes away her sudden tears with the heel of her hand.

"OK, we'll go in Daddy's."

She flings open the door and struggles out. The wind has suddenly come up, and the tamarisk waves on the cliff edge. For a second she thinks she sees a shimmer in the lane over the fault line. The boys scramble out of the car.

"Angel," Andy says, pointing towards the shimmer.

"Stay here, Andy." Caroline grabs his arm and backs towards Frank's car.

"I can't see anything," Jonny cries.

"No," Caroline says, feeling behind her for the Golf. "You can't, Jonny. Just remember that, you can't see anything."

"But..." Jonny says.

"You mustn't," Caroline cries at last.

"Look," says Jonny.

"Angel's come for me," Andy sobs, trying to hide behind Caroline.

"Don't look, Andy." Caroline jabs the keys towards the car.

"Look," Jonny says again. "Look at this wheel."

Caroline looks where he points. The offside back tyre is flat. Completely flat. She steps back and looks at the front wheel. Flat too.

"And that one," Jonny says. He runs round to the other side. "And these."

"Jesus," Caroline cries. "We'll have to go home." She looks down the lane to where she thought she'd seen that faint shimmer. Nothing.

"Angel's gone home," Andy says.

"What?"

"Angel. He's in our garden."

"Then we'll walk this way," Caroline says.

"Why?" Jonny asks.

"We'll walk to the village."

239

"I'm cold," Jonny says.

"I'm sorry," Caroline says. "Walking will keep you warm."

If we can just get to Mullion, she thinks. I can leave the boys at someone's house. A friend from school. She can't think what emergency story she can concoct; she doesn't care. As long as the boys are far, far from the cliff.

"I'm still cold," Jonny grumbles.

Andy keeps turning round to look behind him.

"Is he coming?" Caroline asks.

"No." Andy's voice is trembly.

The track is bumpy and rough underfoot. Caroline is cold too. She never thought to grab coats when they left the house. She glances across the bay. The thunder clouds have swept in, darkening the sea to indigo. White horses are breaking further offshore on the underwater skerries. Caroline can taste the rain that's about to come. A soft, low rumble of thunder. It's not close, it's not loud. It's a warning.

They walk round the final bend. Caroline's already exhausted. She wonders if she'll make it to Mullion without falling down. The road to the village slopes up on the right; to the left is the steep track down to the beach.

Suddenly the air judders. That shimmer again. At the top of the cliff path, barring the way.

"Angel," Andy cries, pointing ahead.

~

Jack has seen the signs for Mullion. It can only a few miles away now. The sky overhead is dark with cumulonimbus clouds. Rain splatters the windscreen, and Jack turns the wipers up to fast. Sometimes there are sharp flashes of lightning in his peripheral vision. The lane is narrow and twisting; the hedges on either side are beaten down by the rain to a dark green pulp. Cars coming the other way are moving fast, hitting the standing water at speed, sending giant fans into the air.

"They're all running away," Jack muses, swerving into the hedge as another car shoots past in a mist of water.

Another flash to the right, over the sea. Jack flinches. He glances at Tim. Tim's still and pale. He looks really unwell. For a second Jack thinks he sees bones and flesh moving under Tim's shoulder. He doesn't see the black film of water, and the car screeches across the road.

Ahead the trees sway together forming a dark tunnel. Jack rights the car, and accelerates down the hill. Headlamps coming the other way, pale and spectral, bouncing up towards them. Lightning through the branches. The other car lurches past them in a grunt of gears and a spray of water. In the darkness Jack briefly registers the red triangular sign warning of a ford, and brakes. The road narrows and bends at the bottom of the slope. There's a deep swathe of water running across the tarmac. In his headlamps Jack sees a figure crouching at the roadside. She has dark hair hanging over her face. Her long skirt is heavy with water. In her hands is a soaking cloth. Jack slams the brakes. The girl is only feet from him. She turns to look up at him, as he stares through the rain-washed window glass.

"It's Verity," he cries, and wrenches off his seat belt.

"No," Tim shouts, grabbing him by the arm. "Drive on."

"It's her. Look."

Verity holds up the soaking bundle. It's a dirty white, stained rusty red. Her eyes are hollow and her skin waxy. She doesn't look alive.

"Do not get out of the car!" Tim commands.

"Let go!" Jack cries. He's taken aback at Tim's strength. His arm throbs. "Verity!"

"Just drive on," Tim says again. "It's not her."

241

Verity staggers to her feet. Her long gold skirt unfurls to the ground. It's torn, bloodstained. She steps through the water towards Jack. He could open the window and reach out to her. His fingers fumble for the window release, and the glass slides down. Cold air, rain and something else. Jack gasps and gags on the smell of decay.

Tim lunges across Jack to reach the window control, as the girl's hand stretches towards the opening. The window shoots up. The girl snarls, showing brown feral teeth. She howls and scrapes her long ragged nails down the glass.

"I fucking told you," Tim says, as Jack shoves the car in gear.

"Who – what – the hell was that?" Jack asks, revving fast.

In his rear view mirror, he sees Verity – the girl, the creature – stumbling through the water after them, in her bedraggled gown, holding out her wet linen.

"Haven't you heard of the washer at the ford?" Tim asks.

"No. Yes."

"She washes the shrouds of those about to die," Tim says. "That was what she was washing."

"Are we about to die?"

"Why can't we go home?" Jonny cries. "I'm cold, I'm wet, I'm frightened."

"It's not safe there anymore," Caroline mutters.

"Where are we going?" Jonny asks. "Why are we doing this?"

Caroline shivers. Rain is slanting down onto them. None of them have coats.

"Angel's in our garden," Andy says, slipping on the muddy stones.

"Quickly then," Caroline says, walking on, over the fault line.

On the right is Carrag Luz. The giant boulders are running with rain. The grasses are flattened and grey. In ten minutes we could get to the harbour, Caroline thinks, but she knows now the futility of this. Lucifer can move as fast as light.

"He's here," Andy sobs, pointing, crying, rain running down his glasses. His hand in Caroline's is icy.

Caroline has already seen the shifting light on the narrow cliff path in front of them. As the sky explodes into lightning the shimmer intensifies. Soon I will see his face, Caroline thinks. She backs away. The shimmer disappears.

"He's behind us now," Andy says.

"Don't speak to him," Caroline snaps.

"I can't see anyone," Jonny wails. "Please let's go home."

"We can't."

Caroline senses the shimmer all around. There's only one way they can go: through the wet grasses to Carrag Luz, to the edge of the cliff. She finds her feet moving of their own accord towards the crag.

"No, no" Andy cries.

"We'll be safe," Caroline says. "The rock will give us shelter."

She slithers on the wet muddy grass. The rocks are silver-white before the dark sky. On the horizon, sea and sky blur in anger. She cannot see the Land's End peninsula through the film of rain. When she reaches the base of the crag, she pushes the boys down.

"Sit on the ledge," she tells them. "It will help keep you dry."

"It's wet," Jonny says.

"Please Jonny," Caroline says.

From here she can see the arc of the cliff road. She can see her house, and Verity's, the glistening scribble of the fault line. Below, the sea rushes into the two bays. The waves are high, jagged. She can feel the force even this high up.

"Where is he, Andy?" she says.

"Don't know," Andy says.

"Stay right where you are." Caroline takes a few steps back through the grass towards the cliff road.

"Mummy, no, he's there!"

That shimmer once more, only feet away from her. She stumbles backwards and the shimmer dissipates. There is nothing else they can do. They will have to wait on the crag, hostages huddled into the cold wet stone, until Tim and Jack arrive. If they arrive.

Caroline eases herself onto a higher ledge. She's so cold her hands are shaking. Rain lashes the side of her head, and stings her eyes. Jonny and Andy clap their hands over their ears at the thunder that cracks overhead. Caroline places her hands on the rock, feels the hard coldness, the prickle of lichen, the slime of the rain, and suddenly a powerful warmth seeps into her hands. Like when she was laying the circle. She inhales the rain and wind, and slowly stands, visualising the earth beneath her feet.

Her body warms with the heat of the earth. She can see the individual blades of grass, the raindrops, the hiding insects and snails. She lets her gaze travel to the cliff road. The fault line is wavering. As lightning and thunder blast the sky together, the crack splits open with a boom.

"Mummy!" the boys cry together.

Caroline feels their hands grasping at her, but she's beyond them now. The earth's pain is her pain. Her womb contracts and she almost falls with the burn.

"Mummy, what's wrong? What's happening? Mummy?" Jonny's voice from far away.

Caroline steadies herself, biting her cheek against the pain. The fault line cracks again, and the cliff above the second bay crumbles, vomiting soil, rocks and roots into the swirling water below. Caroline's eyes follow the fault line as it judders and cracks under the water, splitting the seabed. Through the dark water she can see the twisted fronds

244

of seaweeds, the silver fish, the tiny creatures, all hurled around in the maelstrom. Lightning spears the sky and hits the water with a crash of sparks. There's a cry from the earth itself, as its muscles are torn further to open up the dark, dark chasm offshore.

The birth of the gateway to Hell.

~

Black and white chevrons on a roadsign warn Jack of the hairpin bend. Rainwater streams across the carriageway. The bend is on the edge of an abyss, hugging the cliffside. Above the chevrons, through the needling rain, is the opposite flank of the valley.

"Jesus," Jack says, as the car aquaplanes round the bend.

"What the fuck?"

Jack brakes again. The road yawns down to deep bay with black rocky cliffs. The sea is sucking backwards across the sand, further and further, exposing the dark bones of submerged rocks. Jack inches forwards, wipers on fast. He opens his window, leans out to look.

"It's a tsunami," he says at last. "The water retreating before the wave…"

"Move it!" Tim cries. "We have to get through before it comes back."

"It'll fucking kill us. There must be another way to Mullion."

"We don't have time. Quickly."

~

"Don't look."

Caroline moves in front of the boys, blocking their view over the side of the crag. Below her the water surges back out of the two bays, stripping the silver sand with it. The cliff above the second bay has split in a giant cleft. As the water recedes, Caroline's eyes follow the

245

wound in the sea bed. Smoke and flames spit from the gash. She can smell sulphur. There are rocks never seen before, tangles of weed and bones, and then the gaping hole, the screaming mouth of Hell. Flames shoot up from the tumble of rocks surrounding the pit; lightning fractures the sky. With a roar the sea rises into a dark column, black and monstrous. Caroline clasps her abdomen; pain floods her body as the wave surges towards the cliffs, crashing over the skerries, swallowing the giant fissure. Sparks crackle as the flames are engulfed. The great wave is funnelled into the narrow tidal bay below Carrag Luz. The water churns in, black and oily, bearing on its back foetid seaweed, dead fish and slime, and explodes on the rocks below. Foam ejaculates with a crack, splattering Caroline's face in an icy salty smack.

As Jack swerves round the second hairpin bend at the bottom the cliff, the wave roars in toward the valley mouth.

"Jesus, fuck," he gabbles. "We've had it."

The wave crashes onto the beach, and a dark flood of debris surges up the valley. Water hits the car, and it shakes as the tsunami sweeps past it. Icy seawater splashes through Jack's open window.

Jack can't speak. He wonders for a second if he's shat himself, but the foul stink is coming from the water. He fumbles with his seatbelt and the door catch. When he opens the door, cold air and rain hit him in the face. The air is thick with sulphur and sewage. The car is stained brown-black. Jack's legs shake and he grasps the car roof. Tim gets out. Together they walk the few yards to where the water lies. There has been no backwash; the flood has saturated the beach and flooded the valley. The road disappears into black water.

"I can't drive through that," Jack says. "I don't know how deep it is."

Lightning flashes and Jack instinctively steps back from the water. The drumming rain pockmarks the surface. Jack shivers.

"We'll have to leave the car and wade," Tim says.

"We don't know the way." Jack says. "We're not even in Mullion yet. It could take hours to find her."

The greasy water slaps at the tarmac. A few yards away something pale is floating. He catches the glint of an eye. It's a dead gull, white and malevolent.

"He told me to call him if we needed help," Tim says.

"The piper? He said to call his name."

Tim turns his face to the rain and cries aloud, no name, just a cry – ancient and potent – that makes Jack shudder again and, for only a second, he recalls a bar of the piper's tune, and then it's gone again, and his brain is rushing to catch it.

"Where is he? Will he come?"

"He gave his word. He said he would help us."

Thunder growls round the cliffs. As it fades there's another noise: a click-click. Jack and Tim turn. Across the flooded road a horse canters up to the water and stops, watching them.

"Where did he come from?" Jack asks uncertainly.

"I think he's come for us."

"We've got to get on him?" Jack gazes at the huge russet stallion. "I can't do that."

The horse steps into the water, moves towards them.

"He's our guide," Tim says. "He's showing us how deep the water is. Come on."

He splashes into the dark water. Jack glances back once to the car, left skewed across the road on the bend, and follows Tim. The water is viscous and icy. His jeans slap against his legs. Ahead of him Tim is up to his thighs in water. Jack drags his heavy legs past the floating gull, past other nameless, faceless objects dredged from the deep. As Tim reaches the horse, it turns and canters out of the water. The sky flares with lightning, and Jack stumbles on quickly. He's gasping with cold as he steps out on the other side. The horse starts up the cliff track. Jack can hardly see with the rain driving into his eyes. His clothes are soaking but, as he hauls himself up the slope, he feels a burning on his chest. It's the red cross of blood, of St George. Strength and warmth suffuse his body. He straightens his shoulders and lengthens his stride.

They won't get here in time. They'll never get here, Caroline thinks. Her body convulses with pain again.

"Are you having the baby?" Jonny's teeth chatter when he speaks.

"Yes," Caroline says.

"Can't we go home?"

"We can't get home." Caroline points at the jagged slash in the cliff path where the mauve vein of the fault line used to be. "We're waiting for Tim and Jack. They'll help us." But they won't get here.

"Tim?" Jonny asks. "The man on the phone?"

"Yes. He knows about the Angel. He's coming to rescue us."

"He'll hurt Angel." Andy says.

"Where is the Angel?" Jonny asks.

"Don't know," Andy says.

"Will the baby come here? On this rock?" Jonny demands.

"Yes," Caroline gasps again, as a contraction surges through her.

Pain flares in Tim's shoulders. It is almost time. The cliff path is uneven and slippery. Rain and wind are blasting in off the sea. Tim's eyes run with water, and he can hardly see. The glossy russet stallion never falters on the path, sure-footed and swift. The path slopes steeply down to another bay. Tim stops, looks out down the coast.

Jagged black cliffs rise up on the opposite side and at the very top is a tortured crag, glowing white in the stormy darkness.

Tim cries aloud and nearly falls. Jack grabs him and steadies him with frozen hands.

"What is it?"

"There." Tim points to the crag.

"What?"

"That is the place. That rock there. That is where we shall meet tonight."

Ahead the stallion has stopped and turned, regarding Tim with intelligent eyes. As Tim steps forward the horse moves on. This beach is flooded too at the apex of the bay. Tim plunges into icy water beside the horse, his eyes on the dark shoulder of the opposite cliff, and the spectral crag on the very top.

"Caroline," he cries aloud. "Where are you? Caroline!"

~

"They're coming," Caroline breathes the words as a mantra.

"Tim and Jack?" Jonny asks. "Where are they?"

"I don't know," Caroline says. "I can feel them close. I know they're near. They're coming to save us."

"Angel's coming too," Andy says.

~

Tim is running now beside the horse. Coming round the bend in the cliff path the crag glows. Tim can feel the burn of energy in his limbs. The rock is calling him. Lucifer is calling him. He is only vaguely aware of Jack stumbling behind him. The rain stabs his face, and his clothes are so wet they stick to him but he notices none of this, only the power of the rock, of the battleground, tugging him closer and closer.

The horse throws back its head and whinnies. Tim slithers to a halt. The path in front of them is torn open. Smoke and steam rise from the chasm. Tim can hear the shrieking of the torn earth far below. He stands on the precipice to Hell. Somewhere, down there, in those dark tortured caverns is Verity.

He raises his eyes to the rock, that sacred ancient place that has haunted the dark places in his mind all his life. There are three figures huddled against its flank. One is bent over as if folded in pain; the smaller two are crouched together on the stone ledge.

"Caroline!" Tim cries, and his voice is deeper, older.

The twisted figure stands, looks at him through the rain and the wind. Tim cannot hear her answering words but he does not need to.

"We can't get over that!" Jack gasps. A scree of loose stones skitter from under his feet into the dark abyss.

"You won't have to," Tim says, his eyes on Caroline, the Empress, Mary Moses, guardian of all living creatures and plants. "You must go down."

"What?"

"Into Hell. You must bring back Verity. She's down there."

"But..."

"I will call him out. He will come and challenge me. Your part is to save her."

"I can't."

"You can. You are no longer that Fool. You know who you are now, St George."

Beside Tim the stallion howls again and leaps across the smoking chasm. As it lands on the other side it vanishes. Jack is shouting, but his voice is fainter and fainter. The pain in Tim's shoulders rises and his skin splits beneath his shirt. He feels the heat of blood with the cold of the rain, and he knows the time is here, now. This is the battle of Heaven and Hell. With a cry he plunges across the wounded cliff and, as his feet leave the ground, it seems to him that his whole body is tearing apart, but he does not fall.

~

"Tim!" Caroline cries, as he leaps into the air.

He stays there, suspended a moment above the chasm, hovering, a tiny figure in the dark night. Then, in an instant, huge wings unfurl from his shoulders. In the furious flash of the lightning Caroline sees the dark eyes of peacock feathers on the wings. Tim is soaring larger and larger, his wings obliterating the sky. In his left hand he holds a silver sword, on his right arm a shield. A peacock blue cloak streams behind him.

"He fell in the hole!" Jonny cries. "Was that Tim?"

"He didn't fall," Caroline says, and she's crying tears of cold and fear and joy all together.

"Look, look!" Andy's pointing to the huge figure above them, swirling before the clouds.

"Where?" Jonny howls.

St Michael lowers his sword towards the sea. Its shining tip is only feet from Caroline's face. She can hear the crackle of its energy, the heat and the power. He draws the sword in a line with the underwater chasm. The sea gurgles and roars and sucks back across the sand.

"The sea's going away again," Jonny says.

The dark flood slides like mercury, and the earth's wound is exposed once more, running jaggedly, angrily, down the tidal bay and out to the very mouth of Hell.

"Angel's coming," Andy says.

The lightning is so bright Caroline's eyes burn. Behind her closed lids she can see the pulses again and again. Thunder roars around Carrag Luz. Caroline hears the boys crying and reaches out blindly for them. When she opens her eyes, the sky above is aflame with light and she recoils.

"It's him, it's him," she gasps.

"Angel," Andy cries. "He's so big."

"Don't look," she says.

"I can't see anything!" Jonny wails.

Lucifer shimmers with white-gold light. His sword flashes with gold and his pale hair sparkles with stars. Caroline chokes at his beauty, feels tears in her eyes.

"He's got wings, he's got wings," Andy says. "I knew he had wings."

The two blades clash, silver and gold, and a trident of lightning shafts towards the cliff. Caroline is breathless from the pain in her womb, but she cannot take her eyes from the two giants battling in the sky.

~

The ground shifts under Jack's feet. The fault line – the abyss – is crumbling. He cannot see the bottom of the chasm, but he can hear the moans and screams of the earth. A series of ledges lead downwards into the darkness. He jumps off the cliff path and onto the highest step. It rocks and breaks.

Jack shouts aloud as he slides into the dark, bruising his shoulders and knees on jutting strata. He scrabbles blindly for the sides of the gorge, but they heave and split, and he tears his hands on the rocks. He lands with a crack and a metallic clang, almost falling. Far, far above, he can see the thin incision in the earth and a flash of white lightning. His head feels clumsy and heavy, and he guesses he has hit it. He reaches a tentative hand to his temple. Metal hits metal. He cannot see much in the red-black light, but he flexes his fingers.

He's wearing chain mail, and on his head is a metal helmet. He runs a hand over his chest and legs. Armour. He trips on something heavy on the stony ground. He can just make out the scarlet cross on white. A shield, and beside it a sword. St George takes his arsenal, holds up the shining blade.

The cavern snakes away under the sea. Smoke billows out of the red darkness. St George strides towards the toxic breath, his spurs ringing on the broken ground. As his eyes grow more accustomed to the strange glow, he sees twisted arches on right and left leading to further caves and tunnels. Sometimes he catches a blast of ozone from the ocean. The smells of the elements are overpowering: water, fire, earth and filthy air. There's another sound, under the clang of metal on stone. He stops, and can feel his shooting pulse. The noise again. A whistling, a high keening.

Jack gulps.

Could it be the sea? No.

Suddenly, he can hear the melancholy cry of a hunting horn, and the keening rises, and the whistles become more frenzied, and there's screaming, and the fiery shadows on the rocky wall jump and shudder, and he can hardly inhale through the stink of death that enfolds him. Out of the tunnel before him comes a horde of crones, hardly human, but with skeletal hands, toothy grins, sunken eyes. The creatures are dressed in tattered gowns. Grave clothes. Jack slashes wildly with his sword.

They laugh – a high, crazy sound – and pluck at him. He imagines he can feel their talons through his armour. The horn again, nearer. More and more forms come from the darkness. A huntsman somewhere raises the horn to his lips. A drum thudding down the passage, like the blood in Jack's arteries. He slices in vain with his sword, as the crones surround him. He can just see the dead flowers in their thready hair, and the maggots crawling in their vacant eye sockets. The air is thick with death and corruption: odours he's never breathed before. The corpse-creatures are strong; they spin him around, pushing him, clawing for his face beneath his helmet, pushing him, stumbling, into one of the branch tunnels.

The tunnel is too narrow to swing his sword; it jars on the stone wall with a clang. No, no, Jack thinks, as the ghouls push him further and further into the darkness. He has no loaf of bread to crumble to make a trail. This passage is dark, so dark, and he cannot see anything. Still, they push him onwards. Still, he can hear the horn and the relentless drum, driving his heart rate higher and higher. Somehow, some of the crones have got beyond him; they tug him as the others push him. His shield rings on the wall as he is roughly shoved down yet another side tunnel, pulled and pushed, darker and darker and he can no longer see his assailants. He tries to stop moving for a moment, but they are upon him, faceless horrors, shrieking and clawing, spinning him round. And still the horn and the drum. Into another tunnel and another, this one so narrow and twisted Jack cracks his helmet and arms on the rocks. He is running out of air. He's blinded in the dark. The drum is so fast now he can hardly distinguish the beats. And then, he hears it. The elusive, ancient tune of the piper.

Jack gasps.

The drum slows its beat. The horn is silenced. The melody drifts nearer and nearer, cutting a swathe through the foul air. Jack can no longer sense the crones around him. He reaches out a shaking hand. Nothing but rock. His tormentors have gone. The piper's tune recedes through the passages.

Come back, Jack tries to cry, but his mouth is stiff and he cannot form the words. He does not know which way he has come, which way leads him back, or where Verity is. He is trapped under the sea-bed, alone in the stifling darkness.

Caroline cries as another contraction squeezes her womb into an angry fist. She shudders against the cold clammy shoulder of Carrag Luz. Overhead, St Michael and Lucifer clash swords, and lightning flares between the ragged clouds. Caroline's aware of the boys crying out for her, but there's another voice in her head, deep, ancient, powerful. *Hold back the sea. Hold back the sea for St George*, the Archangel commands her. She turns to the bay below. The tide is surging – turbulent, frustrated – sucking at the edge of the crater to Hell. I can't do it, she thinks, twisting in pain, and the sea splutters forward towards the dark hole. Caroline straightens, her hands on Carrag Luz. She feels its power charging into her palms. Pain flares again in her womb as the tide rocks forward. Jack's down there, St George is down there. Verity's down there. When the sea flows back across the sand it will flood the crack, the way to Hell. St George and Verity will be damned to Hell for eternity.

Jonny and Andy are sobbing beside Caroline. As she hears their voices, the waves rear up again. She presses her hands so hard to the crag she imagines she could fall through into its cold heart. The wave drops, unfulfilled.

Jack takes a few hesitant steps in the direction he thinks the piper's tune came from. He is clumsy in his armour, with his sword and shield. He stops. He only imagines the piper was this way. He does not know. If he does not move from where he is, he will never find Verity; either the fires of Hell or the flooding waters of the sea will kill him down here, and no-one will ever find his skeleton, clothed in its armour. He uses his sword to gauge the walls of the passage, and

255

stumbles onwards, straining his ears for a bar of the piper's tune, or the terrible drum.

The air changes. Jack stretches his sword. It does not meet rock. He guesses the tunnel has opened out into a chamber. An air pocket. He does not remember this. He must have taken the wrong passage. He is hot and encumbered in the armour, but the air is strange. He can actually breathe. Maybe it is only because the stinking creatures have gone. Jack moves onwards slowly, cautiously. Something isn't right.

He taps the ground before him with his sword. Rock. Still rock. He can feel cooler air, movement. His head spins with disorientation and fatigue. He stumbles, shouts aloud, and drops his sword. But there is no clang, just a rushing of air, then nothing.

"Fuck, shit, fuck."

He has no weapon, and no way of testing the treacherous ground. Tears burn his eyes. He cannot go on. He has failed. He is no knight in shining armour. He is only a Fool and now he will die a Fool.

"St George."

Jack knows that voice. Suddenly the darkness lightens with a blue-white glow. His eyes burn at the change.

"Where are you? I'm here. Mum, Mum!"

Now he can see the lines of strata on the rocky wall beside him. He was right: he is standing in a cavern. As he raises his eyes he gasps. His mother is only yards away from him, and between her and him is a gaping black hole that stretches right across the cavern.

"St George," the woman says again. "Pick up your sword."

"I..."

"Walk to the edge of the pit," Rosie's shade flickers in the strange light.

Jack shuffles forwards to the dark mouth. He wants to reach out, touch her, hold her; somehow he knows if he did this she would vanish. His sword glows fiercely. It appears to be suspended in the air, out of his reach.

"I can't," Jack says.

"You can. I have woven a web across the pit. Walk to your sword, and I will guide you."

"You might be a trick," he cries suddenly, remembering Verity hunched at the ford. "You might not really be…her, you."

Still Rosie watches him across the chasm. "I will not allow you to fall. Find Verity and then I can find my peace."

"Where is she?" Jack says.

"In great danger. Only you can save her. But you will need your sword. The next test you will face alone."

Jack steps forwards, though he has no awareness of moving his feet. As he steps into the abyss, a silver web forms beneath him. He feels like he's stepping on the surface of water, something fragile and viscous, holding his weight only by the thinnest membrane. He's hardly breathing. He stands in the middle of the pit. The web behind him has vanished. He reaches for his sword; its weight feels reassuring in his hand. He steps onwards, and the silver threads sparkle in the half-light. He reaches the other side and finds solid rock.

"Do not look behind you," Rosie says. "Behind you is the Fool. Before you is a saint."

Caroline's whispering a mantra, though she does not know the words she utters.

Below her the sea churns, unsated, impotent. How long can her earth's strength hold back the fury of the water? The air above her rings with the thunderous clash of blades and the searing, burning flashes of lightning. A jet of flame erupts from the gateway to Hell. Caroline can feel the boys' hands on her clothes, but she cannot lift her hands from Carrag Luz. If she does, the tide will roar into the bay, engulfing Hell once more.

～

St George follows Rosie through tortured, twisted passages and caves. He can just make out her pale figure before him. The air becomes thicker, foetid with sulphur. He freezes, listening for the drum, but there is nothing. He's sweating inside his armour, from his exertions, from the rising temperature, from the joy and pain of finding his mother. He can smell burning from somewhere ahead and, as the passage turns, he sees red flickers on the rock strata.

Smoke belches towards him, and he coughs on the foul air. As his vision clears, he can see only the vague red-gold flares. Rosie's shade has gone.

"Mum," St George cries, but he knows she has gone for ever, absorbed into the smoke.

It is not just that he now stands alone, he can sense she has left him, that she has found peace, that Verity must be nearby.

He strides on in the eerie glow. Red light, stronger, ahead of him. The rocky cleft twists, and suddenly opens out into a chamber, ringed with a circle of fire. In the middle of the cavern Verity is lying on the ground. The flames turn her ragged gown to amber. She's turned away from him, her dark hair spilling onto the ground like seaweed. He strides forward to snatch up her inert form. As he reaches for her, there's a thunderous snarl and the whole chamber is filled with flames and smoke. A fanged golden dragon hurls itself from the heart of the fire towards St George.

The dragon's breath blasts St George's face with death and foulness. He raises his sword again and slices towards the creature's scaly neck. It leaps back, vomiting more flames into the cave. St George's eyes are watering behind his visor; his lungs are stinging with smoke.

He stumbles as the dragon lunges towards him. He sees four rows of jagged teeth. The smoke almost knocks him to the ground. The dragon tramples past Verity, its claws tearing her gown, and ripping her pale skin. St George roars and slashes his sword into the dragon's underbelly. It shrieks, and the distorted echo rings round and round the rocky walls. Black blood pumps out of the wound, and St George gags on the stench. The dragon's blood falls onto Verity, staining her gown dark.

Still, she does not move.

St George wonders fleetingly if she is already dead, then the bleeding dragon is turning on him again, its tail whipping Verity, its mouth open in a howl of flames and teeth and pain. St George drops his shield, and with two hands on his sword he cleaves the air with a flash of light and slices the dragon's head from its neck. Foul blood spurts on to him, hitting his armour with a sickening, thick crack. The dragon's death-cry still reverberates round the chamber and, below it, another sound: the sound of the sea.

St George seizes Verity. She's lifeless in his arms. He throws her across his shoulder and snatches up his weapons. Sometimes she knocks against the rocky walls as St George runs back along the abyss, but she does not speak or wake. St George can taste the salt-semen of the sea behind him. He drops his sword and shield, stumbles on. The cold force of the water knocks him flat. The last thing he remembers is the burn of his head on the rocks, but still he holds onto Verity.

~

Caroline's cry fractures the night. She falls back from the crag. As she lands on the damp grass, she hears the orgasmic roar of the sea under her. She turns her face to the grass. A few inches from her face she can see a tiny snail creeping up a blade of grass. Caroline curls into herself like a snail.

She could not hold the water.

She has failed the Archangel.

~

St Michael's sword slices into Lucifer's wings. Gold feathers and sparks whirl away into the night. Lucifer roars and dives down to the rock, his gold sword flashing with lightning. St Michael sees the three figures at the base of the crag: Mary Moses curled on her side, her body twisting in pain, Jonny terrified, gazing into a sky that for him is filled only with thunderclouds and lightning, and Andy, open-mouthed, blinking as Lucifer catches him up on the end of his sword and throws him high in the air. St Michael soars down, but Andy has fallen on Lucifer's back. His glasses have gone and his mouth is open in a cry of fear or excitement, as he tugs on the Devil's long pale hair. St Michael veers away to the clouds: he cannot destroy the Devil if the child will be destroyed too.

Lucifer is wheeling over the crag, the tiny speck of the boy dark on his white-gold wings. Below, Jonny is jumping and waving, pulling at Mary Moses, who rolls in the wet grass. She could not hold back the tide; her own tide was too powerful. A child will be born on the crag this night, into a world of goodness or of evil. St Michael raises his blade. Lucifer must be banished for ever and the boy must live.

~

Jack opens his eyes. Lightning flashes overhead and he gasps at the pain in his head. He reaches up and feels his hair, wet and sticky with blood. His helmet has gone. So has his armour. He's wearing his own clothes, and they are heavy and icy with seawater. His skin feels burnt in places, as though a dragon has breathed flames on him.

"Verity," he says. "Verity."

He sits slowly. He remembers the wave, the tsunami, which knocked him flat as he ran from Hell. He has been washed up on a rocky scree. Below him is a narrow cove, churning with dark turbulent water. When he looks up he can see the ragged, distorted face of the crag and, above that, two giants in the sky, blades clashing in explosions of silver and gold.

"Verity," Jack says again.

She must have been torn from his grasp. He grips onto the slippery rocks. One slip and he'll fall into that foaming water. And then he sees her. She's lying on a rocky slab a little further down. She's no longer wearing the gown she had in Hell; she is back in her own clothes, soaked and blood-stained.

Jack moves unsteadily towards her. Spray arcs up into his face, stinging his eyes, almost knocking him off balance. A rock gives way beneath his touch and falls into the dark water.

"Verity."

Jack reaches out to her. She lies very still; her long hair covers her face. Gently he rolls her over, shakes her. There's blood on her face as well as her clothes. There's a dark bruise on her cheekbone. Her hands are freezing. At last, she opens her eyes and stares at him, glazed, unfocussed.

~

Hampered by the child on his back, Lucifer shakes himself. Andy rocks for a moment, then spirals off the Devil's back, his arms outspread like tiny wings. St Michael surges under his laughing adversary, feels the gentle thud of the boy landing on his own back. With a roar of rage he plunges his sword upwards into the flashing gold creature above.

~

261

"Andy's gone, Andy's gone," Jonny cries and shakes Caroline again.

"Gone where?" she gasps.

"Gone. Like Verity. What's happening?"

Caroline never saw Andy go. Andy has gone, and she feels strangely detached, her thoughts centred inwards on the child pushing her way into this crazy night.

"There's so much lightning," Jonny says.

Caroline forces herself to look up and cries aloud.

Molten gold and feathers are pouring from Lucifer's bright figure. Sparks hit the rocks with a crackle. St Michael slashes his sword once again, and more gold blood spurts from the wounded Devil.

"What's happening? What's happening?" Jonny cries again. "I can't see anything."

"Then stay blind for ever," Lucifer roars, and a jagged fork of lightning sears into Jonny's face.

Jonny screams, hands to his eyes, stumbling in the grass. Lucifer falls through the sky, a dying comet with a glittering trail of stars. A few more sparks, one rumble of thunder, then quiet.

~

St Michael throws down his sword and shield. He has no more use for them. His time as a warrior is done. He flies down to the crag below. There are two giant boulders balanced on the top. He lifts one of these in his huge hands and hurls it out to sea. The gateway to Hell is marked with a few golden sparkles on the water. The boulder hits the surface with a crack, sinks through the depths, sealing the void for eternity.

~

Jack sees the tumbling golden figure, disintegrating and bleeding. He sees the huge pale rock searing through the air to the sea. He feels the reverberations of that descent in the cliff face.

"Verity," he says.

Below him the sea surges again. The falling rock will create another wave. He tugs her to her feet, ignoring her cries of pain. The cliff above is springy grass up to the crag.

"We have to get up the cliff," Jack tells Verity. "Don't look down."

If she replies he does not hear her, as a second wall of cold water hits him in the back.

⁓

"I can't see! Mummy, help me!"

"Jonny, it's over now. We're safe."

"I can't see! I'm blind. It's all white. Everything's white."

"I can't do anything," Caroline gasps. "The baby's coming."

⁓

St Michael stands high on the crag with Andy on his back. The rock he hurled into the water has blocked the way to Hell. Already the fissure in the cliff is re-joining, healing. The giant wave below slaps the grassy cliff face, depositing two figures on a rocky ledge. Something silver leaps from the retreating water, flies upwards. St Michael holds out a chain-mailed hand. The fish slithers into his grasp.

⁓

This time Jack does not lose consciousness. Somehow, he's landed on a jutting ledge of rock just below the crag. It's only a few feet to climb. Next to him is a straggle of dark hair. Verity's hand reaches up to brush it from her face.

263

"Jack," she says at last, and slides her hand into his.

~

St Michael's strength is failing. He can feel the soft flutter of peacock feathers falling from his wings. Soon he will be merely a man. Gently he shakes Andy from his back, catches him in his hand and sets him on the grass. He leans down, turns Andy's myopic gaze to his face.

"This fish is a gift to your brother, Jonny, from my brother, Raphael," he says. "Take this fish and place it on Jonny's eyes and he will be healed. My brother is a healer of blindness. Then throw the fish into the air and it will land in the sea. Do it now."

He watches Andy stumble towards his brother, who is crying in a ball on the ground. He should help Mary Moses , but she takes her strength from the earth itself and there is nothing a warrior Archangel can do for her now.

The fish glints in Andy's chubby hand, as he lurches about, seeking Jonny. When he blunders into him, he shakes him, prods him, tugs his clothes. Jonny rolls over to Andy, words falling incoherently from his mouth. Andy lifts the fish, softly draws it across Jonny's eyes. Jonny stops crying, rubs his eyes. Andy turns back to St Michael, smiles at him, and lifts the fish, but instead of throwing it back to the sea he wipes its wriggling silver body across his own eyes.

St Michael raises his hand in benediction, as the fish leaps from the boy's hand and tumbles over the cliffs to the dark sea below.

~

Tim does not remember falling to the rock. He remembers the fish and Andy's smile, and no more. His shoulders are aflame. The rock is cold and hard beneath him. He looks to the sky. The storm has gone, the clouds have gone. He traces the ancient patterns of the stars.

A cry from nearby. The cry of a baby.

Nestled in the grasses below him Caroline holds her baby daughter in her arms. Verity crouches beside her, stroking the child's damp head.

Jack has led Jonny and Andy away, one in each hand. He lets go of Jonny a moment to point at something in the sky. The two boys turn their faces to the stars.

Tim stands on Carrag Luz. The sea is black and calm, sucking and pulling on the sand as the tide ebbs. Across the giant bay is the amber straggle of Penzance and, further out, the pulse of a lighthouse. Tim rests his hands where the giant boulder once lay, feeling the last tremors of power from the rocks.

At last, he turns away and climbs down from the crag. Caroline and Verity are whispering over the baby's head. Tim walks on to where Jack and the boys are standing.

"I can see, I can see!" Jonny says.

"Me too," says Andy. "I can see everything. I don't need glasses."

Tim swallows the treacherous sting in his throat and takes Andy by the hand, leading him back towards Carrag Luz.

"And so, you flew with angels, Andy."

"Yes," Andy says. "But they've both gone."

"Angels never go," Tim says. "The time of the angels may have passed for now, but they will return."

Something's scratching his back. He reaches round and finds the soft breath of a feather. He hands it to Andy, who twirls the stem, watching the peacock's eye flash.

A NOTE FROM THE AUTHOR

Helston Flora Day in Cornwall is a real festival celebrated on the 8th of May. There are street dances throughout the day, and my favourite is the Hal an Tow, which is the mumming play celebrating the victory of good over evil. I danced in it for several years as a teenager and have wonderful memories of racing through the streets with my tambourine, whistling and shouting, jostling the crowds, and – one year – sore feet when the soles of my shoes rubbed through.

Helston's name does come from the legend of St Michael and the Devil, and the Angel Hotel stands to this day on the main street. Whether the chasm to Hell is beneath it or somewhere else nearby is anyone's guess.

The cliff above Polurrian beach is bisected with a fault line where schist meets the Lizard serpentine. The rocks there are unstable. You can see the remains of buildings which fell over the edge in previous rock falls, and only earlier this year (2023) there were several landslides onto the beach below. The coast is a living entity.

Carrag Luz is an iconic rock outcrop on the cliffs, and I have loved it since I was a small child. In spring the rocks are surrounded with drifts of bluebells, wild garlic and campion. From there you can see all around Mount's Bay to Wolf Rock lighthouse on the horizon. You can watch the weather come in, the shape of the rainstorms and the cloud patterns over the sea.

I wrote the first draft of this book when I was sixteen. Since then it has had numerous revamps and changes, and barely resembles that first effort, but it has remained a special book to me. It is set in my home town, and features the places and landscape that I love. I am so happy that I can finally share it with you.

The Hal an Tow Song

Robin Hood and Little John
They both are gone to fair O
And we will to the merry green wood
To see what they do there O
And for to chase
To chase the buck and doe

Chorus

Hal an Tow, jolly Rumblelow
For we are up as soon as any day O
And for to fetch the summer home
The summer and the May O
For summer is a come O
And winter is a gone O

Where are the Spaniards
Who make so great a boast O?
For they shall eat the grey goose feather
And we shall eat the roast O
In every land
The land where'er we go

Chorus

As for that good knight St George
St George he was a knight O
Of all the knights in Christendom
St George he is the right O
In every land

The land where'er we go

Chorus
But to a greater than St George
Our Helston has a right O
St Michael with his wings outspread
The Archangel so bright O
Who fought the fiend
Of all mankind the foe

Chorus

God bless Aunt Mary Moses
In all her power and might O
And send us peace in merry England
Both day and night O
And send us peace in merry England
Both now and evermore O

Chorus

My thanks as always to my family. They have stuck with me and this book for a long time.

To my mother Caroline Matthews. She is always my first reader and editor, and we've probably spent weeks of our lives talking about this one. I hope one day the roles will be reversed and I get to edit her book.

To my late father Chris Hart who always believed in me, but was taken from me before any of my books made it into the world.

To my late grandparents Sylvia and Alfred Matthews – again, huge supporters of my work, again taken too soon. A special thank you to Sylvia for thinking of the title.

And now also to my daughters Rafi and Aelfrida – I love you both beyond imagination.

Huge thanks to Sarah Hembrow of Vulpine Press for taking a chance on me and my books. You have changed my life, and made my dreams reality. And huge thanks also to my editor Jess Jordan who has turned my manuscript into something better than I could have hoped for.

Lucinda Hart grew up in Cornwall and has been writing fiction since the age of three. She has a BA in Fine Art and Creative Writing and a MA in Creative Writing, both from Bath Spa University. The themes in Lucinda's books are often of great relevance to her. Place is also important; she uses her favourite locations in novels and hopes they will interest the reader as much as they have inspired her. She lives in Cornwall with her two daughters.

Printed in Great Britain
by Amazon

32558244R00160